MOHINI

Anuja Chandramouli is a bestselling Indian author and new-age Indian classicist widely regarded as one of the finest writers in mythology, historical fiction and fantasy. She followed up her highly acclaimed debut novel, *Arjuna: Saga of a Pandava Warrior-Prince*, which was named as one of the top five sellers in the Indian writing category for the year 2012 by Amazon India, with *Kamadeva: The God of Desire, Shakti: The Divine Feminine, Yama's Lieutenant* and its sequel, *Yama's Lieutenant and the Stone Witch*. Her articles, short stories and book reviews appear in various publications like *The New Indian Express*, *The Hindu*, and *Femina*. Some of her other books are *Kartikeya: The Destroyer's Son, Prithviraj Chauhan: The Emperor of Hearts, Rani Padmavati: The Burning Queen* and *Ganga: The Constant Goddess*. *Muhammad Bin Tughlaq: Tale of a Tyrant* is her latest work of historical fiction. Her books are available as audiobooks as well.

An accomplished TEDx speaker and storyteller, Anuja Chandramouli regularly conducts workshops on creative writing, mythology and empowerment in schools and colleges across the country. She is also a student of classical dance and yoga.

Email: anujamouli@gmail.com
Twitter handle: @anujamouli
Website: www.anujachandramouli.com
FB page: https://www.facebook.com authoranujachandramouli/

MOHINI
the Enchantress

ANUJA CHANDRAMOULI

RUPA

Published by
Rupa Publications India Pvt. Ltd 2020
7/16, Ansari Road, Daryaganj
New Delhi 110002

Sales Centres:
Allahabad Bengaluru Chennai
Hyderabad Jaipur Kathmandu
Kolkata Mumbai

Copyright © Anuja Chandramouli 2020

All rights reserved.
No part of this publication may be reproduced, transmitted,
or stored in a retrieval system, in any form or by any means,
electronic, mechanical, photocopying, recording or otherwise,
without the prior permission of the publisher.

This is a work of fiction. Names, characters, places and incidents are either the
product of the author's imagination or are used fictitiously and any resemblance
to any actual person, living or dead, events or locales is entirely coincidental.

ISBN: 978-93-89967-26-5

First impression 2020

10 9 8 7 6 5 4 3 2 1

The moral right of the author has been asserted.

Printed HT Media Ltd, Gr. Noida

This book is sold subject to the condition that it shall not,
by way of trade or otherwise, be lent, resold, hired out, or otherwise
circulated, without the publisher's prior consent, in any form
of binding or cover other than that in which it is published.

For Niranjana akka,
who taught me how to take a leap of faith
without falling and to surrender without succumbing

Prelude:
A Hint of Hope Borne on a Dream

The storytellers tended to go into raptures describing her sublime, flawless beauty, waxing eloquent about the perfection of her form and features, not to mention the heaviness of her bosom, supported as it was by an impossibly narrow waist. Captivating eyes with so much depth that most wanted nothing better than to plunge into those twin orbs, exploring the secrets within for the rest of time; lustrous tresses that cascaded in waves of silk, nearly caressing the earth over which she glided with effortless grace; luscious lips that mischievously promised endless delights and so on and so forth.

Though they were mostly males who could not or did not want to look beyond the sumptuous perfection of her physical attributes, none of it was an exaggeration.. For she *was* bewitching and her beauty had a power of its own, which could simply not be discounted. And yet, when it came right down to it, her beauty was almost beside the point.

Ultimately, it was all the things she stood for that really mattered. The tantalizing things she freely offered, all the things that were desired with varying degrees of desperate need and unlimited greed. And unlike what the perverse always assumed, it was not even carnal pleasure, even though a sumptuous smorgasbord of sensual delights was readily available. Mostly it was a whole host of insipid little things that offered transient pleasures and were sought and indulged in repeatedly to the point where they distracted the mind from all else and consumed it in its entirety. She was not surprised that people chose this fulfilling yet ultimately empty state of being over the blandness of nirvana and the promise of eternal tranquillity.

Secure in the knowledge that she would always be chosen, and elusive as a fragment of a beloved dream, she slipped in and out of the consciousness of the fortunate ones who had been either arbitrarily chosen or were part of the intricate cosmic design. These willingly allowed themselves to be bedevilled, consumed by a passion that would not be denied, existing only to serve her will, content to be moulded to suit the purposes of the most enchanting being in all of creation.

Mohini. Mohini. Mohini. They breathed her name. Chanted it like a fervent prayer. Anxious to lose themselves in her, till they were delirious with sheer joy, consumed by a madness from which they never wished to be cured. Who could blame them? A euphoric state of endless intoxication wasn't the worst way to eke out an existence.

The females among the mortals and immortals alike were far less enamoured, although they weren't impervious to her charms either. They muttered darkly about demon magic and shameless hussies who led honest men astray with the promise of unlimited debauchery and sordid shenanigans. Drawing the menfolk into a sticky web of deceit, draining them slowly of their very life essence, till they were little more than desiccated husks who had the vital juices sucked out of their orifices. Reducing the best of men to mindless morons and drooling imbeciles who crawled and debased themselves in the hope of being at the receiving end of a bewitching smile.

In their innermost hearts though, they too wanted to be seduced. Released from the shackles of humdrum virtue so they too could roam where their dreams led them, wild as the wind, blithe and free-spirited. At liberty to sip the nectar of all things delectable, to carouse endlessly in an orgiastic rush of pleasure, swirling in a whirlpool of heady passion. Far away from the senseless spite of conventional morality. Just so they could be as happy as they could be. As happy as she always seemed to be.

Mohini of the unfettered and eternally buoyant spirit, floated alone, far removed from the relentless waves of powerful emotions that surged about her in an endless rush, impervious to the desperate desire and toxic hate that motivated those who sought to draw closer to her, obsessively driven to attempt the impossible task of possessing her.

The Supreme Goddess had warned the Divine Protector about this. And her by extension, of course. Not that she had been concerned then or was now.

'Mohini is incapable of love...' Shakti had informed her old friend.

'How is that a bad thing? She will forever be free from the bondage and tyrannies of the said emotion, the vulnerability and revolting mess that infinite tenderness leaves in its wake as well as the degradation that complete surrender demands.' Vishnu was unperturbed.

'I know...' she replied thoughtfully, 'but even so, it is a pity.'

'Well, she is your creation as much as mine,' he pointed out helpfully. 'Perhaps, even more so.'

She nodded again, 'It used to bother me that you do everything you need to with a detachment that sometimes feels so cold-blooded, almost fiendish. Which is why I suggested the need for Mohini. I was hoping that she would be more emotionally invested in her charges. But she is the same old you in a ravishing new form.'

'You need not sound so disappointed,' he said reprovingly. 'She would be hurt if she were capable of feeling the emotion. Besides, though she was born of my own self, the enchantress possesses the quality of autonomy that is her own. As for the ravishing form, she was made in your image and that is my tribute to you.'

She rolled her eyes at that. What was it with the male of the species and their ridiculous preoccupation with beauty? The females were only marginally better, devoting their limited existence solely to primping, preening and perpetually preoccupying themselves with enhancing their looks, almost as if they needed beauty to be the crowning achievement of their sordid lives, soiled as it was by this commitment to superficiality.

Shakti shook her head in disgust. 'It bothers me that no one can see past her beauty… And I didn't say I was disappointed in her, merely sorry that she herself doesn't get to partake of the gifts she has to offer. It is a tad unfortunate that she is immune not only to the treacherous undercurrents of the tender emotions but also to the more rewarding aspects.'

The Goddess appeared thoughtful, 'The Enchantress is needed. She always will be, particularly as the age grows dark with trouble and strife, brought on by a steady erosion of faith and the gradual dissolution of devotion. In the beginning you had an easier time of it in your role as the Protector. There was a definite pattern—a tyrant or a good soul would accrue more than their fair share of power, deprive the King of heaven of what he feels entitled to, and upset the natural order of things.

Curses and boons would do their share of the damage of course, and consequently there would be mighty duels fought and epic upheavals. Then you would bestir yourself from your prolonged slumber so that engorged beasts of the aquatic, porcine or ferociously predatory variety may emerge from your being to restore things to the way they were. Ironically, it was your obsession with keeping things on an even keel that led to the loss of balance and a sense of proportion. You made it look easy and when the mortals and immortals discovered that a path of moderation was the hardest one to take, they stopped trying.'

'All in a day's work!' Vishnu remarked drily.

'But going forward, it will be different,' Shakti ignored his feeble attempt at humour. 'Things will not be as straightforward. There will be the same old cosmic catastrophes for you to contend with, but their resolution will not be as straightforward. Increasingly, despite your best efforts, you will discover the ascendance of a certain disquieting ambiguity, a dispiriting sense of dwindling dharma, of heroic acts being outnumbered by piffling mediocrity. A gradual dilution of everything of value, leaving piddling inanity and petty issues in place of glorious quests to make a difference.'

He shrugged, 'It will be as you say but that too is the natural order of things. The denizens of the future will be burdened like never before by their actions in the past and the evils of the present. One can hardly blame them for falling from lofty heights, and when it happens once too often, they will not bother to try and right themselves.

'Magic cannot last forever and must make way for the mundane. Powerful rishis will be replaced by shabby aspirants and tricksters more adept at peddling worthless trifles than purveying universal truths. Apsaras, gandharvas and other celestial beings will lose their lustre and with that, the perfection of their sublime arts. The Devas and Asuras, even the Gods and Goddesses, will live on only in the precious stories that will always be the sole things to survive human and divine folly.

'The fabled age of heroes and heroines, warriors and the wise will end. Only the puniest of mortals will remain trapped in a maudlin existence with only the morbid, mundane and monotonous, which will prompt them into increasing acts of desperation to alleviate the sameness and sickness of it all. But there is a long way to go before it all comes to pass. And when it eventually does, it will cease to matter. And we will all carry on muddling along as always.'

'That may be so, but that is hardly reason enough to stop trying to stave off the inevitable…' Shakti lectured Vishnu sternly, 'Wars will be fought for the ostensible purposes of peace and equal rights, but they will only serve to exacerbate senseless slaughter and as a breeding ground for greater injustice. Vice and virtue will remain the equal and opposing forces they always have been, but with an enhanced capacity for propelling countless souls down paths that lead inexorably to their own doom. For such is the design of fate and time with their constant endeavours to create extreme situations with the intention to level the playing field on a universal scale.

'If your avatars are to prove effective, they will need to be a little more effective than the forms of fauna you presently favour, which have fought their way out of the primordial ooze. Noble men and a powerful female capable of interacting with your charges on a more intimate scale will be needed. Beings who can teach, inspire and lead by example to show the mortals a better way. In a loveless universe, leached of light, dreams are more important than ever.'

'I suppose this was your subtle way of insisting that future incarnations could use the assistance of a particularly wrought specimen, infused with the power of the feminine divine…'

'As opposed to the brutish and ham-fisted versions of purusha, yes…' she teased him. 'Which is why your Mohini is special. In troubled times, even knowledge is worthless without bhakti, the highest epitome of love and pure devotion. It is the heart which alone gives impetus to the great deeds that elevate the soul. Mohini needed to emerge from the wellsprings of your own mighty heart. Which is why I worry about the fact that she herself is entirely heartless.'

'It was as you wished,' Vishnu said only half-jestingly. 'I spent the aeons practising tapas to win the grace of a certain great Goddess. Fortunately, she looked upon the venture with favour and bestowed upon me a portion of her power and granted me the fulfilment of a dream, fashioned in her own exquisite image. Living proof that seduction is always superior to carnage, even if it leaves a similar swathe of destruction in its wake. And you needn't worry—in matters of the heart, it always helps not to have one. Mohini will be a troublemaker but the three worlds will benefit from her presence.'

Shakti smiled then. 'I can't see your enchantress healing the land. She may not be the one to make flowers bloom, restore the crops in parched fields, cause dead trees to bear fruits, drain the poisons that befoul the waters or even nurture the wretched. But I daresay, she will do it all and manage something even better.

Even as existence bows down under the burden of protracted sin, Mohini will be the bearer of irresistible flavour, the supreme weapon in the cosmic game of Lila. An exquisite taste of rasa… Perhaps that is what it will take to fix that which cannot be fixed.'

'Now that would be something, wouldn't it?'

Mohini had wandered away from them then, brushing past the tendrils of thoughts and words that swirled around her pleasantly. She walked all the way to the edge of their world, looking out towards the realms of the mortals and the immortals. They would be her vocation. And her prey. She looked away from their incessant demands and pressing problems. It was part of her constitution. It was what she would always do. Wander the three worlds at will, do the needful if she felt the need, and walk away. Without looking back. Vivid and ephemeral as a deeply cherished but forgotten dream.

It had all happened a while ago. But nothing much had changed for her. Or would. Mohini was here to stay. For as long or as short a while as needed. She had emerged from the fullness of his heart and she always faded away into the emptiness of the void. It didn't matter to her either way. After all, it was this that had set her free.

The Inseparables

I am Mohini. And this is my story. But if you are looking for a simple old story with a beginning, middle and end, you are going to be disappointed. That is not entirely true, because no matter what I do, even if I get distracted and diverge from the straight and narrow path of traditional storytelling to meander off the beaten track, taking frustrating detours into the realms of the obscure, fanciful or philosophical, in the end you will be just as enchanted as everybody else. After all, I was meant to be irresistible. And none can withstand my charms. Or so it is said.

But my story did not begin with me. As with most stories, it began with them. The friends. And the lovers. The former were nurtured and nourished by the latter, but in the end, they proved the stronger of the two. Though opinions always vary when it comes to these things.

Their familiar presence has always been a comfort to me. As is the softness of the crimson petals of the pretty flowers against my fingers as I walk past them. The tender stalks and shoots brushing against my bare legs feel like the gentlest of caresses and bring a smile to my face. There is always a profusion of perfumed blooms in these parts, clustered in beds that seem to go on forever. Mercifully, they neither wilt nor wither, not even when I myself fade and flicker from reality to non-reality like a candle harassed by the breeze.

I can't see the duo as yet, but I don't have to. They are in the vicinity. Making my way deeper into the forest, I pretend not to notice the massive trees that lower their branches with a deferential air, revelling in the lingering trace of the myriad things that make me so alluring. They ask for so little, unlike the others who can't help but treat me as an empty vessel into which they can pour the sum total of their dreams, hopes, aspirations, pains and troubles in a torrential outpouring of naked need.

The stolid presence of the stony ridges and ancient ravines is a comfort too. All of it is so familiar and dear. Yet, having traversed it countless times, I know that, like me, this place is never the same, always changing and adapting, ever flowing. There are gardens, streams, waterfalls, hillocks and trees of course, but there are steep drops and mighty rocks rich in ore, to be contended with as well. Birdsong soothes my ears and woodland creatures gambol in my path. Though composed of the physical elements, there is a fluid, ever-changing quality to the place, rendering it something of a dreamscape that has sprung forth from the peace and harmony of a well-ordered mind.

In this case though, it would be two minds. Two hearts. Two souls. Which functioned as one. A single entity. They were there, when I stepped into a clearing that was awash in the brilliance of the joy and quiet tranquillity that emanated from the ancient rishis, Nara and Narayana, in the mountain fastness of their ancient home at Badari. The former was a man. The latter was divine, who contained the finest essence of Vishnu himself. Their eyes were closed but both knew I was there, lost though they were in the remote reaches of meditation. How could they not?

I drank my fill of them. Fair Nara with his rotund belly and skinny legs, clad in the antelope skin they both favoured, uncaring that it revealed more than it concealed. Dark and radiant Narayana, with his messy hair and tendency to place his leg on the knee of his dearest friend. They had always been together. From the very beginning of time. Just being in their presence is soothing and it fills me with contentment.

Sometimes, I am with them when they make their deep forays into the vast reaches of the unknown where time and space have unravelled into unsubstantial wisps. Propelled by their breath, gliding along the streams of their submerged consciousness, merging into their very minds, which have expanded to make room for all things real and unreal, is when I feel the most intensely alive.

Traipsing across the realms of infinity, I go back and forth from the beginning to the end and back again, poring over the pages of their deeds both big and small, which outnumbers every grain of sand, drop of water or gust of wind, revelling in the stories of what has been and what will be. Grand tales of romance, passion, danger, loss and high adventure. The Goddess was wrong. I *am* capable of love, even if it is only for the stories. And the dreams that sometimes come true.

Sometimes I float in the pitch blackness of nothingness. Like the two who are almost one, I feel and hear nothing, adrift on an ocean of emptiness. No images are allowed to inundate the senses and confound the unwary. No memories evoke long dormant feelings. No pleasure. No pain. Merely the sense of being cocooned in layers of warmth and well-being, in a safe space free from all menace.

Then there are times when there are sights, smells and sounds from the frenzied pace and activity of the worlds outside, straining against the gossamer fabric of absolute stillness and serenity. There is the incessant buzzing of overwrought sensation, heated emotions and tempestuous passion propelled thither on the strength of the cries of anguish and voices raised in prayer. The duo are alert, monitoring the gravity of deeds and forbidden thoughts, but with unhurried ease borne of long practice and perennial commitment.

And so I drift. Sometimes with him. Or with them. Or all alone. They are different, the two of them. Yet the very same. I suppose you could say the same about him and me. Each one of us, intertwined inextricably with the very essence of the other, it is impossible to say where one begins and the other ends. It has always been my opinion that these two are the only ones in all of creation that truly deserve to be preserved intact for all of eternity. And it is not only because I love the one and the other too. Of course, such a love of the I, which the wise man would refer to as aham, embodied by Nara, and the self, atman, which is represented by Narayana, can only be accurately described as narcissistic.

It is said that I emerged from Narayana's heart in response to the exhortations made by the Goddess of Vishnu. But Nara had been an inhabitant thereabouts even before me. Always together in times of peace and harmony or terror and strife. They alone have endured. A gentle reminder of what once had been. Of all that has been lost. And all that could still be regained. That is the nice way of looking at it, but in truth both are stubborn louts who refuse to let go of each other. And so the three worlds prevail too. Teetering on the brink, but held securely by the harness of a friendship that transcends all else.

This place, infused as it is with their presence, exudes joy, peace and a radiant calm. Untouched by the turmoil that grips the world of the mortals, Badari holds out steadily against the depredations that have sickened the lands without. Everywhere, life is struggling to assert itself even as death holds sway, firmly entrenched in the rot that has set in deep. From the poisons that have seeped into the world and her waters. Mostly, I have a cynical outlook to how all this is going to turn out. Which probably explains why I firmly feel that dreaming is better than waking even when one is a dream made real and the boundaries between what exactly constitutes the two states is blurred beyond recognition.

The efforts of my favourite twosome in their role as protectors of the Universe is exemplary. Nara and Narayana do what they can to reverse the tide and curb the damage, giving generously of their powers even when their hard work is undone almost as quickly as it is done. The efforts and effects of their goodwill lasts only as long as it takes for avarice and malice to prevail. But they keep at it. Even when the faith, trust and most importantly the bhakti of the mortals, tenuous in the best of times, fails completely, chipping away at all that is left of hope and goodness. They refuse to give up though. And so, neither do I. But my non-existent heart is not in it.

Badari alone prevails, strong and immutable, an evergreen oasis in the treacherous quicksand of time and fate, those perpetual bullies with scant regard and active contempt for dharma. It alone holds out the promise of benevolence, compassion and goodwill for all who seek it. Nara and Narayana watch over mortal and immortal alike from their bastion. They never fail. I am convinced their sincerity and dependability is the reason their charges always feel free to go astray and destroy everything that has any intrinsic worth, complacent in the belief that it will all be restored, because it must.

'You need them to need you…' I had pointed out to him. 'It is why you won't leave them to their own devices and let them clean up after themselves. It is also why they remain spoilt children. And with a mean streak at that.'

'I daresay you are right,' Narayana said, 'but what needs to be done needs to be done. And it does not matter who does it.'

Nara tended to agree. In the end, he always did, even though he had his share of doubts, the same as I. But he was always content to follow his friend's lead and go where he did. Even if it was to a war where a peaceable man and mighty archer would be the instrument of death that annihilated an entire generation. All because his divine friend exhorted him to do so on the killing plains of Kurukshetra and volunteered to charioteer him to his destiny. It was silly of him, but I tend to do the same and so didn't judge him too harshly. My method is more elegant though and involves little or no bloodletting.

It isn't in my nature nor in theirs to worry though. Or care too much about the ways of the wicked. So I skip right along, a kindred spirit of the breeze, rain, rays of the sun, moonlight and time, humming to myself. Tethered to the one, who has tethered himself to the other, I am nevertheless free. At liberty to do as I please. It is the same wherever I go. Because he holds me safe and unchanging, in his head and heart. Securely cradled in the roots of his tapas.

I remember what the Goddess has accused him of. And me. Of being detached to the point of cold-blooded fiendishness. But it didn't really apply to him. Not when it came to Nara at least. Nor me for that matter, when it comes to them. The ancient rishis had been present at the beginning on the Tree of Life, which in turn grew closely entwined with the Tree of Knowledge, two seeds gifted from Shiva and Shakti, back when the worlds were still young and everyone believed their love would survive everything. Two little birds perched prettily on intertwined branches. One munched on a berry while the other kept an eye on him and another out for him.

The trees appeared locked in a tight embrace even though they appeared to be at cross purposes with some of the roots and branches (it was hard to say which belonged to which tree) arching up towards the heavens while the others made their way downward to the Earth. The sap oozed down the barks, shed from the incessant lovemaking of the besotted twosome. They kept at it even when it was readily apparent that one or both would suffocate from a surfeit of amorous activity. As for the birds, they kept at it too. Munching and watching. Awash in contentment.

Time marched on, speeding when there was the need to slow down and savour a moment, and slowing to a crawl, when a moment stretched to better accommodate the experience of agony, as was its wont. Shiva had lost his Shakti, and with her, all that was the best in him. But Narayana would never allow himself to lose Nara. He had said it before and he would say it again, 'I cannot endure the three worlds without Nara and I will tear down all of existence before I allow it to go on without him.'

They are the inseparables and would survive even if nothing else did. After all, hadn't they proved that two souls conjoined in friendship was always superior to the fragile bonds formed by love even of the divine variety as well as those irksome ties of blood everyone set so much store by? I have seen the truth of it in the stories, which remain the only place I can cheerfully inhabit outside of his head and heart. So I keep returning to the fables. Over and over again.

MOHINI

Shiva and Shakti's story is exhausting, depressing and occasionally enlightening. They suffer whether they are together or apart. And the three worlds do too. After her infamous decision to immolate herself over an infamous insult that was best ignored, Shakti was reborn as the Mountain King Himavan's daughters, Ganga and Parvati, water and earth, another of the unnecessary complications that makes this love story so exasperating.

As for Shiva, his mourning ranged across the heavens and the thousand hells of Yama as well as everything in between. His union with Parvati was supposed to be a coming together of excesses that would fix the evils of the cosmos, which they themselves had wrought. But of course, it hadn't been harmonious. It never was. Having tangled with the Destroyer at his most acrimonious, Kama, the God of Desire had been incinerated, sacrificed on the altar of a twisted love story. Desire died with him, relegated evermore to the forbidden depths where Ganga had carried his remains. And there it has remained ever since. In the dark realms of taboos and social stigma.

I suppose this is why even an enchantress has to befriend the shadows and carry out her business in the nooks and crannies of buried desire, far away from prying eyes and envy that has the power to turn dreams to dust. Some would say it is a pity but I don't think so. Some things thrive and flourish only in the secret places where it is not quite as easy to be hunted, maimed, killed, or turned to ashes. It is only the foolish who continue to work towards restoring desire to its so-called rightful place in the sun. Some of us prefer the gentle and tolerant moonbeams to the harsh glare of the judgemental sun.

Having done what he had, Shiva had remained unreconciled to Shakti's loss and was determined to stay that way when the children of the mountain flowed into his consciousness. One, because she was mischievous and bubbling over with exuberance, impatient with his display of protracted grief. The other, because she loved him nearly enough for both of them, and was impatient to be reunited with him, choosing the harder yogic path to win over the adiyogi.

While the love triangle played out, the three worlds with their animate and inanimate denizens limped along, struggling to recover from the deep wounds that had been inflicted upon them with the violent tearing apart of purusha and prakriti. At the time, when Shakti killed herself instead of all those who had galled her, Shiva's grief gave way to wrath and when he hurled his trident in a paroxysm of rage, it tore into life itself, turning everything it touched into ash. None were spared. Not mortal or immortal or flora and fauna.

His implacable weapon, hurtled towards Badari with deadly intent, drawn to the tranquillity of the place, bitterly jealous of the peace enjoyed by its inhabitants, angered by the perennial closeness of the ancient rishis who had inured themselves to the pangs of pleasure and pain which togetherness engendered. It was the sort of savagery and surpassing spitefulness Shiva's ego was capable of, which is not surprising because it was the sum total of every ego that ever was or will be. It was what prompted him to incinerate the gentle God of desire who was only trying to help and which would later cause him to behead his own child.

Nara bristled ever so slightly as the Destroyer's rage hurtled towards them, but Narayana only hummed. It was a sound of deep understanding and compassion. The trident was turned aside briefly but it would not be deterred. Once more, it gained impetus and charged towards Narayana, who smiled but made no move to repel it. Nara wouldn't stand for it. Not even the Destroyer had the right to be a bully.

He picked up a blade of grass and murmured to it, before casually tossing it at their grief-stricken tormentor. Transformed into a fiery axe, it did battle with the trident. On and on, they duelled, winning the three worlds a blessed respite before the Destroyer came to himself and seized both in either hand. He was chastened. Neither mortal nor immortal could prevail over the three-eyed God and the wielder of the trident. But love could. And had.

'The two of you should have put him out of his misery,' I had said at the time, 'and sent him to chase after his beloved in the afterlife. At least that way, we would have been spared the malaise of undiluted misery.'

Neither of them replied. But they didn't have to. Narayana loved Shiva. And so did Nara. And so did I. But not as unconditionally.

It was in this state that Shiva had turned his back on the three worlds and disappeared into the towering flames of penance and rigid austerities. Sullen and smouldering, uncaring that the heat of his tapas continued to sear the three worlds and all who had lived, loved and lost like him.

That was when Ganga had crashed into his head with her almighty waters. The billowing streams, flowing down the dense jungle of matted tresses, doused once and for all the worst of his ardent grief. It seems obvious to me that the River Goddess had not intended to stay. She had only wanted to put an end to the mourning. But to all their surprise, she had chosen to remain with him, content to explore the ceaseless wonders of the Destroyer's head and his matted locks.

I asked her about it once. 'I stayed because he didn't try to hold me captive. Everybody thought he would imprison me in his matted locks. I confess I did too, and had looked forward to defeating him, for my will alone must prevail. But to my surprise, he did not fight. And so I yielded.'

And she would stay forever, letting her waters trickle into the worlds in a thousand little streams, though she herself would dwell forever more on the person of the Destroyer, engulfing him like a second skin. There was a collective sigh of relief. Ganga had stopped his fires from burning creation to cinders. Shiva had held her waters in check before they inadvertently washed away all of life. It was the perfect union, they said. But Parvati certainly didn't think so. Shiva was hers and she would be reunited with him, even if it meant an eternity of enduring kisses that tasted of her sister's sweet and sour waters.

Parvati got her way eventually. There had been a grand wedding and unprecedented celebration. Like the other celestials who must have their voyeuristic pleasures, I was intensely aware of the lovers celebrating their union in a frenzy of lovemaking that sent tremors through the hearts of the wary ones among them who remembered the past and the trees that wanted to remain together for eternity, yet longed to break free.

Conjoined and unwilling to disentangle their limbs, the newlyweds carried on in a ceaseless embrace, not bothering to surface for air, uncaring that they were dripping with their exertions and the emissions of their passions were dripping down their copulating forms, in tiny rivulets of golden amrita that glistened invitingly. The nectar of immortality.

I looked at the shimmering stream, thinking it would be best for the damn thing to evaporate. But like all desirable objects, the nectar refused to disappear, choosing to tantalize instead, and seduce the unwary into fighting over it. The amrita would sustain life after a fashion, I admitted grudgingly to myself, but not before too many had killed each other while fighting for it, in their ironical bid to prolong their lives.

Later, when it all came to pass, I blamed the Destroyer and his consort for the mess. When it came to those two, their passion was every bit as intimidating and ruinous as their wretchedness or wrath. Even so, the world was never as happy as when Shiva and Parvati achieved blissful union. Even the Devas and Asuras, brothers from different mothers, set aside their differences and learned to live side by side. The mortals followed their example and there was blessed peace.

It was hardly cause for rejoicing though. After all, the other side of the coin was that the world was never as unhappy as when the supreme couple engaged in their endless tiffs. The Devas and Asuras went to war then. The humans were not far behind, devoting themselves wholeheartedly to devastation.

They allowed the corrosive flood of their collective anger and hatred to crash into the quiet places, the wild and austere regions, far from civilization and dense with ancient trees and wildlife where the seekers of truth were known to repair in their quest to unearth universal secrets. They hacked at the trees and tore them down, even the ones that were stubbornly entwined and unwilling to let go. They killed the birds for their cooking pots. Both, the ones that munched and the ones that watched. They drove themselves farther and farther away from their humanity and divinity both. Then they wept at their own predicament.

Meanwhile, the divine duo carried on and on. When they were entwined in a torrid embrace, all recoiled from the friction and frenzy that was unbearable. When they were torn apart by death or the polar opposites of their own corrosive personalities, the worlds still reeled.

All would have been lost, if it hadn't been for the two who were actually one. The ones who had chosen friendship over love. I have always wondered what would happen if they chose to let them all careen towards the catastrophes of their own making and follow it through to its logical conclusion. But they never have.

I could feel his eyelids flickering. Naturally, like him, I knew what was coming. His eyes blinked open. He was needed. And so was I. Which is why I stretched languorously and settled in snugly while he went about his business. Even stories have to wait when the dreams beckon. As do the rest.

Ceaseless Conflict

Isn't it annoying, when people attribute the starring role in what was mostly a misadventure to you and associate you forever more with nothing but extraordinary good looks, powerful enchantment and a jar of sap they call the nectar of immortality, though it has nothing to recommend it aside from its qualities as a powerful inebriant? That sort of thing tests my patience, it does. Because you just know that when it comes to certain tall tales, the narrator belongs to the male of the species, with an extremely limited imagination and little or no understanding of the feminine psyche.

These tall tales abound with beguiling enchantresses who transform into insatiable sexpots in the blink of an eye. It is most convenient to worship these improbable creatures who are always attentive, effortlessly exquisite, perennially patient, readily available for sex, and impossibly pleasing. When that begins to pall, the former paragons of perfection can be dragged down from their pedestals to be burnt alive for witchery and whoredom. If that were not bad enough, they are doomed to be shaped ever after by the twisted perception of impassioned males. Even their so-called power to turn men into mush and pull them along like a puppet on a string is merely an illusion created by an indulgent masculine ego.

Mercifully, my creator is a fervent believer in free will and though he isn't above manipulating it to suit his requirements, my will is my own, even if it was originally fashioned from his. Dreams outlast the dreamer in the same way a creation survives a lot longer than the creator. When it comes to not just me, but every immortal in the divine pantheon including the Trimurti—Brahma, Vishnu and Shiva—our very existence comes down to belief, or the willing suspension of disbelief at the very least. The so-called indestructibility and imperishability of the Gods rests on the most fragile of foundations—faith—which is the ficklest of things. It is small wonder then that Indra and his brethren have always been so painfully insecure.

Not me though. A fervent imagination and a mind rank with unfulfilled desire will always have place for me. So I prefer to grouse about less pressing matters pertaining to the limitations of fevered imaginations and messy minds.

Most think I do little more than beguile or bewitch. I do that of course, but it is galling to think that I was created for the express purpose of pleasing men. For most of them, I am the impossible ideal that cannot be possessed in their wildest dreams. Yet, it hardly stops them from trying to force me into their little moulds to be held captive in the prisons of their small minds. Which is mostly why I dance just out of their reach, spread my wings and disappear into flights of fancy and fantasy where the tantalizing tales await.

The Devas and the Asuras were fighting again. You would think they were born that way and that they came out of their mothers Aditi's and Diti's wombs, wrestling all the way, anxious to kill, or at the very least, maim each other. But that wasn't always the case. As children they had played together and of course, there were epic fights where mud cakes, sticks and stones were wielded with deadly intent and there was more than a little drama over who deserved a larger share of the dessert, but no more or no less than is normal for half-siblings.

Even the fights didn't always come down to Deva versus Asura. Sometimes Deva fought Deva and Asura fought Asura for mostly moronic reasons that are nevertheless profound in a child's mind. Some would take sides, thereby exacerbating the conflict, while others would prefer to stay neutral, which meant that the warring factions could be expected to turn on them at any moment. It was all very complicated. Their poor mothers worried themselves sick over this boisterous bunch and spent their days praying for peace.

Contrary to popular belief, the differences between the two sets of half-siblings were not clearly demarcated on the strength of skin colour, beliefs, behaviour or disposition. Even their mothers had trouble telling them apart because there were simply too many of that squalling, irrepressible lot, although that stopped neither Aditi nor Diti from being firmly convinced of the superiority of their own offspring, even as both fed the perpetually hungry lot, wiped noses, scrubbed bottoms, attended to assorted injuries and scolded the troublemakers with nary a hint of partiality. So they grew up higgledy-piggledy, inadequately overseen by Aditi and Diti, jostling for their father Kashyap's attention, although the great man had made it abundantly clear that having dispensed his duty with regard to procreation, he wanted no part of filial responsibility.

All too soon, as their differences became more pronounced, the shenanigans of their shared past were forgotten and all ceased to be uniformly adorable. The only thing carried over from childhood was the same voracious appetite that now extended to all the resources the three worlds had to offer and more. They were all endlessly hungry for everything existence had to offer, but Indra was the hungriest of them all.

The eventual wielder of the thunderbolt and lord of the heavens was used to being adored and having his own way. He was a good-looking fellow, bold as brass, and a master schemer who was charming even at his most intractable. Even Diti couldn't resist his blandishments after all he had done to the detriment of her sons. Later though, his own mother, Aditi, felt a good whipping would have done him a world of good. But by then, it was too late. He had made the decision to ride the lightning to power and there was no stopping him. Before they knew it, they were all embroiled in a ceaseless conflict that would have no end.

'He has a good heart,' Aditi would tell her sister repeatedly, 'and he really wants to make a difference. There is kindness in him, as well as generosity, bravery, wisdom, wit and a capacity for compassion. I wish everybody could see that.'

'He is also greedy for power and the only vision he has is a universe where all have been enslaved in order to venerate his ego. If that were not revolting enough, your son also happens to be a depraved voluptuary, who will stop at nothing to get what he wants, even if it means destroying his kith and kin,' Diti said drily, holding up her palm to cut off her sister's angry protests, 'but my sons aren't without their own flaws and they lack Indra's subtle cunning. Even so, it is a pity that the sons of Kashyap can't set aside their differences because together, they may have had the chance to neutralize each other's shortcomings.'

Aditi said nothing but she hoped in her heart that Indra would find a way to triumph over her sister's sons. Diti seemed to have read her mind, 'Neither my sons nor yours can hope to prevail for good. I don't know for certain whether that is heartening or disheartening but it is what it is.'

Diti was right. It was what it was. And not a soul in the three worlds would remain untouched by their struggle. As for me, I would find myself in the very middle of the maelstrom all too soon...

In the early days, attempts were made towards arbitration, if not reconciliation. The Devas ascended to the heavens and Indra claimed the skies, while the Asuras preferred living deep underground with the roots and rocks, far away from the hustle and bustle of cosmic politics, making their homes in caves, forests and the bottom of the ocean. Here, they reverted to the purest state of animalism in their pursuit of the metaphysical.

The former claimed the daylight hours and made it their own while the latter preferred the silver haven offered by the night to do their best work. Both groups worked with the elements. Both were caretakers of life and all living things. But that was only when the fallout from their endless wars weren't endangering all in existence.

Ever the canny operator, Indra allied himself with Brahma,

the saptarishis and great sages of the age, insinuating his way into their favour. Much to everybody's surprise, the King of Heaven and Vishnu formed a fast friendship. Aside from an innate capacity for deviousness, surely they had little in common?

'You do realize he is completely amoral, don't you?' I murmured into Vishnu's ear. 'I should know; after all, is there anyone better versed in the amoral arts than I am? There is something likeable about him though… The rare moments when he is true to himself and others stand out like precious rays of light in the tapestry of falsehood he is committed to weaving. His complete and utter lack of scruples makes him ideally suited for the power and trappings he craves so much. But I still don't see how he is worthy of your friendship.'

'Don't you?' was all he would say on the subject, preferring to follow up on his unsatisfactory response with an infuriating smile.

I took another look at Indra, studying him surreptitiously. The studious impression he gave of scrupulous contrition and dedication to making the three worlds a better place may have fooled the others but Vishnu would have seen through it in an instant. But observing him with the Protector, it was obvious he had stripped himself of artifice and that his affection for Vishnu was entirely genuine and unfeigned. Feeling my eyes on him, he raised his gaze to meet mine. Not much takes me by surprise but… there was only one other who was that supremely confident of resisting my so-called enchantments to make folks surrender their hearts and very life to me in exchange for a seductive smile or something equally stupid.

Indra drew closer to me in a companionable manner, his love for Vishnu extending to include me as well. But of course. I would have been flattered if I hadn't been aware of the wheels turning in his head, as he tried to figure out how best to use me in the furtherance of his own interests.

'My ambition is a monstrous creature,' he told me candidly, 'and my hankering for the finest things eternity has to offer is a raging fire in my gut. With Vishnu's help, I will get not only every single thing I have ever desired but more... More and more of everything worth having. And even more. But they will prove to be passing pleasures and ephemeral treasures though that is not going to stop me from relishing and appeasing my taste for them for as long as I possibly can. But in the end, the only thing that matters to me and the only thing I will take into the emptiness of the great beyond is my affection for Vishnu. For that alone is worth everything when nothing else matters.'

It was a rare moment of self-awareness for him, I'll admit. When he walked away from me, the very quality of the air had changed, as if it had suddenly been infused with a radiance and tranquillity that only the best of friendships can exude. And that was the moment I knew. Or at least saw the hint of a possibility. For once again, I saw them. It was an image I carried in whatever exists in place of a non-existent heart. An image of two ancient rishis. Two dear friends, who had always soothed and medicated the aches, pains, traumas and wounds inflicted by excessive love, which almost always turns to hate.

'I see it now!' the remark was unnecessary because Vishnu knew I had finally understood. His complacent air irked me and the fact that I was aware that he knew that it would be so, irked me some more.

'There will be much Vishnu and Indra will achieve, for neither of you is either short of cunning or courage, but Nara and Narayana are the superior beings. If anyone deserves to be worshipped, it is them. Besides, I like them better than you two!'

'I know.' It was all he would say.

'But I suppose it will be Vishnu and Indra who will capture the popular imagination by dint of flair and daring. They are the ones who will be remembered, the former with love and the latter with a touch of derision. I still think a lot of the less-remembered stories are the better ones.'

'And the people who seek them, especially the ones who have

need of these, will find them. And they will be treasured. That is more than enough.'

Was it? I walked away, swinging my hips with sinuous grace, thinking that as long as the stories themselves mattered, it would not matter which were remembered and which were less so.

In the meantime, acting on the advice of his powerful new friends, Indra accepted the services of the renowned Brihaspati, son of Angiras, as the preceptor of the Devas. There could be no questioning his credentials or erudition and yet there were a few who murmured of dark deeds and a history of violently abusive behaviour when it came to women. But it wouldn't have been convenient for Indra to give credence to uncomfortable truths so he dismissed them as rumours and helped his new mentor swat them away, both hoping they would disintegrate completely.

Later, it would amuse me endlessly that not only did the allegations refuse to die but they came back to bite both in their pompous posteriors and nearly cost them everything they had unscrupulously accumulated over the years. I will tell you all about it in good time, if you haven't wandered away to more diverting pastimes.

All the pieces were in place. Indra was crowned the King of Heaven in a glittering ceremony in the heavenly city of Amaravati he had built with his brothers. They had gathered all the treasures of the known world and placed it in their capital, which shone with newfound splendour and unmatched grandeur, giving absolutely no indication of the violence, spilled blood, lost lives and treacherous thievery that had gone into its making.

Indra wanted more. He wanted everything—all the adulation, respect and the good things the three worlds had to offer. He wanted to be a god. He demanded worship, rites, rituals and sacrifice. He needed to be admired and feared. So he doled out largesse and death in equal measure, and most fell over themselves in their haste to give him everything he wished for.

Even those who were impervious to his brand of effrontery

and charm couldn't help but be dazzled by his derring-do. He stole a brand from the pillar of light to fashion the lightning bolts that he would use to cow the rain-bearing clouds into submission. Having done so, he convinced the mortals that they needed him for life-affirming rain and they were happy, even desperate to believe, eager to hand over their future to Indra, of the wondrous countenance, impressive physique and powerful aura, accompanied as he was by his luminous brothers. They were as anxious to be tricked as he was to trick them.

Water was everything. It was life itself. They needed to believe that they would never run out of it or rely on the wiles and will of the capricious Goddess of the Waters. Ganga was so caught up in a celestial ménage à trois, she couldn't be bothered with keeping them perpetually plied with the lifesaving liquid. If there was one thing they couldn't tolerate in a female even if she was a powerful goddess, it was a selfish love of the self over service to others. How dare she put her needs above their own, far more pressing ones?

When they poured their hearts out to her, the impudent Ganga of the crooked ways had told them to take more responsibility towards a limited resource, insisting that they do their part to keep her waters clean and free from pollution. And when they ignored her ridiculous ideas, she accused them of violating her divine person and left in a huff. To sulk and brood in the jatas of the Destroyer, uncaring that her galling behaviour would disrupt the happiness of all the inhabitants in the three worlds and the marital happiness of her sister as well. What a shameless hussy! To hell with her! They would be better served by placing their faith in Indra, who seemed to be the very embodiment of reliability.

Indra was the safer bet. He had promised them water and all they had to do in return was to kowtow to his every whim and kiss his backside. And every once in a while, when he threw a celestial tantrum that was nothing less than his divine right and deprived them of rain till the land grew parched and miserable, it was only because they had failed to appease him by scrimping on the grandness of the yagnas and magnificence of the temples he was owed. And didn't the epitome of masculine pride deserve all this and more from them?

Bloody fools! To think they would rather part with a fortune to secure their future by building monuments to the fickle gods they themselves created rather than work towards undoing the damage they have done, which endangers not just their precious offspring (who are innocent as yet but are well and truly on the way to becoming as obnoxious as they themselves are), but all of creation as well! It boggles the mind.

Vishnu says I lack compassion for the foibles of mortals. He is a fine one to talk, especially since he has committed himself to a periodic culling of the human race. Every single one of his avatars will end in mass slaughter and destruction on a scale that would forever be unequalled in terms of sheer savagery. Not that I fault him for it. If left unchecked, the mortals would carry on with their vile gang rape of Bhumi Devi, keeping at it, till she died of her injuries, which included but were not limited to a broken heart and embittered spirit. The Protector will wash out her wounds with blood before helping her descend into the healing waters of Pralaya to recover from the damage done to her.

As for Indra, now that he had been elevated to Godhood by his own will and the weakness of mortals who need to believe in gods to save them from their combined stupidity, he lost no time in assigning places on the divine pantheon to his brothers, insisting that the humans worship the sun, moon, water, fire, wind and earth over which he and his fellow deities presided.

These developments astounded his half-brothers, the Asuras. 'Indra is like a crow,' they laughed at him over mouthfuls of food and drink. 'He can't resist anything that glitters. It is fitting. After all, he is little more than a steaming turd, which glistens when it catches the rays of the sun!'

As one, they guffawed while sharing news of his astounding activities and boundless ambition. They continued to laugh at the monumental folly of those who sought to be worshipped and those who debased themselves with worship. The humans were pathetic, servile creatures who deserved the shackles they were born and died with, they told each other, shaking their heads as they went back to the business of mining and fortifying the foundation of the three worlds, which was ill-equipped to handle the burden of foolishness, false pride and infamy it was expected to deal with.

And people dared to complain when the Asuras occasionally hunted them down, as was their right given their respective positions on the food chain, and feasted on their flesh, drank their blood, cracked their bones to suck out the marrow and fertilized the Earth Mother with their remains. Hypocritical filth! Such self-righteous wrath and accusations of cannibalism levied against them by the humans when they themselves made no bones of the fact that they consumed animals, birds and fishes who were their betters in every way and stuffed themselves so greedily and vociferously that their excesses had endangered the entire animal kingdom. It was disgraceful and this was the sorry lot Indra had adopted for his vested purposes!

As for the sages, their sanctimonious ways could scarce be abided. They used their influence over the mortals to further their own interests and those of their offspring for entire ages. The oppressive caste system came into being so that they could hoard knowledge and deprive the deserving of it. Warriors were given the lion's share of wealth and between these two, they ensured that all else would be the downtrodden. Birth would forever more determine the fate of the mortals. Hard work and merit would be trod underfoot by power and privilege. Far from putting an end to this atrocity, men and women endorsed and encouraged it, doing all in their power to enforce that which would prove detrimental to them all in the long run.

They did these things despite knowing in their flinty hearts that it was wrong. Why did they allow this evil into their lives? Of course it favoured the rich, powerful and knowledgeable, which was why they were more than happy to enforce inequality, but why didn't the downtrodden fight back given their larger numbers? Was it because they had been enslaved for so long they didn't know enough to leave when a pitiful few committed to justice and fairness threw open the doors of their prisons and cast off their chains? Was it because they found it easier to take the path of least resistance? It was hard to say.

Belatedly, the Asuras decided they would fight to preserve their way of life, going to war with their brethren. Ferocious attacks were launched against the holy men who had taken advantage of people's grief over the loss of loved ones, manipulating them to pay exorbitant prices for funeral rites for the ostensible purpose of easing the passing of the soul. These proceedings were forcibly disrupted, as bands of brothers doused the pyres with copious amounts of urine and relieved the sages of their beards one hair at a time. The humans were appalled at this display of bestial and uncouth behaviour, and fled in terror. They spent money they didn't have on grand sacrifices to annihilate the Asuras instead, angered beyond measure that their religious practices were being desecrated. This, in turn, incensed the Asuras further.

Initially, the Asuras fought for the right reasons, to uphold personal liberty and equality. But all too soon, they became blinded by their hatred of Indra and all whom they viewed as his supporters. Their tactics became increasingly reckless and ruthless and blood ran freely in the three worlds. Many who cared neither for Deva nor Asura, were butchered just the same. A clash of this nature always meant that it was the innocent who paid too heavy a price.

It would have been farcical if the entire thing hadn't turned out to be so profoundly tragic.

The Asuras may have had the best of intentions but they had underestimated the power of influential connections, bigoted faith and blind devotion. More importantly, they had underestimated the power of the puny mortals and overestimated their own ingrained righteousness and capacity for survival, given that they were the minority and did not enjoy the popularity and reverence Indra did.

The rigid adherence to rites and rituals, religious frenzy, feverish worship and fanatical adoration of the mortals gave wings to Indra's burgeoning ambition and for a while he was unstoppable. Callow and callous as ever, it wasn't enough for him to be universally loved and feared. He wanted his half-brothers to be abhorred and despised. And they were.

Tired of being consumed and sick of the argument that their deaths were necessary to propagate life on a planet where the resources were limited, the mortals appealed to Indra for succour and he was delighted with the excuse to kill his half-brothers. After all, the Asuras knew all about exhaustible assets and surely their extermination would leave more for the Devas and the mortals who looked to them for protection?

And so it began. The killing of the Asuras. They died in droves, struck down by bolts of lightning and an assorted arsenal of celestial weaponry gifted to the Devas by Brihaspati and the sages. Blasted out of existence for no crime other than just being. And a staunch refusal to kowtow to the bullying demands and dictates of the majority. Those who would have mourned them and celebrated their deeds died too.

Karanja, Parnaya, Vanga, Ahisuva, Virata, Trishiras, Arunavabha, Arpuda, Ahisha, Ilibasa, Shambara, Namuci, Sushma, Uranyu, Svara, Bhanu, Araru... So many names and so little to remember them by, even in the stories that have the longest of memories.

Those among the Devas who helped them were punished, humiliated and stripped of all their property and powers, left to roam the realms of the mortals like beggars. Indra never had any compunction about destroying those he viewed as his enemies. It was madness! And it was just the beginning. The God of Thunder and the King of Heaven was determined not to rest till he had destroyed the threat posed by his half-brothers in its entirety.

The Asuras who had survived the onslaught went into hiding. They roamed the dark reaches of the cosmos and relegated themselves to the shadowy realms. Heartsick, weary and wishing for death, they finally washed up on the shore of a good woman's mercy. Her name was Kavya. Or Kavyamata, as they would call her ever after.

Her story was never widely disseminated. The details are missing and there is much contradiction and confusion. There is no agreement about her name even. But that is hardly surprising, since men have never been overly fond of women who put them in their place.

Taking Sides

The lady of the legendary compassion and generosity was the wife of Sage Bhrigu. Most stories feature stunningly beautiful women like yours truly but Kavya could only be described as plain in the interest of honesty. She didn't seem to mind in the least. And why should she? I never did understand why beauty is prized above all else in the three worlds.

Take my own self for instance. I might have been responsible for the cold-blooded murder of one who wanted to partake of the precious nectar to which he was entitled too, since he played a part in procuring it at great personal cost, and somehow, he became the villain of the piece and it was I who was much revered and admired simply because I was by far and away the better looking of the two of us! It is criminal, the things beauty absolves you of, at least in the eyes of the great majority who don't know better.

Personally, I don't set too much store by beauty and its superficial accoutrements. Which is why Kavya was so refreshing. Not one to bother with silks and jewels or cosmetic aids, there was nevertheless something arresting about her vivacity and overall demeanour and she had more than her fair share of admirers. She seemed to like the attention well enough, though she was far too sensible to let it turn her head and reduce her to a vapid, simpering mess. Blunt and plainspoken, she knew her mind and knew how to get exactly what she wanted out of life.

Constantly on the move, flitting from one task to the other, Kavya kept busy without ever breaking into a sweat. They said she got more done in a minute than most did in a lifetime. What was more, she was radiant, filled to the brim with goodness, infectious energy and a perpetual willingness to laugh out loud.

All of these good qualities were accentuated a hundred fold by the inevitable flaws that peeked out every once in a while from behind the veneer of perfection she so successfully projected with a wink and a cheeky smile. She had a temper that, when provoked, was a violent force of nature that left all in its wake reduced to smithereens and an unassailable belief that she knew what was best and therefore was always right.

The fleeing Asuras threw themselves at this inimitable lady's feet and she adopted them as her own. Kavya nursed them back to health with her own hands. Her husband Bhrigu was roped in to minister to their wounded spirits and she even tried to convince her reluctant stepson, Sukra, to become their preceptor. Neither was as enthusiastic as she was when it came to the Asuras though, much to her irritation.

'Why are you making this so personal?' Bhrigu remonstrated with her, fussing over the wild strands of her hair that were sticking out in all directions as she bristled at his lack of conviction about her chosen course. 'It is never a good idea to get in the middle of fighting dogs. You are the one most likely to get hurt and I couldn't bear for that to happen.'

Kavya was mollified, but her tone was stern, 'Would you rather I stepped aside and pretended not to notice the injustice that has brought them to my doorstep seeking shelter? Do you condone the senseless slaughter of Diti's sons?'

'They are not completely innocent of wrongdoing.' His tone was mild, but she heard the impatience nevertheless. 'If my information is correct—and it is—the Asuras did a fair bit of slaughtering themselves before they were taken by surprise and routed. It was more on account of their carelessness and foolish belief in their own invincibility as opposed to Indra's cleverness.'

I couldn't help but nod in agreement. The losing side in any war usually feel themselves to be the victims of unfair prosecution, while the victors assure themselves that their enemies were evil creatures who deserved to die in gruesome ways. In reality, there isn't much to distinguish one from the other and it is always those who fight in the name of virtue and justice who commit the gravest crimes of vice and injustice. Life's little ironies always make one feel hopeless. Kavya, meanwhile, had turned away in a huff. She hated it when all in the three worlds failed to agree with her.

'They have only themselves to blame for their predicament,' Bhrigu continued his futile quest to make her see reason, 'and their infamous disdain for the mortals is well known. The Asuras viewed them as their inferiors, filthy parasites who had latched onto Indra's backside and felt perfectly justified in treating them roughly. Brutality is always repaid a hundred fold, I keep telling my students, as is kindness, which is why one must always choose the latter.'

'Spare me the lecture,' she snapped at him. 'Of course, there will be casualties in a war and wrongdoing on both sides. I blame Vishnu for tilting the scale in favour of the Devas. Indra's plans would have come to naught without the so-called Protector egging him on. As for the ill-used humans you keep clamouring about, they *are* parasites and a menace who will prove to be far more of a threat to Bhumi Devi than the combined atrocities of the Devas and Asuras. Mark my words, their rapaciousness makes Indra seem like a saint by comparison!'

'Do you condone the senseless slaughter of humans then?' he asked her softly, watching her flaring nostrils and heaving bosom with admiration even as he continued with his measured discourse. 'As for Vishnu whom you are so quick to blame, he is the restorer of balance,' he lectured her in the same tone he used for his pupils when they were taxing him. 'He will most certainly curtail the excesses of the Devas. There is a reason why he does the things he does, even if the meaning is obscure to most of you. He is Bhumi Devi's beloved and her champion and even his sins are to ensure her well-being.'

'That is most convenient,' Kavya snorted. 'Indra did everything in his power to exterminate his half-brothers and Vishnu did nothing to set right this wrong. I am not saying the Divine Protector is the miscreant that his protégé clearly is, but if Vishnu has a weakness, it is friendship, and if he were as committed to preserving the balance inherent in all things as you claim, he wouldn't favour the Devas so blatantly even if it is ostensibly for his darling consort's sake.' Her face was set in the familiar stubborn lines he adored, but this time it worried him no end.

'Vishnu is not partial. It only seems that way. He knows that the Asuras will have the backing of the Destroyer eventually and you will do well to remember that the path to be followed by Shiva's devotees is the harder one to traverse, which is why Diti's sons are having a difficult time at present. But once the wheel of time has turned fully, they will find themselves on top. And believe me, having emerged triumphant, their rule will be no better or worse than Indra's.'

'Be that as it may, we must help them and provide succour till they are ready to face their brothers again. Winning the favour of Shiva takes aeons as you well know, in addition to entailing untold hardships inflicted on the spirit and extreme mortification of the flesh. At best, one or two will manage it and even then, with Shiva it is hard to say whether one has been cursed with a boon or blessed with a curse. Indra, on the other hand, had to endure no such hardship to win himself such a powerful benefactor. Where is the fairness in any of this? We must help the Asuras. Besides, I promised Diti that we will do our best to help them escape extermination.'

Silently, Bhrigu cursed Diti. Why were mothers so ridiculous when it came to their erring offspring? And why did she feel the need to dump the detritus of their deeds right in the middle of his peaceful ashram? Nothing good was bound to come out of this nonsensical affair. Why couldn't his wife see this?

Neither the Devas nor the Asuras will ever be annihilated entirely, Bhrigu wanted to tell her. In fact, some among them will always find a way past the barriers of hate that separate them and remain on good terms with each other, going so far as to take spouses from the so-called enemy camp. Eventually, they would always neutralize each other while time marched relentlessly on, slowly but surely eroding the magnitude and magnificence of their mighty deeds and misdeeds.

He could have told her all this and more, but he felt there would be no point. Her mind was made up. Besides, his son Sukra had just come home and Kavya rounded on him.

'You have been every bit as helpful as your father,' she scolded. 'Why are you refusing to be their teacher and providing them the guidance they so desperately need? They have offered you the sum total of their wealth and I know that you have a fondness for gold.'

'Gold, silver, precious stones, and all the marvels of the three worlds, not to mention every type of intoxicant there is…' Sukra told his mother, noting with pleasure that she was well and truly riled up. 'As father knows and you refuse to acknowledge, this is a war in which the hostilities are never going to end. Why should I get involved? There are more constructive ways for me to keep myself gainfully employed. It is my intention to leave here before you apply your considerable skills to wear me down into obeying you. The study of alchemy beckons to me and I am going to see if I can perfect the formula to produce all the gold my greedy little heart desires.'

'You are just making excuses because you are secretly scared of Brihaspati…'

Sukra refused to be provoked. 'Neither of us harbour any animosity towards the other, despite people's constant attempts to pit us against each other since when we were children hoping to engage us in an endless pissing contest. Brihaspati is welcome to get involved in this business if he wants to. It is far more trouble than it is worth. As for me, I shall continue with my studies and devote myself to doing exactly as I please.'

'A dutiful son would obey his mother without question.' Kavya sniffed in disapproval.

'I agree, but my mother raised me to have a mind of my own and do what I think is right.'

'This is what I get for sparing him the rod...' she complained to Bhrigu but seemed unwilling to press her point.

At the time, Sukra felt he had successfully walked away from the entire unholy mess. Later, when knee-deep in his favourite intoxicants, he would reveal to the Asuras that in that moment, he had experienced relief and had even gone so far as to pat himself on the shoulder for managing to extricate himself from the existence that fate had planned for him right down to the last detail. At the time, he had been certain that he would lead the life he wanted to and not the one he was meant to. Then he would raise his goblet to the skies and imbibe from it deeply before proceeding to eat and drink himself into a state of blissful oblivion. And his charges would do their utmost to emulate his example.

I have always liked Sukra. And I daresay he likes me as well, though we have been at cross purposes for the most part. But unlike the others, he understood that none of it was personal. That I was so skilled in the art of manipulation, simply because there was never any intent to harm, even if my actions ensured that his charges were relieved of their heads because they had either exploded or been severed from the neck by means of a spinning chakra of the purest gold. For in my arms everyone finds what they look for, and it is only when I release them from the embrace that they suffer. But it has to be done. In order for them to get what they need most rather than what they deserve or what they want. Sukra knew this. Not many do.

Angered by Bhrigu's refusal, Kavya took it upon herself to become their preceptor. Under her tutelage, many among the Asuras were indoctrinated into the subtle and mystical occult arts. While they were a long way off from becoming adepts, some were fairly proficient. It did not do their already fearsome reputation any favours, and the humans driven to hysteria with fear and rage, and angered by their refusal to die en masse at Indra's hands, accused

MOHINI

them of demonical activities.

It was asserted that the Asuras kidnapped pregnant women and virgins to cut out their umbilical cords and unbroken hymens to be used in spells of potent black magic. That they drained the blood of the living to drink themselves senseless before fornicating with wild animals and wanton women on top of corpses. That they gathered skulls and eyeballs from the victims they murdered in cold blood to be used in nefarious necromancy. That they ate the flesh of mortal bodies to add the years of stolen lives to their own accursed ones.

As someone accused of being a practitioner of witchcraft and black magic myself, my sympathies lay with the Asuras. Enamoured people often blame the object of their affection rather than their own weakness, which delude them into thinking that the heights of pleasure are fully worth the abyss of pain that always follows.

On the strength of such spurious claims that lacked veracity on account of there being no corroborative evidence, the Asuras were still being hunted down and killed, though no outrage was generated over their deaths. The humans went so far as to celebrate their deaths with festive cheer and elaborate celebration, foolishly convinced that evil had been extinguished in the world, and going forth, their world would be a happy place free of trouble and turmoil. Even when they were proved wrong repeatedly, they continued to believe. That their wrongs could be righted if only they managed to kill the right people who had wronged them.

However, the Asuras had learned their lesson this time around. They were better prepared and with Kavya's support, they struck back with a vengeance.

Pusan, lord of the pastures and friendly guide to the travellers, was the first to fall, cut to pieces by the Asuras. He had not been one of the aggressors but he had done nothing to stop them either. It made him guilty in the eyes of his half-brothers, who suffered nary a qualm when they slew him. Pusan would never rise again. All that remained of him were forgotten stories that nobody cared to recover and half-remembered hymns, barely preserved in crumbling texts.

Others fell in quick succession. Parjanya, one of the Storm Gods belonging to Indra's retinue, was next. It was a terrible affair. Blood rained down from the skies as Parjanya did not fight for the purpose of survival but to take his enemies with him to whatever awaited on the other side of mortality.

The backlash was swift and the reprisals were savage. Even then, the killing was far from over. Aryaman, Bhaga, Sakra, Dhuti, Savitr and Amsa fell one after the other, consigned to the apocalyptic wasteland of total obliteration. Victims of dark arts that would see them eradicated not just from life but memory as well. And still the Asuras were not done and wouldn't be till they went too far.

I have always wondered why people go too far. Is it because that they recognize that it is preferable to tear oneself apart in the hope of being resurrected anew rather than be torn apart with the faint hope of being reassembled in the junkyards of time with an indiscriminate lack of haste? I can't claim to know for certain. Because, to the best of my knowledge, I neither hurtled towards destruction nor fled pell-mell before it. Instead, I slip between being and non-being, uncaring whether I am awake or dreaming.

The half-brothers had no such luck, trapped as they were in the limbo world of a nightmare. Mitra, the faithful companion of Varuna and dear friend to the mortals, was the next to succumb. They said that it was his passing that led to the irreparable loss of goodwill from the three worlds, which he had done much to promulgate. There were always those who said these things. And though words were wind, they remained after all else was gone past recapture.

As for the one who had survived, he was inconsolable. Not even Agastya and Vashishtha, the sons of Varuna and Mitra conceived in jars when the two friends had shed their seed on beholding the beautiful nymph, Urvashi, could comfort him. The two greatest seers and doers the three worlds had seen, were inconsequential when weighed against a lost friendship. They were living reminders of what had been gained rather than what was lost, but that was never going to be enough.

According to the words carried by the wayward breeze gleaned from forgotten fragments and scattered shards of blurred memories, Varuna had been the sterner one in their role as enforcers and protectors but without his friend's benevolent influence to steady him and unable to withstand the great loss, Varuna went berserk. He laid waste to the bottom of the ocean floors with his almighty trident, the points sharpened on his sorrow, gouging out deep trenches and chasms ringed with fire, from whence he released the deep sea monsters that ranged about in a frenzy of fury and pain that mirrored his own. Forever more, these desolate parts would remain uninhabitable, a testament to his overarching grief.

As for Mitra, he escaped total obliteration, but barely. In the faint echoes of remembrances and recollections of an abiding friendship that harkened back to an earlier time when two birds perched contentedly on the branches of two trees locked together in a perpetual embrace, where the only thing that mattered was the comfort of each other's presence.

Mitra's fate makes me shudder. If friendship cannot prevail forever, then what can? Why then should anybody bother about anything at all? Not even the nectar of immortality can restore that which is lost. It can merely prolong that which is preordained; not help anybody escape the inescapable. And yet, I did my part to put it within the reach of grasping powers. Most choose illusion to escape the harshness of existence and I am not cruel enough to deny them their comforts even if it is little more than inert medication wrapped in an elaborate confection. It is this deceptive delicacy that, powered by belief, acts as a mind-altering drug that can bend the rules of reality just as long as the charade can be maintained, before it crumbles into the sickly sweet nothingness that went into its making.

Soma's end was even more distressing, if that were possible. He too died under mysterious circumstances. Indra blamed the Asuras of course, but that goes without saying. The charming God of the heady sap, who had refused all truck with the violence that had torn the half-brothers and much of the three worlds apart, had been recognized as the distiller of intoxicants, healthy beverages and healing potions.

During the great wars, he had gained infamy for the dreaded crime of remaining utterly neutral and impartial. By ministering to the needs of all who sought him out, Deva as well as Asura, he earned the ire of the powerful on both sides and the eternal regard of those who had thrown themselves upon his mercy and been blessed with his skills. Indra had conscripted Soma's services for his own use but he remained available for those who managed to make their way to him. Soma's overlord accused him of betrayal.

Somehow, he had run afoul of the Asuras too. They were convinced that Soma was pretending to nurse the wounded and fallen among them back to health, when in reality, he was euthanizing them to help Indra's cause.

Soma's personal motivations behind the risky decision to take the middle path in perilous times remains a mystery. He may have genuinely tried to do good or was merely committed to saving his skin regardless of which side prevailed. All that is known is that he disappeared for good. All that remained was the thirst for the intoxicating beverage he had so painstakingly gathered and the need for vengeance. Blow for blow. Blood for blood.

The Death of a Good Woman

It was without doubt the worst thing he had ever done.

Nara disagreed, 'He did what needed to be done...' was what he said in defence of his friend. 'The female of the species keep harping about equal rights, and yet when they are treated just the same, they can't handle it. In his role as the Protector, Vishnu has snuffed out the lives of good men for the greater good. And so it must be for good women as well. He does not deserve to be excoriated for it. And it isn't fair that he has to endure a curse for it.'

Nara held my withering gaze. He liked being the only man who dared to, and took great pride in his ability to withstand the allure of enchantment. It amused me. Narayana had warned him that it was impossible to conquer Maya. Even Shiva, Vishnu, Brahma and every enlightened soul of every age had succumbed to it. But he still liked to think that he was above being ensnared or seduced by beauty, love or power. I knew that he would succumb too, to Lila, the game of the gods, but in that particular reality, I would be too much of a lady to rub it in his face, especially since he would be nursing a broken heart till the spell was lifted. But that is a story for another day.

'I didn't say he deserves to be judged or punished...' I told him patiently, though it was annoying when he tended to treat me as the enemy merely because I happened to be the voice of dissent, 'but it is still necessary to point out that while he felt he was acting in the best interests of the future, his ego did come into play because a female not only defied his express wishes but held her own against him.'

He looked none too pleased with my rejoinder and glanced protectively at his friend, who as always had nothing to say on the contentious subject and liked to pretend that we were talking about someone else, which as a matter of fact we were, since it was Vishnu who had been guilty of the transgression against womanhood. But weren't they a part of each other too? Didn't one have to answer for the sins of the other?

Nara spoke again, 'Bhrigu was wrong to do what he did. But Narayana will take the bitter with the better and create something beautiful even from this most sordid of situations. The three worlds will benefit from his sacrifice. And he will not be alone. I will be with him every step of the way in spirit and flesh.'

'As will I,' I pointed out gamely, 'but none of it alters the fact that he was most foolish to do what he did. Good men are an anomaly but a good woman is an irreplaceable treasure.'

'Now who is being sexist?' he grumbled, rising to take the bait.

But he really shouldn't have killed her. And certainly not in the way he had.

The fallout from all the fratricidal killing was not pretty. Indra wasn't happy about the losses he had sustained. Nor with the fact that the mortals were no longer fully convinced about his infallibility. It felt like their loss of faith was the reason the aura of invincibility he had so carefully cultivated was being chipped away.

'If the Lord of the Heavens cannot keep his fellow celestials safe, then what hope is there for us?'

'Why should we bother with the punishing expenses incurred by elaborate rites for worship, building grand temples and the rest of the ritualistic rigmarole?'

'We might as well cast our lot with the Asuras and raise altars to appease them. Perhaps if we were to sacrifice virgins or whores depending on their preference, we could coax them into sparing us from their cooking pots.'

The humans are an amusing lot. When they are not raising gargantuan monuments to their folly, they are razing the very same to the ground. Indra had to act fast and he rose magnificently to the occasion. Even as his enemies and would-be foes circled around him, he distracted them with the razzle-dazzle of scurrilous scandal and the promise of a fallen woman they could tear to shreds with teeth, fang and claw. Skilfully he directed their attention to Kavya, the woman who had dared thwart his will. She would pay for the lapse. But not before he had relieved her of the armour of respectability she dared to wear with impunity despite her colourful past.

'The Asuras think they are safe hiding behind the skirts of a so-called virtuous woman!' he roared. 'But I will tear it apart to reveal that it is nothing but a stinking sepulchre for vice!'

Indra did keep his word, though he didn't actually rip off her garments, and that was only because Vishnu would never have condoned, let alone supported, such infamy. Instead, he encouraged all and sundry to dwell obsessively on Kavya's 'far from spotless history,' poring over every unseemly detail they could dredge up, not caring that their own pasts were not free from its share of disgraceful conduct and dirty deeds.

'Her lover's name was Puloma and he belonged to the same ilk she has taken under her wing. Bhrigu's wife bestowed her favours freely on him.' *Puloma. Puloma. Puloma.* The wind carried the name to her and she brushed it aside impatiently. *Puloma. Puloma. Puloma.* It hovered about her like a swarm of mosquitoes, buzzing and circling. Eager for an opening to sting.

Puloma. Puloma. Puloma. They all started whispering the name behind her back, some going so far as to refer to her as Puloma. Like an invective that could be hurled to wound and draw blood. Soon there were more barbed words. And more missiles.

'In return for the access he had been granted to her not so sacrosanct body, he taught her the secrets of powerful black magic so potent that whores and witches who sully their hands with it can easily pass themselves off as wives and virtuous women.'

'The wily creature sucked him dry of his arcane arts before carelessly discarding him, having emptied the fool of his usefulness.'

'It wasn't enough that she had mastered the black arts. The vile woman decided she wanted respectability.'

'So she used her ill-gotten powers to draw Bhrigu into her web of deceit and trapped him there to use in a similar way till she gets what she wants, which is everything that is worth having. That woman's appetite is voracious!'

'Her husband's ashram is a den of horrors, full of unspeakable atrocities that are every bit as vile and wicked as she herself is. For shame!'

'She has built a stronghold for the Asuras, many of whom are her lovers, and Bhrigu foolishly protects those who would cuckold him and defile his wife.'

'She was defiled to start with!'

The sneering and sniggering went on and on. Until Bhrigu could stand it no longer. Kavya herself paid no heed to the slander and went about her business with customary good cheer. Words were wind. And she would not dignify their vileness with a response or by allowing them to make her feel bad.

'Ignoring this problem isn't going to make it go away,' her husband insisted.

'I ignored Puloma and he went away, remember?' She smiled bitterly at the memory. Her former lover had refused to accept that their relationship was not the sweeping saga of grand romance he had imagined it to be, but merely a brief and only vaguely interesting couplet. The fool had stalked and harassed her, even attempting an abduction when she was pregnant with her chosen mate's son.

Kavya had been furious. She remembered the feel of his burly arms and how entitled and possessive they had felt while she was being dragged, protesting and struggling, to his chariot. He had been so convinced about his own righteousness and genuinely believed he was doing what was good for both of them. It had been the last straw.

'If you attempt to hold me against my will,' she had said

through gritted teeth, the vehemence in her tone clearly taking him by surprise, which made her angrier still, 'I promise I will spend every waking moment plotting your demise, and when I strike I will miss neither your impotent manhood nor your worthless life!'

She saw the hurt that ravaged his features as though he had been unable to believe the cruelty she was capable of, instantly replaced with the blinding rage that poured forth from the stab wound to the ego. In a fit of pique and fury, he had hurled her from the skies, before leaping to his own death. No doubt he thought this was a fitting epitaph for their doomed love story.

Fortunately a tree had broken her fall. She had grabbed a branch and nearly wrenched an arm, but managed to land safely. Her gritty little baby, Cyavana, had also survived the fall and she had delivered him then and there. It was truly a miracle and she had felt that under the circumstances, she had been truly fortunate. Other women forced into the same position seldom fared as well. But of course it wasn't enough for the judgemental fools who surrounded her.

The murmuring began in earnest when Kavya returned home triumphantly with her son. Questions were raised about the child's paternity and her own virtue. Many were convinced that a powerful rishi's wife could not be assaulted and abducted from her home in broad daylight without her active consent and participation. And since the offender was a former lover, surely she must have tried to elope with him?

Kavya would neither defend herself nor refute the rumours, much to Bhrigu's chagrin. When he brought it up, she became impatient, 'Do you know what it feels like to be kidnapped by a brute you imagined yourself to have been in love with a long time ago? Have you known the agony and guilt you experience for having put your unborn child in peril even if it is through no fault of your own?

'Mercifully, it was a brief episode, but when it happened,

every moment was packed with the excruciating agony of entire lifetimes spent in the darkest of Yama's thousand hells. I cannot change what happened in all that wasted time but I refuse to spend a single moment more, dwelling on or discussing it for the macabre satisfaction of others. What happened to me happened and I choose not to relive it over and over again, thereby prolonging the unendurable misery of that wretched incident. I will not give my deceased tormentor that satisfaction. Mercifully he is gone and I refuse to let the ghost of his memory haunt me and hold me hostage in my own mind and body. I'd rather find a way to be happy and productive. And that is the last thing I have to say on this subject.'

Unfortunately, her husband who meant well, had respected her choice every bit as much as her assaulter had. Bhrigu couldn't bear the calumny and he doggedly worked his spells with words to reconstruct the unhappy incident, working hard to spread the 'truth', charging his disciples with enforcing it with repetition. His charges were happy to oblige. They all loved her well enough to commit themselves to doing something she hated.

Together, these men conjured up images of the impossibly perfect wife, which only they could conceive of—that incredibly pure, improbably auspicious woman who lived solely to serve her husband and devoted her lifetime to fulfilling his every need.

> Of course, Kavyamata (she loathed the honorific every bit as much as she had loathed being called Puloma) had known no man other than her husband. Puloma had been a former suitor who had sought her hand in marriage but had been firmly rejected by her father. Unable to accept this, he had become obsessed with Bhrigu's unsuspecting wife and with the help of an unwitting Agni, the Lord of the Flames, Puloma had carried the hapless object of his affection away.
>
> But her chastity and virtue were the unassailable

fortress and the armour that kept her safe. Puloma had been reduced to ashes and Kavya had floated to safety, made buoyant by the power of her purity and delivered a radiant son who shone with the same undeniable incandescence. As for Agni's role in this affair, he was cursed to devour everything irrespective of whether it was wholesome or not (which was what fire did anyway!). The story was supposed to serve the dual purpose of inspiring women to aspire towards chastity in perpetuity and deterring overly amorous men from assault and abuse.

It irritated me no end. Naturally, all this did was put the pressure on the female of the species to aspire towards a faulty notion of perfection that was impossible to achieve and entirely unnecessary. As for men, they remained men, because hardly anything ever deterred a man caught in the throes of his baser needs. So when women who were kidnapped, raped, and repeatedly abused did not succeed in turning the perpetrators to ash and floating away to safety, they were blamed for their suffering. When in truth, it was the falseness kept alive in a made-up story, passing itself off as the truth that was to blame. And every single male who refused to take no for an answer, of course.

Kavya had hated the elaborate masquerade and was known to comment that men who tried to protect a woman's so-called virtue were nearly as bad and twice as irksome as those who sought to assail it. But she stuck to her own course and refused to dwell on or agitate about any of it. Now that submerged truths, half-truths and outright falsehoods had been dredged up by Indra, she was cast adrift on the tides of calumny yet again.

Bhrigu was furious and more than a little worried. He decided the Asuras were to blame for the evil that had been ushered back into their lives. 'You can't continue to harbour the Asuras here. Not after what they have done! Even you will admit that they have gone too far. Killing Soma and Mitra who had distanced themselves from this infernal conflict and endless bloodletting, simply because they made easier targets when compared to the rest of the bellicose brethren, is unforgiveable. Theirs is a lost cause and they will disappear into the quagmire of ugliness and dark deeds that is of their own making. I will not let them drag you down as well.'

'They claim they had nothing to do with it and that is good enough for me.' She retorted. 'It is not the first time Indra has killed one or two of his own for personal gain and it won't be the last. Besides, I will not turn away those who have come to my doorstep requesting my aid. It is the very least I can do for a good cause even if it is a lost one.'

'That is all very noble of you my dear, but I care more about my wife than a lost cause that serves little purpose. Indra has already started a vicious campaign to smear your good name and hitherto faultless reputation. I am doing everything in my power to undo the damage, but as you know, when it comes to a woman's honour, the slightest hint of scandal is sufficient to ruin entire lifetimes of good conduct.'

'I am aware…' her voice was flinty and there was so much fury in those flashing eyes, Bhrigu stepped back despite himself, 'and you are to blame every bit as much as Indra. I never asked you to take up the hopeless task of championing my virtue! With your excessive efforts to paint me as the perfect woman, all you have succeeded in doing is to validate the vicious rumours because even the stupidest of mortals can sense that a faultless reputation is little more than a carefully constructed facade. I have never felt the need to justify my choices in order to win the approval and approbation of hypocritical males or spiteful females. They can do their worst and I wish them the joy of their ugly words and uglier minds. I refused to be bogged down in the muck with the miserable and the moronic.'

'All that is besides the point at present,' Bhrigu was stung by her retort but he pressed on, 'Indra cannot let the deaths of Mitra and Soma go unavenged. The Asuras know this and it is cowardly of them to use you as a shield against his wrath. They have brought war to our doorstep. Can't you feel the trouble brewing even as we speak? The very air we breathe is heavy with the hint of danger and I can feel it rasping against my insides. Even Indra dare not risk killing a Brahmin or a woman, but I would feel better if Sukra were here.'

'I am here,' Sukra came into their presence, 'to offer what comfort and support I can. Which is why I shall refrain from pointing out that Indra has killed a Brahmin before, unmindful that he incurred the dreaded sin of Brahmahatya in the process. Or that he did attack with the clear intent to kill Usas, the exquisite Goddess of the Dawn, and drove her away from the very heavens that she had ruled over.'

'Is that supposed to scare me? Let the wielder of the thunderbolt show up here if he dares. He will find that unlike Usas, I will not be an easy target.' Kavya's voice dripped with scorn, even as she gathered her son in a tight embrace. 'But it does me good to see your dear unwashed face with the scraggly beard stained with wine and uncombed hair that could easily pass for a nest of serpents.'

Sukra was ready with a witty rejoinder, when Bali, the king of the Asuras, respectfully sought permission to enter. Bali was one of those hulking giants you would expect to stomp you underfoot without warning, but in reality, he was that rarest of souls who combined strength, kindness and a ferocious intellect in equal measure. A veritable gem among the Asuras.

'I seek your apologies, Guruji,' he bowed respectfully. 'We should not have bothered you with our troubles. But it won't be for long now. My people are on the move. In good conscience, I cannot allow these hallowed premises to become a battlefield and a smoking funerary ground. Our scouts have reported that Indra plans to launch a major offensive. The good news is that Vishnu refused to support this endeavour but the bad one is that the serpent King Takshaka has lent his support to Indra. We will draw them far away from here and make an end of this bloody business once and for all.'

It was all very sweet and reassuring. I daresay things would have turned out very differently if only Vishnu had actually followed through on his firm decision not to support Indra in this endeavour. And he *had* been firm on the point. I ought to know.

'I cannot let the deaths of my brothers go unavenged,' Indra thundered. 'By the time I am done with bloody Bali and his bleeding brutes, the vicious manner in which they brought about the deaths of Pusan, Parjanya, Aryaman, Bhaga, Sakra, Dhuti, Savitr, Amsa, Mitra and Soma will seem merciful by comparison.'

Vishnu wagged a finger at him. 'You know very well that I know the Asuras had nothing at all to do with the deaths of Mitra and Soma.'

Indra somehow managed to look discomfited and defiant at the same time but Vishnu was relentless, 'I am not one for apportioning blame but if anyone were to be held responsible, it would be you. As long as Soma was gathering the sticky elixir and brewing his potions for purposes of healing, it was all well and good. But all too soon he discovered that it had other properties too when taken in certain amounts, or mixed with specific ingredients... The blessed nectar could throw open the portals to endless vistas of pleasure so that some among you could submerge yourselves in a delirium of delicious sensations.

'It was just the thing, wasn't it? When the pressure from all the politicking, warring and overindulgence of your appetite for the good things the three worlds has to offer, be it wealth, women or wine, got to be too much? All you had to do was turn to Soma and he could slow things down for you so that you could sedate the senses till they swirled languidly and soothed your frazzled nerves. Or he could amp up the pace to speed up your enjoyment, ramp up your taking of pleasure, all so you could scale the peak of ecstasy and cram in gratification painstakingly gathered over the aeons into a single beautiful moment. Soon you were all addicted to the highs to escape the lows and the lows to escape the highs, with no way of escaping this vicious cycle.

'Before you knew it, even that was not enough. Soma figured out how to further intensify your emotions and enhance the reckless consumption of pure delectation by distorting your reality till it was sublime fantasy that felt far more real than anything ever could, including all that was actually real, till you had dissociated from everything that kept you tethered to the truth, content to drift endlessly on tidal waves of euphoria.

'The warning signs were all there. A crippling numbness of feeling, bouts of delirium and blank states of pitch blackness that threatened to swallow up every memory you possessed whole. An endless see-saw between extreme joy and debilitating sorrow. Sluggish thoughts that urged you to take your own lives and yet none of it nudged you towards caution. Rather, it recklessly prodded you along a path that promised nothing but doom and despair.

'Some among you managed to keep it together, even if barely. Killing is its own intoxicant, as is incessant pleasure-seeking after all, but Soma and Mitra were the unluckier ones. Both died pitifully. The former drowned in the poison he had forced down his throat, which his beleaguered body regurgitated while he was sunk in a coma of deep oblivion. As for the latter, he threw himself from the heavens and plummeted to his death when the rotting bits of his infected brain convinced him that giant rodents had taken his body hostage and were devouring him from inside. Don't you dare place the blame for this monumental folly on the doorstep of the Asuras.'

Indra was seething. 'What happens is never as important as what is perceived to have happened. All that matters is the correct narrative, which can be manipulated into masquerading as the irrefutable truth. It was the Asuras who murdered the blameless Mitra and Soma in cold blood and they will pay for it with their own blood. This is the only truth that shall be peddled. The three worlds and its denizens shall never be allowed to know better. The Devas are infallible. They are the physical manifestation of pure perfection, which not even time shall erode. And so it shall be.'

'Time triumphs over everything,' Vishnu looked at him pityingly, 'and those who seek the truth shall find it despite the best efforts of deceivers. You should let this matter rest. The Devas have killed too many Asuras and the reverse holds true as well. Walk away now while you still can.'

'You know I can't...' Vishnu looked away into the distance. The tiniest of frowns marred the serene tranquillity of his face, rippling across the deep blue of his features. He did know. I have always wondered if he knew the rest of it as well. Knowing him as I do, he probably did. Or not. All that I know for certain is that nothing ever disturbed his equanimity. Except for that one time when he thought he risked losing his inseparable friend and promised to destroy the three worlds in retaliation.

'With you by my side, everything will work out for the best. You will see.' Indra's simple faith in his friend even in the face of his overweening ambition and arrogance was always touching.

'Except I will not be by your side this time,' Vishnu said firmly. 'It is bad enough you attempted to shame and dishonour a brave woman who is simply trying to preserve the balance—the same as I—but you seek to humiliate her further, by destroying the sanctity of her home by drenching it in blood. I will have no part in this.'

'So be it,' Indra shrugged with his trademark insouciant smirk, 'but as you keep pointing out, none of us are in complete control of these things, if at all. War is a bloody business and it was not my idea for Bhrigu's noble-to-a-fault wife to stick her nose in my affairs. Since I can't tear her apart from limb to limb, which is my preferred way for dealing with antagonists, I tore her reputation to shreds instead. It is all fair and above board in the business of killing and the game of power we find ourselves entangled in. And despite what you think, I have no intention of invading her home and tarnishing my reputation or her's further. Mahabali fancies himself too noble to risk it at any rate. We will hash out our differences on the battlefield in the time-honoured tradition and Bhrigu will never allow his precious Kavyamata to risk her life there. It will all be very civilized. You will see.'

There were good intentions all around, given that the concerned parties were fully intent on butchering each other. I may have even been amused if it hadn't turned out to be the carnival of carnage it was!

The half-brothers launched themselves into their preferred sport of war with typical gusto. At this point, let me clarify that the storytellers, in the interests of brevity and simplicity, tend to give the impression that these pitched battles were fought between the Devas on one side and the Asuras on the other. In reality though, over the years, the purity of their bloodlines had proved impossible to maintain, despite the best efforts of hardliners on both sides. Deva and Asura alike had intermarried, choosing spouses from among the rishis, mortals and Nagas. And there was the odd instance of inter-species coupling, which infamously saw the rise of the Buffalo Demon, who had been the scourge of the three worlds before he surrendered at the feet of Durga.

Hence, when it comes to these epic instances of war, it would be more accurate to say that it always comes down to two opposing factions who had more in common than either cared to admit, with both lacking Bhumi Devi's magnanimity when it came to sharing her resources among all who required it with a semblance of fairness.

I always find myself escaping into my thoughts when confronted with the stomach-churning spectacle of violence unfolding before my very eyes. The sight of all those aggressive warriors with their impressive battle regalia locked together in furious combat as the convulsions of battle tore through their ranks in repeated bursts often makes me wonder if even golden peace is worth all this trouble. They remained this way for the longest time. Every move was countered and neutralized, with neither side giving an inch as they fought with everything they had, gaining nothing and refusing to yield anything in the protracted process.

They reminded me of the time Shiva and Parvati remained glued to each other in a passionate embrace with neither remotely inclined to crown their consummation with an explosive climax that would match the frenzy of their lovemaking and hasten it along to a logical conclusion, leading to the bliss of sweet release and blessed sleep. No wonder the denizens of the three worlds had grown restive and breathed freely only after the amorous couple were made to cease and desist from the friction of their incessant coupling and mutual stubbornness when it came to resisting surrender.

The battle would have gone on forever and destroyed everything in creation if it had not been for Indra's canny instincts and his need to manipulate variables in his favour. It was Takshaka, Indra's ally and his serpent hordes, who shifted the tides of battle in favour of the Devas. The shape-shifters and sorcerers confounded the Asuras whose own skills in the dark arts were not sufficient to win back the edge. Felled by the toxins released from bared fangs and befuddled by the effects of the killing spells cast on them, the Asuras began to give ground.

Mahabali was doing his best to rally his warriors when Takshaka engulfed him in his mighty coils. The Asura king fought back with a vengeance, slashing and hacking at those odious coils and scaly armour. Takshaka reared back, bellowing in pain and nearly suffocated his victim with his toxic breath.

Meanwhile, crucial as this event was, with two kings going hammer and tongs at each other, the outcome of the battle would hinge on a fight to the death being played out a good distance from the battlefield. At that precise moment, the naga spy made his move.

Kavya had been monitoring the situation with the help of Bhrigu's yogic vision, which she had appropriated for her own use. He had indulged her whim as always, when his warning that she was better off not seeing or hearing the evil unfolding all around them was ignored.

'Those blasted Nagas are using their foul powers indiscriminately to prevail over the Asuras. They are refusing to give quarter or spare even those Asuras who have thrown down their weapons in surrender. Indra's orders, no doubt. Damn the Lord of Thunder! He never fights fair. Sukra, you must go to them and...' she began, but stopped as he dissolved before her astonished eyes. Even Bhrigu stood slack-jawed with shock and horror for long seconds he could not afford to spare in light of the crisis.

A monstrous creature remained where Sukra had been standing. Faster than thought, the monstrous reptile had incapacitated Bhrigu with a blow of a mighty tail to the unsuspecting head that stunned him, before tightening its coils around his person. Its scales glistened, as the coils worked slowly, squeezing the life out of him even as a fang the size of a mighty sword and dripping with venom appeared poised to sink into an exposed vein on her husband's neck. The powerful sage's eyes were glazed and unseeing, helpless against the enchantment that held him in its thrall. Cast by the traitor who had insinuated himself into their home in the guise of their own son!

Kavya felt the same dread and cold terror she had experienced on the day Puloma had abducted her, not for her own safety but on behalf of someone she loved more than anything else. For a long moment, it held her paralysed before dormant rage exploded out of her in an overpowering rush.

The magic painstakingly gathered from accumulated studies, discipline and devotion came alive within her then and she could feel it bubbling and surging in her blood, pouring forth from the white heat of her rage, dissolving the fear, uncertainty and hurt. Kavya shuddered with revulsion when she realized that she had held the imposter in her arms with gladness in her heart as she took in well-loved details of her son, which the shape-shifter had carefully replicated.

She expelled her breath in a hiss and the serpent started in surprise. It was the last thing he did before exploding into a billion pieces, torn apart by the power of her dark arts, which left him reduced to less than nothing. Shockwaves reverberated across the three worlds from the impact of her fury and the power she wielded.

The very heavens recoiled as the full extent of her magic boiled forth from the molten core of her rage in a burst of deadly smoke and vaporous fumes, storming into the world outside their little haven with furious intent. The inky tendrils overwhelmed the sun and plunged them all into pitch darkness. Having absorbed the light, they surged over the heaving mass of bodies and writhing snakes, expertly passing over Kavya's adopted sons and their allies to wrap the Devas and Nagas in a somnambulant trance as they were paralysed mid-action—engaged as they were in hurling missiles and inflicting all manner of hurt—reduced to a frozen tableau of terror.

Mahabali was the first to respond, infected by the vicious intensity of his Kavyamata's unstoppable anger. He sounded the battle call and led the Asuras in a renewed charge against their helpless foes. Hefting their weapons, they hacked the heads off the offending snakes and their not-so-dear half-brothers. Some tore out fangs and used it to gouge out eyes stiff with horror. They chopped off limbs and drenched themselves in the sprays of thick blood even as mouths remained locked in the rictus of a silent scream. The Devas remained frozen and impotent. Unable to defend themselves, surrender, plead for help, or beg for mercy.

Kavyamata witnessed it all and she couldn't desist, driven by the demons she had denied and buried in the fathomless depths of her unacknowledged pain. Her masterpiece of rage and vengeance was all that mattered and she would complete it. No matter the cost.

Stop it! Stop it! Stop it!

Was it Bhrigu who was screaming at her? Was it the voices in her own head that were clamouring so shrilly that her head hurt? Either way she refused to listen.

Kavyaaa! Stop it! You have lost all control. They are helpless as children. You can't allow them to die like this. It is not right. She would not listen.

Stop it! This is madness! She didn't want to listen.

You are the bitch everybody accused you of being! Butcher bitch! That made her happy; she wasn't inclined to listen to the voices from within and without, urging her to stop.

Indra's teeth were bared in a snarl. How ferocious he looked! How filled with hate! Yet he was so handsome and strong. Mahabali looked demented as he raised his battleaxe to make an end of him once and for all. How good it would feel to kill him, the rabid cur that he was!

She could smell his despair. Feel his terror. His helplessness. He deserved it. Oh, how he deserved it! The time had come for him to die and disappear into the deep pit of damnation where he belonged. Women would be safe from the likes of him. They wouldn't be attacked and chased away from their own homes. They would no longer be maligned or have their reputations besmirched with vicious rumours to justify the atrocities they had been made to suffer. The likes of him would no longer stalk, harass, abuse, violate or use women as puppets in their games of power. Women would no longer be afraid of running afoul of the almighty male ego.

Indra had to die. Die! Die! Die! She wanted to spend the aeons killing him so he would never rise again.

'That is enough, Kavya.' The voice shattered her euphoric reverie. Why was this one different from the rest? Why was she listening to this one alone? The voice was calm and even. She recognized it. Why did it make her happy even as she could feel herself bristling with outrage? Far in the distance, she saw the whirring of a golden orb. The slow spinning of the deadly, serrated edges was mesmerizing as it got closer and closer. Closer and closer. She felt time slow down.

'You are right. He deserves to die. But not today. I will not allow it.' His voice was soothing but the words... He would not allow it? She felt the unspeakable rage flare again. Another bloody male who dared think he could stop her but couldn't be bothered with curtailing the excesses of his foul friend. How they stuck up for each other! Why couldn't they ever do the same for the women and children who needed them more?

'We all do what we can for each other. No more. No less. We are the sum total of good deeds and bad. Even Indra. Spare him, Kavya. His time has not come. There is no peace at the end of foul deeds, even if it is justified. Or necessary.'

Why was she listening to this charming charlatan? How had he managed to make her stay her hand? Why hadn't Mahabali's battleaxe made an end of things? Why had time slowed everywhere save the inside of her head?

What was it he had said? Yes! She remembered. He would not allow her to kill Indra the way he deserved to die... She would see about that.

The rage flared and erupted out of her in a final burst of absolute power. Thick palls of smoke descended on the frozen Nagas and Devas, tearing them to bits and pieces. She ignored the dying. It was Indra she wanted. But something was blocking her vision. Kavya gnashed her teeth in frustration. Damn Vishnu! Damn him to Yama's thousand hells. She would kill Indra and his accursed brethren if it was the last thing she did.

'I told you to stop! I pleaded with you to stop!' The voice was sorrowful over the incessant whirring.

'Make me!' She was surprised to hear the pleading note in her own. Where had the defiance gone? Where was the anger? She needed both to see things through to the end. What was he doing to her? And why was she surrendering?

The golden disc sliced her throat cleanly. It was surprising to note that there was no pain. It merely felt like she had been opened up to release the floodwaters of her anger. An outlet for the pain to gush out of her in a torrential outpouring of red blood to relieve the pressure that had built up inside her to such unbearable levels. Already she was feeling better.

She saw her husband's face. His arms were outstretched. He was crying copious tears and seemed to be pleading with someone. She wanted to comfort him. *It is not as bad as it looks. I feel better now.*

Then she spotted Sukra! It was really him this time. He was tearing across the distance to reach her side. He was weeping too. The sight tore at her heart. If only she had been allowed to really hold him in an embrace and take in the sight of that dear unwashed face with the scraggly beard stained with wine and uncombed hair that could easily pass for a nest of serpents. How grateful she was for having had the privilege of being his mother!

They cradled her in their arms tenderly. So many tears. She wished she could wipe them away and console them. Mahabali was howling with grief like a wild animal, 'Mother! Forgive me! This was my fault!' *Of course it was your bloody fault! You should have swung that battleaxe when you had the chance! Quickly and unerringly so that it would have been Indra's head that was rolling in the dirt.* She was glad he couldn't hear her. And she didn't mind too much about Indra either.

The Asuras were all wailing in unison. Even the Devas were crying over her remains. Indra looked pained. Before he regained his perfect composure, his handsome face was flushed with shame and regret. *Get a hold of yourselves! I am going to be just fine. And it is nobody's fault. Not even Indra's. Or Vishnu's.*

Kavya could feel the rage building in her husband's chest and her son's. *No! Don't let the anger gain control! It will consume you the way it did me. Believe me! Not even revenge is worth it.*

'Vishnu!' Bhrigu spat out the name. 'This foul deed will not go unpunished and you will rue the day you killed a blameless woman. For this gravest of crimes, you shall make atonement. Ten times you shall take birth among the mortals and suffer the same vices and vicissitudes of fate that we all do. Forever more you will be condemned to search futilely for peace even as you engage in the darkest of deeds, trapped in an endless circle of mass murder, bloodshed and rank destruction that will preclude the passing of the ages. Doomed to float on an ocean of tears and angry recrimination till the cycle begins anew.'

Her husband's serene features were contorted with bestial rage unlike Vishnu's, which was as perfectly serene as it always was.

His composure seemed to gall Sukra no end. 'Don't think you can escape punishment just because you have perfected the art of detachment and are no slave to desire. Over the course of the incarnations, my father has condemned you too, it shall be your lot to sup from the same cup of suffering and loss that the rest of us are condemned to!' Sukra's chest was heaving with the weight of the crushing sorrow and rage.

Don't do this on my account. All who pronounce a curse suffer as much as the one who has been cursed. Let go of your pain. I will come back to both of you. Our love is too strong. We will not be parted forever. Believe me!

None of them could hear her. But her words would not be uttered in vain. They would find their way into their hearts and comfort them, till the blessed moment when they would all be reunited.

'So it shall be!' Vishnu's tone was unchanged.

Vishnu turned to her with a bow, seeking her forgiveness.

You did what had to be done. I would be the first to admit it.

'I wish I didn't have to.'

I wish he hadn't too. There would never be another like Kavya. I remember thinking that as I watched her husband and son cradling her mangled remains rendered unrecognizable by the blood, dust and tears in the middle of a formerly peaceful haven that had been lit up by the radiant presence of an extraordinary woman, who cared too much and too deeply about fixing broken things.

Crime and Consequences

Amrita. What was it about the nectar of immortality that exerted such considerable allure for the Devas and Asuras? But they felt the same way about me as well—Mohini, the enchantress they all wanted to imprison within the narrow confines of their lives so they could grow fat on a surfeit of pleasure and fulfilment. Their desperate need was so great that they were prepared to chase after this impossible dream for the rest of time. In fact, it was the only thing ever before and ever after that would convince them to set aside their differences in order to unite for a common cause—to possess and hold the key to lasting life and its attendant pleasures in the palm of their hands.

Some assume that this obsession began when they began their games for total dominion and realized how evenly matched they were, forcing them to acknowledge that when death and decomposition claimed them, they stank as badly as the lowly humans. Others claim that the search for a magic elixir that could fix all ills after a delicate sip or two began with a dastardly deed that claimed the life of a good woman who was only trying to help, and triggered off a chain of events that would have far-reaching consequences for the three worlds.

I believe it is a little of both, but also the incontrovertible fact that they were running scared, terrified, despite themselves, of their capacity for ruination not just with regard to their worlds but for self-destruction as well. Despite their bravado, the Devas, Asuras and the mortals are like children who are scared senseless of the dark. Except the darkness that terrifies them is death, Mrtyu. They even deal with it the same way that children do, by creating imaginary friends who would stand by their side, every moment of every day, across the yugas, ever ready to battle monsters, chase away the encroaching darkness, offer unconditional support and endless comfort, listen to the minutest, most boring, petty, insipid and intimate details of a humdrum life with total absorption and share in the laughter as well as the tears.

The warring half-brothers were keen to take this further though. Both sides sought to make real this imaginary companion from the dream world in which their champion against approaching death had been conjured up. After all, the entirety of creation had emerged from Brahma's mind, simply because he had managed the divine feat of willing them into reality, by blurring the borders between all things that stood at opposite ends of the spectrum—light and dark, sanity and delirium, sleep and waking, life and death—while seated comfortably on a lotus blossom that sprang forth from Vishnu's navel.

It seemed obvious to them that such a smudging of hitherto clearly defined boundaries, which would enable them to make an imaginary character real, would also allow them, the dreamers, to escape into the dream where the rigid concepts of time and space were permanently relaxed, within the confines of which they could live forever. And best of all, they need never worry about dying in gory ways with ruptured bowels, smashed skulls and ripped-off appendages.

The half-brothers arrived at the same conclusion from opposite directions. One lot remained convinced that all they had to do was churn their consciousness till it yielded up the sticky discharge, the precious Amrita. It was this philtre that animated all of creation, sparked the flow of life across inert nerve endings and greased the wheels of existence itself.

Soma had gathered it for them before, using his skill in divining the silent trickle of this special substance inherent in all living creatures with disastrous results for himself and his brothers. But if the same substance was manifested from the mind, then they could imbibe it safely without risking addiction and a painful, ignominious death.

The others felt that their saviour had to be the lost mother

MOHINI

figure, their Kavyamata, who had kept them safe without a care for her own safety. If they could bring her back to life, she would have managed to elude death and live forever and usher them towards eternal life as well. All they had to do was to gather the best bits from every woman in the three worlds and create a composite of stolen perfection, for that was what Kavyamata had been in life. To them at least.

They throbbed with the excitement of it all and patted themselves on the back for finally having figured out a way to triumph over the looming spectre of death that had previously dogged their every footstep in life like a particularly relentless ghoul. For the first time since the passing of Kavyamata, they all dared to feel the tiniest bit better. It was a definite improvement over how things had been when she had fallen, claimed by a merciless golden discus wielded by one whose role it was to protect and in which capacity, he found it necessary to kill. Perhaps the quest for immortality did begin with the death of a good woman.

There was a suspension of hostilities as Mahabali and Indra called for a truce. They agreed to go their separate ways and have as little to do with each other as possible. No mention was made of the fallen among them, though neither had made their peace with their losses or forgiven each other for inflicting said losses upon them. But for the moment at least, they would bury their grievances and give themselves time to rest. Neither side said it, but they needed to prepare for the next great confrontation that was inevitable.

'It is an exhausting business to take birth, live and die among the mortals.' I tried to be sympathetic, though I did feel Vishnu had earned the curse. 'What's worse is that Sukra was most insistent that you be made to suffer. Until then, I was concerned that the curse was a mere formality, neatly aligned with the role you have been chosen to play in preserving the cosmos.'

Vishnu didn't answer at first and I was expecting one of his non sequiturs. He didn't disappoint. He hardly ever did.

'Given your love for stories, let me tell you one of my favourites. As you probably know, love that burns with too intense an ardour and too bright a flame burns itself out all too quickly. But there was once that rarest of lovers who mastered the miraculous feat of loving each other to perfection with just the right degree of all things needed to sustain such a rare and precious state of pure bliss. They lived their immaculate romance for millions of years. Entire kalpas passed but their love remained fresh without ever fading. Their love was such that it was all that was needed to sustain them forever and ever, it seemed. Even merciless death softened in their presence and could not bring itself to claim either life. And yet nothing lasts forever. Not even the rarest of rare love stories such as theirs.'

He fell silent. And I waited with bated breath, impatient for him to finish contemplating whatever it was he was contemplating and get on with it. Later, I realized he was giving me time to compose myself. It was strange but hearing that wondrous tale made me feel things I didn't know I was capable of feeling. It made me yearn so achingly, so desperately, it actually hurt. I felt the pain as a physical pang. In fact, of all the stories I have loved and lived in, this one had become my favourite even as I heard it. Forevermore, it was my fondest hope that this would be the one story that would claim me, swallow me up whole and never set me free. I loved it so much I didn't ever want it to end.

'It did end,' he said with the detachment that was so often tinged with cruelty. 'They lived their dream and even got their wish to die in each other's arms. A light had gone out and the entire cosmos was suddenly a sadder place, colder and with less hope. The three worlds with their inhabitants mourned their passing, the elements sang a lament in their honour and gathered the ashes they were reduced to with the intent of preserving their essence across the annals of time.'

MOHINI

'What happened next?' I asked him urgently, not daring to breathe, for I feared I already knew the answer.

'Nothing. Time claimed their remains and left not the faintest trace behind. It was the greatest love story the three worlds had seen and it had defied time to last as long as it had. But time marched on anyway till nothing remained. No names, no charming quirks, no particulars, no remembrance. Not even in the archives of ancient memory. Now it is merely a forgotten story I barely take the time to remember.'

I said nothing. 'Imagine that? All the love in the world and it disappeared as if it never had been, exactly the same as violent hate, kindness, generosity, sacrifice, heroism, or even an epic struggle for immortality or mere survival. It makes you wonder, doesn't it?'

Bhrigu was inconsolable and utterly distraught with grief. Sukra was desolate as well, but he remained resolute. 'It is not enough...' he mused aloud to his father, who looked at him with dull, grief-stricken eyes that suddenly hardened with fury.

'Yes, I could have done more to keep her safe. I should have done more than slap Vishnu on the wrist with a curse...'

'In retrospect, it seems the curse serves his purpose better than ours. Which is why more is needed. Mother wanted me to become the preceptor of the Asuras and I have decided to honour her wish. Mahabali is delighted with my acceptance of the post.'

Bhrigu shook his head vehemently, 'It may have been what she wanted, but Kavya was killed because she allowed herself to get sucked into this ceaseless conflict that shall never end. I couldn't bear for the same to happen to you.'

'It won't happen to me,' Sukra reassured his father, 'For one thing, a peace has finally been brokered.' But he didn't sound too convinced. Of course, his very existence would hitherto be defined by the clash between Deva and Asura but he was determined that it would still be his own.

'A temporary truce,' Bhrigu pointed out.

Sukra nodded in acknowledgment. 'But it is a valuable respite from war and I shall use it well. For the moment, I will devote myself to my students and teach them some of the things they need to master, if they are going to survive against the might of Vishnu and Indra. At the very least, they won't make for such gullible targets in the future. Mother would have liked me to do at least this much for the Asuras before I leave…'

Something in his voice made Bhrigu look up. 'Leave? Where will you go?'

'I will go where none before me has managed to go. It is a path none dare take because in all of living memory, none have returned successfully. Those who seek death inevitably find it, but they have never managed to conquer it.'

'Mrtyu…' Bhrigu breathed the word with dread. 'Brahma created her in a bygone age, at the suggestion of Rudra when he feared for life itself because there was no death. None of his mind-born children would die, and time stretched out in an endlessly, barren landscape that offered little to savour. The beings he had created grew bored, and in their restlessness were meaner than was usual to each other and themselves.'

He took a deep breath. 'Brahma had to save his creation. So he created Mrtyu. Her job was only to kill without exception and arbitrarily. In the beginning, she wept. Her's was a thankless job and she hated the grief, loss and tears she left in her wake. But now she doesn't look back as much. Nor does she cry. She knows now that death is inevitable. And there is nothing anybody can do about it.

Thus Brahma saved all of his beloved creation. And it earned him little more than the resentment of his children who have hated him ever since. For giving life and releasing death among the living. Because it is Mrtyu who rules over us all now. With an iron fist. Why would you seek her out?'

'You have told me this story many times, Father. And it was

you who told me about Mrityu Sanjivani. I will go in search of this marvel, Shiva's most closely guarded secret, to resurrect the dead, and I will learn this craft even if it takes my life.'

Bhrigu shook his head wearily. 'Perhaps I should have emphasized that sometimes a story is just a story. I could urge you to give up this poisonous dream. I could go so far as to point out that there is no certainty that this mysterious craft exists. That if it did, Shiva would have used it to resurrect his beloved Shakti… But I can see your mind is irrevocably made up. Kavya would not have wanted this for you. Or for herself. I beg you to remember this if nothing else.'

Sukra blinked away his tears. And he went on his way. Bhrigu watched him with a heavy heart. But he understood why Sukra felt he had to do this for her. Their Kavya.

I didn't. Everybody dies. It is best to accept the fact. Instead of determinedly going after that which is gone. For good. Besides, if it hadn't been for Sukra's grit and stubbornness, Indra wouldn't have felt the need to embark on his own quest for the nectar of immortality and dragged Vishnu along with him. Or me.

Bringing Back the Dear Departed

Later, they, who always insist they know what they are talking about, even if they don't, said Sukra regretted the destination he had chosen for himself. It was one of the many reasons he tried his darndest to drown himself in wine and just about anything that was its equivalent. But I don't think he regretted the journey he undertook to chase down death. After all, it was a merry dance that Mrtyu led him on!

Thousands of years passed in a feverish bout of frenzied activity interspersed with soul-cleansing stillness. Pain beyond endurance, pleasure that consumed him whole, and peace that transcended both. He journeyed through rocky mountainous terrain, ascending the highest peaks into the very hearts of the storm clouds feasting on flesh, fish and the strongest of wines.

He cavorted his way through shady vales of abiding beauty that he defiled by dancing drunkenly with woodland nymphs and carousing with all who came to join in the debauched revels. He roamed the ocean floor, communing with the creatures of the deep, and the weird, deformed beings who had made the punishing depths their home. Long years passed as he lived with them and learned their ways, teaching himself to endure every kind of hardship and forego all want.

When he returned, the humans worshipped him as a god, for his powers had grown considerably. Sukra had accumulated vast stores of treasure, amassing a fortune the likes of which had never before been seen in the three worlds. His love for filthy lucre was well known but he distributed every single thing he had painstakingly gathered among the Asuras as well as the humans, keeping nothing at all for himself.

Then there were the stories of unbridled passion. Having emptied himself of need, he proceeded to fill himself up to the brim with personal fulfilment and sensual satisfaction. He spent a thousand years sporting with the nymph Visvachi to his heart's content, unwilling to disentangle himself from her embrace. Their overindulgence in carnal delights saw them burn through even his vast stores of ascetic merit and the lovers plummeted from the heavens to the harsher realms of the humans trapped in the body of a lamb and a man, respectively. Even so, their passion continued unabated and they carried on with their frenzied lovemaking, uncaring of the censure and infamy till it finally burnt itself out and left them cold. To the best of my knowledge, neither of them regretted a single moment.

His voracious appetite was legendary but so was his capacity for enduring extreme privation. He roamed the deserts naked and exposed to the elements without a morsel of food or a drop of water to sustain him. The flesh melted off his bones and he hung himself by the heels with thorns, dangling over enormous pyres that devoured the dead, remaining that way as the years rolled on.

How keenly alive he felt as he grappled endlessly with death, his mind freed from the limitations of his body, which had been wracked with gut-wrenching agony and dragged to the final frontiers of pain, beyond which it succumbed to blessed numbness. In the heat of the towering flames and the thick palls of smoke, he finally danced with Mrtyu, balanced on the knife edge between salvation and damnation.

There was a lightness to her movements as she spun in tandem with him, her tongue darting out, teasing and ruby red, as she drew closer to him, her lips grazing his, before pulling away and dancing just out of his reach. Always she stayed clear of his grasp. But he wouldn't give up. And they twirled round and round even as the funerary smoke swirled around the duo, concealing little and revealing a lot.

'Everybody runs away from me...' she told him seriously. 'Not that it does them any good. Why do you persist in this foolishness? You do it for love, which is the best of intentions, and yet, it will lead to the worst of consequences. If you are wise, you will walk away with everything you have won, having accepted your loss.'

'I am not wise,' Sukra insisted, seeing himself from a great distance. A scrawny creature with dangling genitalia perspiring from the flames, caked in his own filth, breathing in the suffocating scent of death and decomposition, blathering on to himself in a feverish delirium. It was not a pretty sight. 'And I will not walk away. Not when my loss hurts worse than I can bear and robs the sweetness from every one of my successes.'

'Do you love her that much?' she asked him curiously. After all she had seen, she no longer felt anything. But Sukra had made her feel something. And she was so happy it was pitiful. She would have taken him, if she could have kept him. 'It happens with mothers and sons. But you are no longer doing this for her. This is mostly about yourself. And your ego. Time has dulled the edge of your pain and too much water has flowed under the bridge. But you stubbornly insist on persisting, simply because you will not be denied your urges. Even the worst of them.'

'I have to bring her back. It was a promise made when I arrived too late to help her. But it is no longer only about that. This is what I was born to achieve. I can feel it in my bones. And I am going to succeed. For I cannot go back without fulfilling my life's mission.'

'Are you sure about that? Death will ensure that you move forward at any rate, instead of spinning around in circles. Everybody is scared because they don't know what awaits them on the other side. Nobody does. But I do know that it is no better or worse than life.' Her hypnotic gaze dwelled on him for a long moment. And then she disappeared in a puff of smoke.

'Wait…' he cried out, but it was too late and he found himself falling into the gaping chasm that opened beneath him, straight down the gullet and right into the belly of the unknown beast. Rank terror engulfed him as the blackness closed about him in a suffocating embrace.

In all of his journey, that was the closest Sukra came to breaking. He would have too, if he hadn't been so consumed by his compulsion. Besides, he realized he wasn't alone. It took him a while to understand. But he did. Once he allowed the panic to ebb and focused on the many shades of black he was engulfed in, deep in the heart of Shiva. The Destroyer. And sole possessor of the secrets of Mrtyu.

What am I doing? And why am I doing this? Why is it so important that I bring my mother back? He wasn't sure he knew. All he knew was that he hadn't saved her once. And he had promised himself that there wouldn't be a second time.

She hadn't been the perfect mother. There were days when she had been overwhelmed. When she had lost her temper. When she had threatened to give him away to the first passing beggar. And meant it. And yet, she had been his mother. Not once had he been made to feel that he wasn't the son she had carried in her womb. She had always been *his* mother, though many felt compelled to point out that she was the stepmother.

The memories surged through him.

The little boy with the skinny legs and the determined chin ran like his very life depended on it. He ran faster than he ever had before, despite knowing that he could never hope to catch up with the man who had carried away his mother. The stranger who had barged into their home and dragged her away as if he had all the right in the world.

She had been serving him a meal. Rice with brinjal and a chicken gravy she had simmering on the stove for hours, making his mouth water. It was his favourite. She had urged him to have a second helping and had been fanning him while he ate. It was her way of making it up to him after giving him the sharp edge of her tongue. He had been bitterly jealous of the unwelcome baby who had staked a claim to his mother's body. The damn thing kept her up at nights with his incessant kicking and made her sick. Poor mother was so tired and miserable all the time. 'You would feel better—we would all feel better—if that baby were to go away.'

He had only said what they were all thinking. But she had frowned at him. 'You are never to speak that way again, unless you want me to whip your buttocks bloody.'

He knew she felt bad for hurting his feelings and this was her way of making it up to him. The food was so good, he forgave her immediately. She was not so bad, his mother. Tired though she was because of the baby that made her stomach so bulky, she had still made the time to cook him his favourite meals, play with him and tell him all the stories he demanded. It made him happy when she led him to believe he was his whole world. Even if it wasn't true. There were others in their world. His father, his students, her assorted friends and relatives and now this idiotic baby. He wished he didn't have to share her with anybody.

And now there was this loathsome stranger, who had boldly demanded that she leave them all. For him. The nerve of that man! With his barrel-shaped body, thick arms that looked like tree trunks and that ugly bushy moustache that barely hid his fat lips. He wanted to get up and beat him to death.

'Sukra! Concentrate on your food and finish every bite!' She was speaking softly, in order not to alarm him. 'I don't want you to waste anything, do you hear? Everything is going to be just fine.'

He had been angry with her then. She was lying. But he felt compelled to listen and obey. So he ate every mouthful. It always made her happy when he savoured every bite and polished off the entire meal she had prepared for him. His fingers were shaking but he chewed through mouthfuls of food. And swallowed. There were snatches of conversation. There had been a struggle.

'Take your dirty paws off me before I chop them off and hurl it into the flames...'

'You are mine. You always were...'

'Don't you dare do this...'

'...another man's child... you belong to me alone.'

'Don't... not in front of my son...'

'...not yours...'

He continued eating. Swallowing the food, forcing it past the anger and the lump of tears. He stopped only when he had finished. By then the monster had dragged her away from their home. She was struggling and fighting. But her oppressor was so much bigger and stronger. He held her easily. The man forced her into his chariot and it rose into the heavens.

He ran. Even though there was no point. He would never be able to keep pace. He would never be able to catch up. He ran anyway. He knew he wouldn't stop running even if his heart burst asunder, the way it was threatening to. He knew he wouldn't stop till he found her.

He was determined to keep on running. For thousands of years, if that was what it took. Something told him he would find her if he kept looking. So he did. And he had been right. He did find her. She lay still and unmoving. He couldn't move. Then something moved. It was a tiny fist. She was holding the ugly creature it belonged to close to her chest. He heard the sounds of suckling. Ordinarily it would have made him angry. But he was so happy to see her, he didn't even mind the ridiculous, mewling thing latched to her breast.

She had been happy to see him too. And had stopped

crying immediately. 'Did you finish eating?' she asked him. He nodded. She was pleased. He could tell. They walked home together. He handed her the cloth he had tied around his waist when he noticed her shivering. Her garments were torn. And covered in blood. She thanked him and used it to swaddle the stinking brat in her arms. 'Your little brother has arrived safe and sound. His name is Cyavana. Aren't you glad to see him?'

'Yes.' He lied. But it was okay. They did that now. He was glad to see her. Even if it was with a baby.

'Mother had a fall,' she told him consolingly, 'and I was a little hurt. But mostly it is dirt.' She was lying again. But he forgave her. She had placed her hand on his shoulder. And she didn't take it off till Father found them.

The memories comforted him and gave him strength. Where had the doubt come from? It was all so simple. He would just keep going till he found her again. He had to.

Sukra never talked about his time in the Destroyer's belly. Some say that he continued with his austerities and focused his entire being on the Three-eyed God, till he earned his favour. In an unparalleled act of generosity, Shiva had released him and taught him the secrets of the Mrityu Sanjivani craft and rewarded him with all the precious stones in the world when he mastered it perfectly, as a mark of his high regard.

Those who like their stories to be messy and complicated say that Shiva was not remotely pleased to have Sukra wondering about his insides, swimming in his blood, and clambering into his cavernous mind to explore and study its most intimate and closely guarded secrets. The Destroyer forcibly ejected the alien presence through his penis and would have killed him, if Parvati had not interceded and insisted he spare his life.

'He is a part of you, now that he has emerged from your being. In fact, he is like a son and it would never do for you to kill another one of those.' She was referring to the time when Ganesha, who had been created by a defiant Parvati after a marital spat, had been relieved of his head when Shiva lost his own in the extreme throes of rage.

Now, thanks to her intercession, Shiva had given in and spared Sukra. The former resident of his insides had been released along with the precious knowledge he had sought.

It is hard to be certain about the veracity of either version, but I do know that the incendiary Mrityu Sanjivani he had come for was something that required careful handling and a whole lot of soul-searching. Sukra remains the only one who balanced on the knife-edge of life and death, going as far as he needed to in order to achieve the impossible and relegate the inevitable to the distant future.

'Irksome little thing, aren't you?' the Destroyer's voice boomed in his ear. But he sounded kind. Quite unlike one who had once ripped off Brahma's head or turned Kamadeva, the gentle God of Desire, to ash.

'I have to do this...' Sukra tried to find the words to explain, but Shiva interrupted.

'What is it that you think the Mrityu Sanjivani does? I'll be disappointed if you think it merely brings the dead back to life, nice and easy with nary a consequence.'

Sukra hesitated. Was the Destroyer trying to scare him? All he knew was that he wanted his mother back. A nagging worry gnawed at him. He would get her back and it would be just the way it had been, wouldn't it? And that was not all, he would use his newfound skill to help others as well. His was a worthy cause. Wasn't it?

'Why didn't you use this craft to bring your lost Shakti back?' he asked him instead. That was the question. Why hadn't he? Everybody knew how he had gone berserk and demented with grief when she had self-immolated. Surely it would have been a simple matter for him to restore her to life?

'Because it would not have made a difference,' Shiva told him simply. 'Death's work can never be undone in perpetuity. Shakti made the decision to leave me, leaving me with no choice but to accept her decision even though I railed against it with every fibre of my being. And even if I had used the Mrityu Sanjivani to bring her back to me, it would have been at best a temporary measure and at its worst, stolen moments of togetherness before the sword fell and tore us apart again. The mantra merely appropriates the years from another life and in subsequent lifetimes, my time with her would be cut shorter than was preordained and I would have lost her all over again.

'When the irrevocable working of death or time is tampered with, a heavy debt is incurred and it must be paid back in the future with a crippling interest. That was not something I could allow or bear. All I had was hope and her promise that we would be together again. So I held on to that and waited, even when the pain of parting was so great that I died a thousand deaths.'

The words sank in. But Sukra was obstinate. 'I have lived a hundred lifetimes and will live hundreds more. All I know is that it is not wise to remain bogged down by the deeds of the past or imperil my entire existence by investing only in an improbable future that is yet to be determined and is, therefore, insubstantial as smoke. That is no way to live. In this lifetime, this life and its requirements are all that matter. The problems from the past must be fixed in the now in order to prevent them from spilling over into subsequent lifetimes. As for the future and the implications you pointed out, they can always be dealt with in good time.'

'Aren't you the clever one though?' Shiva was sardonic. 'You have it all figured out. But whether you choose to acknowledge it or not, all things in creation are weighed down by the accumulated deeds of the past. Every action is the result of the one before, and the future is only that which is shaped by the present.'

'Be that as it may, I can live neither in the past nor the future, and therefore, I care solely for the present. If my actions do lead to further loss in the future and I have to undo them all over again over the course of infinity, then perhaps I shall find a way to do so. Whatever it takes, over and over again.'

'That is easier said than done. Rare feats are rare simply because they cannot be replicated at one's convenience. Remember that, if nothing else. And if you feel inclined to think you will be welcome in my insides whenever you see fit to trespass, allow me to issue a fair warning.'

Sukra heard the mocking laughter and braced himself for impact. But he was falling. Hard and fast. Dropping through space, like a stone. His stomach gave out under him and he found himself pinwheeling wildly. Just when he was convinced that he was going to plummet to his death with his remains splattered across the Earth Mother, the storm winds snatched him up and cast him into the eye of the storm where the forked lightning and thunder, with the aid of high-velocity winds, threatened to tear him apart even as fiendish apparitions shrieked, till his eardrums, unable to stand it, burst asunder and blood gushed out in copious streams from every available orifice.

The staggering shock and damage from the relentless assault on his person should have killed him. But pain was an old friend and Sukra knew that if you gritted your teeth and rode it out, you would not only survive the worst but may just be rewarded for your fortitude with all the treasure and pleasure there was to be enjoyed.

So he gritted his teeth and endured. Even when it got too much. The gale winds had done their worst but they were far from done with him and he was dropped without warning into the towering walls of flame that had sprang up out of nowhere, scorching hot and ravenous. Sukra screamed as the heat burned through every inch of him with unseemly vigour. He smelt his flesh roasting before it was burned and reduced to scorched cinders. He longed for death but all that was there was the excruciating agony that consumed him entirely, till it was all that was left, having obliterated every other memory or good feeling he had ever experienced, leaving nothing but the unbearable anguish of the pain that had been inflicted on him, the ghastly torments of the flesh, which were being meted out to him, and the searing trauma of torture and mortification of the body and spirit that still awaited him.

It went on long after he could bear it no more. Even when it ended, there was no relief or succour in sight. The shock from the plunge into the icy waters and the impact from the fall jarred every bone in his body and the cold bit into him like a thousand daggers. There was an acrid stench to the cold stream and it burned him every bit as badly as the flames. The tides dragged him over and under, bashing him against hidden rocks that turned the water red with his blood, toying with him mercilessly. In a final rush of surging currents that filled his lungs to the brim, Sukra saw the blessed end and waited for merciful release.

Instead, he woke up in a shady glen where he had once sported with the celestial nymphs in a distant past. Everything felt intact and nothing hurt. He was covered in so much filth that he was unrecognizable and he reeked so badly that he vomited copiously all over himself, feeling its corrosive burn against his throat. Gasping and feverish, he hugged his knees to his chest, as excitement and the joy of being alive flooded through his being. He was alive and well. Not only that, he was now the master of the Mrityu Sanjivani. And most heartening of all, he had finally found a way back to her.

Resurrection and Rewards

The news spread like wildfire. Sukracharya had mastered the Mrityu Sanjivani under the tutelage of none other than Shiva himself. He was now the worker of miracles. Using his hard-won skills, he had brought his late mother, Kavya, back to life. She had been reunited with Bhrigu and her son and it was as if she had never left. It was extraordinary and the curious and the morbid seekers of the macabre thronged to the ashram in droves, hoping to have a glimpse of the vile apparition and the indescribable horror that had surely been wrought using the blackest of arts.

But they were bitterly disappointed. There was nothing of the spectral about Kavya. No signs of decay or anything else that reeked of the despoiled, indicating the handiwork of death, were visible on her person though she was subjected to the most intense scrutiny. The more perversely inclined amongst them had hoped she had been rendered into something of an abomination, a foul creature that would revolt the senses, having been reduced to a haggard crone by the ordeal she had been through and which she had no business surviving.

Kavya was as vibrantly alive as she had always been, fresh-faced and full of verve as she bounded about, bubbling over with energy and enthusiasm, ever ready to smile as she went about doing the hundred unremarkable things she had always done. To the annoyance of everyone present, she did entirely normal things like eat, sleep, burp and belch like everybody else. It was all most astounding!

Without doubt, her resurrection was the most marvellous event in living memory, if not of all time. Truly a thing of wonder. And it made the rest of them bitterly envious. They had all lost loved ones too—blameless children, good wives and decent, hard-working menfolk. All lost to disease, war, natural disasters and arbitrary accidents. But they wouldn't ever get them back. How was this fair? It was so typical that the so-called great souls hoarded their knowledge and secret crafts for personal gain or to be used in favour of those who could afford it. As for those who didn't have the good fortune to defecate gold, they were left to suffer the cruelties of fate and wither away.

Sukra and Bhrigu were too happy to care about the incessant outrage that was being generated by the embittered folks who envied their good fortune. Their world was more beautiful than it had ever been, now that Kavya was back in it where she belonged. Having lost her once, they had a fresh appreciation for all the things they had previously taken for granted, including her sharp tongue, tendency to scold and erratic cooking skills.

Enhanced by her very presence, their humble ashram was transformed into the finest abode in the three worlds. Enlivened by the richness of her indefatigable spirit, the simple edifice was a sublime presence amidst the natural beauty of their surroundings, which included tall trees and swaying grass, bubbling brooks, wildflowers, hundreds of species of insects, animals and birds, making it a paradise from which none ever wanted to leave.

Yet, not even their peaceful home could remain untouched by the malice of what lay outside. Sukra was unwilling to bother with those who sought to wreck their happiness and who were up in arms about the fact that he had upset the natural order of things, which would have devastating consequences for the rest of the three worlds. Or something like that. All were convinced that they needed to agitate endlessly, for this was a righteous cause and they were determined to grumble and grouse to their last breath, casting the net of their collective malevolence, far and wide.

Naturally, as with most powerful ideas that drove them, they had little actual understanding of the Sanjivani mantra or what it actually entailed.

'Do *you* understand the consequences?' Bhrigu asked his son. 'I hope you won't misunderstand because I am happier than I can stand, to have the love of my life back. You have my gratitude and I couldn't be prouder of your achievements. But sometimes, I worry that it is all too good to be true.'

Sukra merely shrugged. 'Even if it is too good to be true and there is a price to be paid, I am more than willing to pay it, given the happiness we have gained.'

Kavya bustled in just then and she heard the tail end of their conversation. She took her son's hand in hers and squeezed it gently. Naturally, they had been curious about the afterlife and taken it in turns to quiz her about it, but she didn't have much to say.

'It felt like waking up after a long, dreamless slumber,' she had told them. 'There is a vague memory of something troubling, but for the life of me, I can't remember the things that had made me so angry in the past. Or sad. It is like my memories have been scoured clean of unpleasantness. All I know is that none of the things we insist on clinging to are worth it. What we have right now is a gift and I intend to cherish it till the moment I draw my last breath.'

She had wiped a tear from her eye and in the same motion tucked an errant strand behind her ear. Her smile was mischievous. 'Of course, when I am slicing onions, peeling potatoes, scrubbing floors or washing soiled loincloths by the dozen, I am less inclined to be grateful for little blessings but overall, I have no cause for complaint.'

Sukra knew the value of rare moments of perfect bliss too. And given the nature of the almighty ruckus that had been raised on account of his recent achievements, there could be little doubt that he would be embroiled in the eye of the storm sooner rather than later. But for the moment at least, he wished to savour the peace and quiet.

He glanced back at the unobtrusive presence who seemed to have blended into the shadows. She had been following him for what felt like forever now. He sighed. She was trouble. Had he been wise, he would have fled. Fortunately, he was anything but.

'She is persistent, I'll give her that...' Kavya murmured. 'And she seems to genuinely care, even though her orders were to destroy you.'

'Love seems to bring out the worst in people,' Bhrigu grumbled. 'Those under its baleful influence do the most abhorrent of things and feel perfectly justified in doing so. Hate is more honest.'

'It is not love that has led her to me,' Sukra grimaced, 'which is probably why I trust her more than her father.'

The Devas held their breath as Sukracharya practised his craft with impunity and could only watch with chagrined helplessness as the ranks of their fallen—half-brothers who had been decimated in battles of yore—were restored to full strength. They sprang up everywhere you looked. Like Kavya, all had been regurgitated from the nether end of death and none seemed the worse for wear, which was a pity. Having been reunited with their loved ones, they went right back to the business of living and killing.

Revivification had not made them wiser, the Devas were displeased to note. They still behaved like the goons and loons they had always taken pride in being, pissing on the heads of holy men, desecrating holy rituals, toying with humans, and picking fights with their half-brothers. From having faced extinction, the Asuras now threatened to overrun the three worlds in terms of sheer numbers. Indra took note of this run of good fortune bestowed on his hated adversaries and he was ready to do whatever it took to reverse it.

'He is like a child with a new toy,' Brihaspati muttered balefully. 'Mark my word, no good will come of such unnatural acts. Sukra thinks he can do as he pleases but when the cosmic creditors come calling, he will have nowhere to hide and his temporary gains will amount to nothing when compared with the mounting losses he has incurred for himself as well as others.'

He continued to murmur dire imprecations to himself about those who overreached themselves and spread misery in the three worlds. Indra was impatient. He was tired of vague predictions of doom prophesized to take place many yugas later. As their king, it was the present that concerned him and for the time being at least, nothing seemed to touch Sukra or the Asuras while he practised his unholy craft.

In the meantime, Brihaspati seemed to be at his wit's end. The limitations of his preceptor had become annoyingly apparent to Indra. There was nothing in his arsenal to match Sukra at present and Brihaspati was not exactly making himself useful. Indra had bought the Devas some time, when Sukra burned through stores of ascetic merit while he consummated his great passion for Visvachi who had been artfully placed in his path during his grand quest at Indra's instigation. But that hadn't been nearly enough.

So, Indra had assigned his lovely daughter, Jayanti, with the task of keeping Sukra too busy to use his boon to its fullest potential. His daughter was beautiful, wilful and proud. Unfortunately, a sense of duty was not among her many virtues. Even so, she had agreed to do his bidding.

Much to his annoyance, despite the best efforts of his spies, it was hard to ascertain whether she had followed his wishes in the matter. Or not.

Normally, he would send apsaras for missions like this and Visvachi had succeeded in Sukra's case, though things had not worked out as well for her as it had for him. Intent on his pursuit of total mastery over the Mrityu Sanjivani, Sukra had regained his lost lustre after his disgraceful affair with her but she hadn't been as lucky. Devastated and alone after he left her, she had returned to Amaravati and flitted from one bed to the other, trying to recapture the magical all-consuming romance she had experienced and lost.

Indra knew he would have to try something different to ensnare the preceptor of the Asuras before he successfully achieved his goal. That was when he thought of Jayanti. She was unschooled in the arts of love and yet, there was something about her, a certain innocence coupled with a fiery spirit, that made her irresistible. He thought long and hard before sending for her.

His instructions had been explicit. 'I am sending you on a mission of the utmost importance. The fate of the Devas will rest in your hands. You must take yourself to the side of the Acharya, Sukra, and serve him respectfully, with a sense of duty and affection. His moods will be mercurial but you must attend to his every need. At no point should you allow yourself to feel the slightest twinge of irritation. When you have succeeded in winning his favour and he grants you a favour in return, ask him to make you his wife and devote his attention solely to you.'

She glared at him, exactly the way her mother did when she was furious with him for spending his leisure time in the arms of his favourites among the apsaras, not realizing that it was the very same look in her eyes that had killed his desire for her in the first place and sent him scurrying towards warmer beds.

'You know how I feel about the shabby treatment meted out to the apsaras,' she bit out. 'They may be the most beautiful, desired and accomplished women in the three worlds who are sought after and loved by all. They may have their pick of the heroes, saints and kings of the age. But in the end, they are bound to your will. You keep them like bitches on a leash, deciding all who are to be the recipient of their favours, for vulgar purposes that are not worth mentioning. They have been little more than vessels for sages to pour their lust or fury into, and they have been condemned as whores, turned to stone or stoned to death, all because they were carrying out your orders. In the meantime, you use their misery as the building blocks for your empire and lose no sleep on their account unless they are engaged in pleasuring you...'

'Is that any way to talk to your father?'

She ignored his deceptively jovial tone. 'It is bad enough that you have done this to the apsaras. Must you compound your errors by pimping out your own daughter? And to the same man who took everything Visvachi had to offer and left her emptied of her very essence, leaving her doomed to spend her days with nothing but a life she no longer cares for! This is a new low even for you, Father!'

Indra took a deep breath and waited for the mounting fury to subside. He knew she certainly wouldn't be cowed by his infamous temper, especially since she had inherited her own from him. Besides, Jayanti was his favourite and knew she could get away with just about anything where he was concerned.

He rubbed his temple wearily. 'Sukra has given the Asuras too big an advantage over us. If we don't do something about it, our race will be entirely decimated. As the King of the Devas, I need to do whatever it takes to avert a catastrophe of this magnitude.' He met her gaze squarely. 'Even if it means pimping out my daughter, although I feel it is necessary to emphasize that I asked you to make him marry you, not seduce him. It would never do for the King of Heaven and the champion of virtue to come across as a procurer.'

She threw up her hands in a gesture of impatience so like his own. 'Marry, seduce, same difference! As for the Acharya and his Sanjivani craft, I think it is only a matter of time before you find a way to neutralize the threat. Vishnu will show you the way and then everything will go back to being just the same as it always was. Why are you so terrified that the Devas will be wiped out from the three worlds, or cower in fear that the day will come when your powers will be lost to you?'

Indra would not reply but he frowned. It was just like his daughter to get straight to the heart of the matter. Of course, there were days when he wished he had nothing. But he had worked hard to accumulate his power, wealth, the devotion of the mortals, fabled wonders and most marvellous treasures of the three worlds. And he could not regret that. Of course, someday he would lose it all. He did know that. But he would be damned if he sat around twiddling his thumbs, waiting to be overwhelmed by the irrevocable dictates of time. While he was still the undisputed king of his domain, he would do what it took to preserve his hard-earned possessions and add to them, the scruples of his own flesh and blood notwithstanding.

Undeterred by the chilly silence, Jayanti went on, 'As a child, I worshipped you because my father was the bravest, boldest and strongest of them all. Even now it holds true. Which makes it all the more sad that you have allowed your fears and insecurities to determine your every move. In fact, you are consumed by it. Accept that nothing lasts forever. Make your peace with it. Only then will you realize that the irksome issues plaguing your every waking thought will unravel of their own accord and that your efforts are mostly unnecessary. Perhaps then you will be happier and less susceptible to the influences of the corrosive elements that have burnt away your best qualities.'

Indra had been a typical father and had sheltered his daughter from the madness of the realms he ruled over. This was the result of his excessive protectiveness. She knew little of the three worlds outside, save the imaginary one he had built her with its attendant privileges, pleasures and endless pampering. A hopeless romantic and idealist, she genuinely believed that ideas and well-thought-out arguments could resolve all the problems in the world. And yet, she was brave, bold and strong too, to say the things she did to his face. Of course, she was never one to be afraid of punishment but she had always hated hurting anyone, even him. Because it always hurt her more. Even so, she had said what needed to be said. He hoped she knew how proud he was of her.

'We can keep arguing till the end of time but my mind is made up and you will do as you are told for the sake of your people!' He sounded colder than he intended and he knew he had hurt her, because his own heart was in agony.

'You are the lord of the heavens and your every wish is my command!' Her voice was soft and she had kept her eyes lowered as she bowed. Yet, there had been a defiant gleam in her eye and her scorn was a palpable thing, as Jayanti swept gracefully out of his presence. She was truly a magnificent creature. He hoped the odious Sukra would treat her with the love and respect she deserved. If not, he would have a good reason to blast him into oblivion with his thunderbolt. And no, not even Sukra had mastered the art of bringing his own self back from the dead.

Their union woke me up from a deep sleep. It was a rude awakening and I was annoyed, for it felt like an unpardonable intrusion. But to come awake is to know that one is alive. For an uninterrupted slumber, undisturbed even by dreams is death. Or nirvana. Which is why I am convinced people cannot be bothered with things like moksha or salvation. Once you cut away the chaff from all the philosophical pantomiming, deliverance from the so-called hellish cycle of birth, rebirth and karma seems to entail little more than putting in entire lifetimes worth of effort only to fall asleep and never wake up.

Folks understand Karma though. Cause and effect. In fact, most are obsessed with the intricate detailing and gorgeous patterns of Karma and are forever working their way through mazes raised on innumerably tangled threads to decipher its secret workings and find an explanation for the inexplicable. It is almost as if they can live with gaping wounds that can never heal only insofar as they can somehow figure out why it was inflicted on them. Almost as if they were convinced that an acceptable answer is the only medicine worth taking because though it may not heal, it can certainly lessen the pain.

'How did they wind up together if Jayanti was keen to defy her father, and Sukra of the formidable intellect was very much aware that she had been sent by Indra to persuade him to find some other means to keep himself occupied, which included the mind-numbing minutiae of the householder's existence and excluded the use of the Sanjivani mantra?' Nara enquired of Narayana and I listened because it was something I was curious about too.

'In her heart and from the realms of dreams that are more receptive to the mysterious workings of that which is preordained and therefore inexorable, Jayanti always knew that every path she chose to take or not to take would invariably lead her to Sukra. Her father had less to do with it than even he realized. Even as a child, the Deva Princess, who was raised on a diet of stories that focused solely on the grandeur and glory of her people, listened and remembered mostly the ones that involved Sukra in one way or the other.

'She knew the one where Sukra lost one of his eyes, when the divine Protector took the avatar of the dwarf Vamana, to destroy the good king, Mahabali. Jayanti had argued that it was Sukra who did the right thing and that Vishnu had been guilty of trickery and deceit, much to the chagrin of all present.

'Sukra was part of her earliest memories. She remembered her father carrying her in his arms when he went to visit the great man with a view to persuade him to be their preceptor. Sukra had refused on account of the fact that Indra had killed Trisiras who had previously occupied the post. They had talked and laughed a lot for two powerful players on the stage of existence whose thoughts and needs were not in harmony with each other's.

'She had been a mere child then, but Jayanti remembered the day she met the one who was to be her fate. It stood out stark and clear against a sea of vivid images from the past. She remembered the feel of the uncomfortable garments of gold and the heavy jewellery that she had been forced to wear for the occasion and the indifference of the wizened old man with the shabby beard who had paid scant attention to her after perfunctorily bouncing her on his knee and offering her sweets. His lack of awareness about their shared destiny had galled her.

'Why had she wandered into his stories more than any other? Why is a certain lover of stories and colourful dweller in dreams drawn to their love story to the point where her peaceful slumber is interrupted? It all comes down to the stories that resonate with us more deeply than the others because they are somehow relevant to our own lives, and to the stories that will be eventually told about us.

It took Sukra longer, but he too knew that he must bow before the ineluctable and he was happy to rest from his labours with a wife who, like him, knew the importance of allowing oneself to be sucked into a whirlpool of inequity and sinful indulgence in order to fortify oneself for the eventual ejection onto the placid plains of righteousness.

'I suppose you are saying that the universe conspired to bring them together because the daughter born of their union will propagate a mighty race that will have a definitive role to play in the myths, legends and sagas of the three worlds? Isn't that the simpler explanation?'

Narayana only smiled in response.

He was right. I was drawn to their story and not only because it impacted my own. Stories make you feel as though you know the characters. As if they are an actual part of your own lives. Even Sukra's motivations were obvious to me.

He had undertaken a mystical journey into the very heart of the metaphysical, and emerged, even if it was not entirely unscathed. Now his entire being was a beacon for the parasitic beings who clung to him with desperate need, feeding off what he had to offer. Latching onto his very essence and leaching him of so much energy that even his overly brilliant radiance was dimmed.

Jayanti had come to him like the very breath of life, even though she was listless and disinterested. She had taken the path of least resistance and hadn't been entirely happy about fate's decision to lead her towards a decrepit old man whose gluttonous appetite and aversion to personal hygiene had been most unsettling. While it was true that she had been revolted by his carnal obsession with Visvachi who had been casually discarded after the flames of his passion had died down, there was no denying her fascination with his exploits. The strange odyssey to revive his mother had bordered on incestuous love in her opinion, and yet, she had been strangely moved.

For Sukra, she had been little more than an irksome presence by his side he wanted to swat aside. And yet he had not given voice to the curse that had formed on his lips. Ordered to thwart him, she had never once violated his space but had seemed content to remain in the vicinity, taking off on her own private journey while anchored to his presence. Both were taken by surprise at how fond they had become of each other.

She liked being with him. It felt natural and she couldn't imagine how she had lived as long as she had without him by her side. She hadn't wanted him to stop using his craft. He did. And he didn't do it for her. He did it for himself. Deep down, he could feel the tectonic shifts across the sands of time, every time he brought the dead back to life. He had sworn he could deal with the consequences but he knew now that he could not. So he turned to her and away from himself and the crippling burden of his deeds.

When they became lovers, there was space in their respective worlds only for each other. Neither wanted more. They disappeared into each other, invisible to prying eyes and grasping arms that would seek to tear them apart. The years rolled by and they refused to release themselves from the sweet bondage they had chosen for themselves.

Sukra ignored his duties for as long as he could, but all too soon, they were too pressing for him to ignore. He did return. Jayanti would not follow him back. She chose to remain behind with the memories and she stayed there till they both faded. But for the longest time, the lovers endured. And they were happy.

There is something about the union of two souls, even if it is only briefly, that leaves all who witness it buffeted by bittersweet feelings—envy, joy in the reflected radiance, hope, and mostly, longing for the same. Sometimes, in the presence of sublime love, even the eternal dreamer finds the courage to leave behind the simulated reality of the dream for reality itself, the bitter pill that was coated with such sweetness that one couldn't help but wish for a tiny taste.

The Churning of the Ocean of Milk

It was the greatest undertaking of all time, which Deva and Asura had undertaken together. As always, they nearly came to blows while hashing out numerous details on an alarmingly regular basis but in the end they did manage to find a way to work together. For the first time in forever, the half-brothers had reached an accord and were willing to set aside their differences for a common cause.

How their mothers Aditi and Diti rejoiced along with the rest of the three worlds! Even I was touched, though sentiment is not really my forte. Later, I was mildly annoyed because, of all the tall tales and fables out there, this was the one I became the most closely associated with—an enchanting apparition who bewitched the Asuras into allowing the promise of immortality made real to slip away from their grasp. Be that as it may, it happened like this.

Indra had come to the awful realization that he and his brothers had become far too dependent on the humans. They had grown fat on the faith and fear he had carefully cultivated among the mortals, but they could no longer count on it. Modelling themselves after the gods, mankind and womankind had learned their lessons well. It was might that prevailed over morals. Every single time.

A simple enough observation and yet, by flexing their muscles in the manner demonstrated by the wielder of the thunderbolt, they worked their way relentlessly and ruthlessly to the very top of the food chain. The only thing that stopped them from taking on the gods themselves were the remnants of an ancient fear of being smote down by merciless bolts of thunder, devoured by ravenous flames, ripped apart by high-velocity winds, being buried alive or cast asunder into the lonely reaches of space. As well as their increasingly fragile faith, which they nevertheless clung to. Out of habit.

Well-loved stories that they had preserved in the realms of memory and imagination reminded them of a time when they had been at the mercy of the elements and the gods had walked among them, giving them their succour and rescuing them from monsters that fed on human flesh. Besides, it was the gods and demons both who had unravelled the secret of immortality, if the stories were to be believed. The humans were much further behind in the race to conquer death, though they too were obsessed with the idea of shattering the linear passage of time, turning base metal to gold and precious stones, unearthing unlimited sources of energy, and in the process, retaining their youth and lives.

When the age was just beginning, humans had been little more than animals, grateful for the gifts of the gods. The animal skin and bark they covered themselves in and the caves, trees and hovels they lived in granted them clemency from the fierceness of the elements governed by the gods. Most of all, in indirect proportion to its actual usefulness, they were thankful for the rites and rituals they had been taught by the kindly Brahmins, which would earn them the protection of the celestials and keep death, disease and every other kind of doom at bay. But how quickly they had evolved!

Progress became the precise mantra they swore by. They learned to make and use tools. Soon they were emulating the Devas and Asuras and took it many steps further when it came to ambition and avarice. Like the former, they made a lifelong commitment to accumulating and hoarding all the good things the Earth Mother had to offer. Dividing themselves into ever-increasing factions along innumerable lines of colour, caste, creed... Fighting and killing each other over everything, including the surreal stories. It didn't take them long to figure out that if they didn't consume, they would be the ones who would be consumed.

Deva and Asura alike had bullied and cowed the humans into

submission. They followed suit with all living things below them on the food chain to establish their superiority, hunting and killing the four-legged, winged or finned creatures for their meat, teeth, skin and bones, domesticating them or enslaving them to serve their needs. Even the wildest beasts that resisted them were brutally decimated, endangering the very species, or were locked up in cages to be displayed, their broken spirits a chilling reminder of the savagery of man.

Their thirst for knowledge and the sciences was insatiable. Unlike the Devas and Asuras who had made inroads into immortality and therefore found themselves with more time to indulge their follies, the humans, with the limited years left to them, did the utmost to cram in all the foolishness they could. They were making rapid advances and calling it civilization and had neither the time nor the patience to pursue the secrets of the universe with penances. They became obsessed with the shortcuts that led to their goals and couldn't be bothered with the arduous journey towards self-actualization. Soon there would be no room for the magical and mystical in their lives. Indra would have to act fast if he wished to stay ahead of them…

As for the Asuras, they couldn't be bothered with the humans, but they didn't like being dependent on their Guru either. It was most tedious to be subject to Sukra's increasingly idiosyncratic whims and fancies. Of course, they were grateful to him for raising them from the dead, but it was hard to appreciate him when he made it a regular practice to disappear for thousands of years together at a stretch, depriving them of his counsel and skills, while he was off canoodling with a chosen apsara or enjoying marital bliss with their enemy's daughter.

Didn't his latest escapade make him a traitor? After all, he was consorting with their foes, in a manner of speaking. Weren't they better off with someone more dependable? Or better yet, wouldn't it be for the best, if they could somehow manage to evade death altogether for good, using simpler and quicker means? Perhaps a nectar, an elixir, or an ambrosia that they could brew and sip from out of golden chalices… It was a worthwhile pursuit and by freeing themselves from the cruel constraints of time, they could devote themselves to achieving enlightenment and spread the doctrine of goodness across the three worlds.

It was Vishnu who put the germ of an idea in their heads. They could churn the ocean of milk for the precious nectar of immortality. After all, hadn't it all begun with the waters—life, consciousness, everything? And it all ended in the waters as well. With Pralaya. The great dissolution. After the great wars and Shiva's dance of destruction had consumed all of creation, the remnants of life and death were buried in the waters. The little and big things, the profound as well as the profane, good and bad, fragments of thoughts, scraps of memories, slivers of feelings, and bits and pieces of beloved stories, all of which would endure forever, caressed by the watery embrace of the Great Mother.

In the healing embrace of the Goddess of the Waters, all was carefully preserved. In the end, nothing was ever created or destroyed for good. All that happened had already happened and would happen again. Again and again. In a perfect circle that had no beginning. And no end.

So they would turn to the waters, the endless ocean where everything that mattered from previous lives was housed along with entire worlds and existences that had been chewed up whole and regurgitated by the ravages of time. And there they had remained. Until now, when it was time to rebuild and create something new from the materials that had been carried over from the past, to be revived in the present in order to pave the way for the future.

If the Devas and Asuras sought to brew the ambrosia to serve as their infallible weapon against death, it was to the ocean of milk they needed to go to. Getting there wasn't going to be easy, but it was made easier and harder by the fact that they were going to do it together. The males were going to do it all by themselves, but that was before they realized that they couldn't do it without the support and wise counsel of their femalefolk. And also because the ladies insisted, withholding all manner of services that had hitherto been taken for granted till they got their way.

So they journeyed forth together in a joyous odyssey, filled with the spirit of adventure and the boundless optimism of those who truly believed in their own nonsense. An exodus, which led them away from the rigours of rigid routine and monotony that had always made war seem like a good idea, towards something they believed in.

What an experience it was! There was good food, music, singing, dancing and endless bonhomie. They forgot the umpteen grievances they had long nursed on account of each other, their troubles and even managed to live together happily for the moment if not ever after. It was the best of times without even the foreshadowing of the worst to come.

The half-brothers devoted themselves to gathering the precious sap from vibrant green plants and tall trees, nectar from beautiful flowers, juices from luscious fruits and vegetables, wild honey from the beehives, blood, bones and lymph from their natural prey and burnt offerings. These were poured into the ocean of milk. Even as the three worlds groaned, they went on filling the watery void with everything they could get their hands on.

The ladies felt it wasn't nearly enough.

'How foolish the Devas and Asuras are! They want to expend all this time and effort on a lousy drink that will make bigger sots and fools of them all. What is the point of defeating death if life lacks the many things it always has lacked?'

'How like these ne'er-do-wells to want to spend eternity in a state of inebriated stupor! What a waste of such gargantuan effort…'

'We need more than an intoxicant or a happy juice! The ocean of milk needs to yield medicines and healers to save the sick and diseased amongst us.'

'Food has always been hard to come by… We can use a

mammal that will nourish and sustain us without intoxicating the senses.'

'We work so hard. We should have gems with magical, curative and wish-fulfilling properties. That will shore up our strength and supplement our efforts as we kill ourselves day after day to keep up with the tedious demands of endless chores, childcare and the effort to strengthen the bonds of family as well as community.'

Thanks to their efforts, more oblations were offered to the milky waters. So much more. Medicinal herbs, the nine noble foodgrains and roots were dumped into the depths. These were followed by milk, curd, butter, ghee, buttermilk and rosewater in copious streams. Chanting hymns and singing together, they tossed in prayer and promises. Then they poured out their wishes and dreams, hopes and desires, sincerity and goodwill, little pieces of their hearts and souls were generously given, plus all the things deemed necessary to make the three worlds a better place.

Of course, there were other suggestions. So many more. Most agreed that eternity would be impossible to endure without an endless supply of wine, potent spirits, and pleasure-givers belonging to both sexes blessed with beauty, brains and proficiency in the sixty-four noble arts. Of course, they would need weapons and armour to protect themselves from each other and their enemies.

I watched as the aeons rolled by in a flash, while they planned and prepared for immortality. Those were heady times, filled with excitement. It was the time for dreams and their fulfilment. A historic moment when many minds merged into one another to make manifest their strongest desire. They fought and argued over everything, but so great was their desire to live forever that, for once, they didn't kill each other over it. Instead, they determinedly befriended each other and meant it. In furtherance of a common dream, they worked hard together and had fun doing it. How the heavens rang with the sound of their laughter at the end of long days of hard labour!

They feasted, drank, sang and danced in a frenzy of careless abandon and jubilant spirits, ecstatic in their fervent belief that they would soon be spared the dread of encroaching death. Delirious with delight and soaring expectations of an everlasting life filled with nothing but all things bright and beautiful that existence had to offer, they convinced themselves that a happily ever after was well within their reach.

It didn't occur to any of them that they may be overreaching. If it had, doubt would have raised its ugly head and the bubble that housed their aspirations would have burst. Such enterprises were always fuelled by reckless hope that was needed to ride roughshod over caution and concerns as well as help blind one to the seeds of doom, which were inadvertently sowed along with the very best of intentions.

'How can you simply stand by and allow them to deceive themselves to such a degree?' I couldn't help but ask Vishnu.

'They are happy, aren't they?' came the sanguine reply.

'But they wouldn't be if they only knew…'

'Which is probably why they don't and it will be an act of cruelty to lay the truth before them without warning.'

'But if they knew the outcome of their actions in advance, would they still choose this course, which you so adroitly have nudged them towards?'

'In all likelihood, yes, because all are conditioned to choose happiness, as most live with the knowledge that sadness is just around the corner, waiting to pounce on them. The former is believed to make the latter bearable, though in reality the greater the pleasure, the more terrible the pain… But that is neither here nor there, because one can only guess at consequences. Especially since effects lead back to the cause as often as a cause produces an effect. We are, after all, the origin of the sacred mysteries that go into our own creation and the architects of our own destruction as well. It also explains the importance of personal choices as well as an unwillingness to choose to act when in the process of hurtling towards the inevitable.'

MOHINI

'Your love of paradox is most childish!' I told him tartly, before turning my attention back to the unfolding folly of such an endeavour.

Of course, it wasn't all fun and games once they got closer to their goal.

They had uprooted mount Mandara, the strongest of beaters, to churn the ocean of milk, in order to make it yield the things they sought and desired above all else. Years and years were spent propitiating the great mountain. So many flowers were used to garland its circumference, so many trees were uprooted for construction purposes, so much of the countryside was stripped bare of its flora and fauna, so many of the people living there were enslaved and overworked to death, the place became barren, depleted of its resources and natural populace, becoming uninhabitable in the process.

'Sacrifices have to be made if we are to succeed in this noble endeavour!' was all Indra had to say on the subject. As if the three worlds needed the wretched humans with their parasitic ways? He simply couldn't understand the fuss raised every time these useless creatures were killed in droves. It was not as if their numbers weren't constantly being replenished, given how much time they devoted to fornication and making babies by the dozen, burdening Bhumi Devi with an ever-increasing number of mouths to feed. He was sorry about the ravages endured by Mother Nature, but once this business was successfully completed, they would work hard to remedy the situation.

While the Asuras weren't too fond of the humans, Mahabali had been sympathetic and he promised restitution to survivors. The next task was to dig around the implacable mountain, deep into the core of Bhumi Devi, to uproot and lift it free. And they paid a steep price for it.

As always, death did not discriminate. Devas, Asuras, men, women and children died in droves, under piles of falling rock, and sudden storms or natural disasters when the ground beneath their feet gave way as tremors rocked the region, dragging them down below to a gruesome end. The ocean lapped up the offering of blood, bones and bits of flesh with alacrity, while the survivors wiped their tears, gritted their teeth, and carried on. They had come too far to turn back.

Lubricated by the blood of the fallen, and the tears of the survivors, they proceeded forth, carrying their monstrous churning rod to the ocean of milk, even as it crushed many more beneath its bulk. Vishnu took pity on them and sent his mount, Garuda, to their aid, though initially, the mighty eagle wanted no truck with an ill-advised quest for immortality.

When time escaped its moorings and rolled back from the straight and narrow path that most falsely believed it took, it laid bare its secrets, which could prove most illuminating for those who sought out the patterns that governed all in the cosmos. Which was how it revealed the occasion when Garuda stole the precious elixir and carried it in his beak to free his mother, Vinata, from her bondage to his serpent half-brothers.

Not a drop was imbibed by him though, for he was one of the few souls in all of creation who was free from greed and the desires it engendered. Indra had been in hot pursuit with the view to kill the interloper, but even he was so stunned with the magnanimity of the great bird that he had blessed the one who had stolen his most prized possession instead.

So, while Garuda did not really care about the nectar of immortality and the joys it promised, he did understand rifts between half-brothers and was happy to oblige any endeavour that did not involve war and mass slaughter. The Devas and Asuras cheered raucously as he carried Mandara as though it weighed nothing. With fresh heart and bated breath, they watched as Vishnu raised it from Garuda's back with his hand and lowered it into the swirling waves, anxious to begin the churning.

Mandara was less obliging than Garuda and promptly sank to the bottom of the ocean, taking their hearts along with it. Just like that, the lot of them were plunged from the heights of happiness into the very depths of despair and sorrow. In a fit of temper, Indra kicked the waves like one possessed and hurled thunderbolts into the depths in a steady succession and the others followed his example till Mahabali grabbed him by the scruff of his neck and hauled him back from the brink.

Like my own self, Mahabali was perceptive. Despite their best efforts to purify the ocean of milk and fill it with nothing but the so-called good things, they had inadvertently contaminated it with their own impatience, rage, despair and death. He took in the sight of the bloated carcasses of the decimated sea creatures that floated on the surface and shook his head sadly. Even if they did achieve their goal, eternity would be filled with the very things they sought to escape. He couldn't dwell on it though, nor turn back the tide.

'You will poison eternity with the detritus of your rage if you keep this up,' he admonished Indra.

'I would prefer it if you would refrain from manhandling me,' Indra glowered at him, 'and I would appreciate it even more if you could offer a viable solution to our current predicament instead of lecturing me about the merits of keeping calm.'

'As a matter of fact, I do have a solution,' Mahabali replied evenly, holding up his hands in a placatory gesture. 'If you would kindly refrain from attacking the ocean and killing the harmless creatures in the depths, I will send a delegation to King Akupara, the sovereign of the turtles. In the past, when you chased us away from your domains and drove us into hiding on the ocean floor, he offered us refuge. If we ask him nicely, I am sure he will not only restore Mandara to us, but hold it in place as we go about our business.'

Indra was all smiles again. 'I have heard that the Turtle King is a sacred vessel for the essence of the divine Protector. There can be little doubt that he will assent and help us see our quest through to fruition.'

He glanced curiously at Mahabali who had no trouble divining his thoughts. 'You are wondering why King Akupara helped us, though the general belief is that Vishnu as the champion of righteousness always sides with the Devas… I understand your confusion but it must be pointed out, that though it doesn't always seem that way, given how subtly he operates, Vishnu's allegiance is only to his beloved consort, Bhumi Devi, and what is best for her. Which is the upkeep of balance in the three worlds.'

Indra shrugged. 'These things always come down to perspective, don't they?'

They settled down and made themselves comfortable after sending representatives to King Akupara with instructions to enlist his aid. Attendants laid out a meal for them to share and they enjoyed it in companionable silence.

'I have been watching you…' Indra began. 'You seem wary and nowhere near as excited as our dear subjects.'

'I have been watching you too…' Mahabali smiled. 'And you are not exactly very happy either for somebody who is on the cusp of getting something he has plotted, planned and even killed for.'

'You have to answer first, because I asked the question first…'

They grinned, feeling suddenly like the boys they had once been. Where had that time gone?

Mahabali was silent as he gathered his thoughts. 'These rare moments of accord, even when we don't entirely see eye to eye, are valuable and I suppose I am grateful. It is nice that we are doing this together. I suppose I want it to last, even if it probably won't. Besides, it is a little too simple, isn't it? After all this time, if there is anything we know, it is that the inscrutable forces that govern the three worlds are committed to maintaining a stable equilibrium while forcing us to adapt to changing variables. I find it hard to believe that we are going to overcome the host of obstacles that still await us, share the amrita peaceably, and verily become the very epitome of filial love and affection while ushering in a new age that is free of the evils that plagued the ones before it.'

Indra rolled his eyes. 'The problem here is that you worry too much over the things that are not in your hands. I know you are thinking that as a child, I never really liked sharing my toys, but we are not children anymore. Who would have thought that the Devas and Asuras would embark on a joint venture after all the acrimony and bloodshed in our past? If we have managed this much, then perhaps we can find a way to negotiate the rest of time together.

I also feel inclined to point out that you haven't exactly felt compelled to share Sukra's Sanjivani vidya with us. Not even when we suffered severe losses that left us devastated or when Durvasa cursed us for not falling over ourselves to kiss his backside and left us shorn of our powers, forcing us to look for ways to supplement it. Whereas it was I who invited you to join us in this endeavour.'

'It was kind of you,' Mahabali was sardonic, 'to include us as a favour and not because, as you pointed out, Durvasa left you shorn of your full powers and you simply can't do this without us. As for Sukra, he makes his own decisions as you well know, and he would have shared his precious craft with you if you hadn't tried repeatedly to steal it from him or devoted yourself to doing whatever it takes to stop him from using it, thereby depriving us of his invaluable knowledge as well.'

'I daresay you are right,' Indra grinned, 'but even if it is improbable that we will do the right thing by each other, isn't the merest possibility of such a scenario worth working towards?'

'I daresay you are right,' Mahabali grinned back, 'and it is good to know that we are too evenly matched to destroy each other for good, irrespective of which one of us triumphs or loses.'

'Vishnu would say that victors don't necessarily win and the vanquished don't always lose.'

'Not that it is going to stop either of us from striving to win.'

They sat together for a while before rising to their feet, embracing each other warmly and retiring for a bit before they returned to the momentous task at hand. There was much that still needed to be taken care of.

A Treasure Trove

King Akupara had responded favourably and Mandara now rested firmly on his back. All they needed was a churning rope. The Naga King Vasuki's aid had been enlisted and he had come with hordes of Nagas. The great serpent had agreed to loan his gigantic scaly body, which they were now tugging at, with the Asuras holding the head while the Devas held the tail as they sought to churn the ocean and cajole it into parting with the wondrous troves of treasure in its depths and yield to them the most valuable one.

Time came to a standstill as the brothers, aided by Vasuki's serpent-subjects, toiled endlessly. The base of the mountain was churning away beneath the waves while they gripped the slimy scales of the Serpent King and tried to breathe, as poisonous fumes swirled about their heads. The poor creature gasped aloud from his exertions as they pulled him this way and that, ripping out entire chunks of skin and scales in the process. He shrieked in pain and the toxic blasts of his breath made his tormentors' lot every bit as bad as his own. The Nagas absorbed as much of the poison as they possibly could and became glutted with it.

The process was endless, with the snakes interrupting constantly to attend to their King's wounds, apply healing salves and poultices while feeding him potions to rejuvenate him and restore his strength and vigour. The interminable delays coupled with the laborious churning process chafed, but the brothers refused to give up, though everyone couldn't help but wonder if immortality was worth so much toil and trouble.

They kept at it even when they started vomiting blood, and viscous fluids spilled out of their nostrils and ears. Their womenfolk stepped up and gave the Serpent King as well as their beleaguered lords draught after draught of breast milk to revive them and keep them fighting fit with the stamina to go on, long after they no longer wanted to.

And still nothing happened, though their faith was certainly stretched dangerously thin. It was perilous, for this entire enterprise had been set afloat by the power of conviction, belief in the impossible and the purported ability of the mind to prevail over matter. So they kept at their labours in a bid to distract themselves from doubt and allow exhaustion to stop them from questioning the wisdom of their choices.

The ocean was a tricky customer full of distractions and sought repeatedly to drive them off course even as they struggled to relieve the water body of its valuables.

Surabhi, the Cow of Plenty, emerged in a wondrous spray of silvery foam. She was beautiful with delicate, polished hooves and eyes so kind that battle-hardened veterans wept to see her and threw themselves at her feet. And it wasn't a moment too soon, for all the breasts in the vicinity lay fallow and drained of milk. The divine cow blessed them with all the food and drink they would need to sustain them through the long hours of their labours. More importantly, they were so blessedly full, it felt awfully close to fulfilment and they would have given anything—even given up on their precious quest—to have the luxury to bask in the well-being that a full belly affords for the rest of time.

Memory kicked in through the pleasing mists of their contentment—incessant and prodding. Stubborn tentacles of persistent thoughts that reminded them repeatedly of the marvellous things to be dredged up from the ocean. And they were far superior to a mother's sublime offering of sustenance. Greed was a powerful motivator and it pushed them outside the food-induced torpor. And they returned to their labours somewhat reluctantly but spurred by the prospect of finding further marvels.

Their untiring efforts were rewarded. The flying steed Uchaishravas was the next to arrive. It was the most marvellous beast in all of creation with its noble head, mane and wings of silver, strong legs, well-proportioned body, graceful neck and eyes that flashed with the fire in his heart. Indra and Mahabali took turns riding it bareback across the three worlds while their subjects joined in the experience vicariously. How wonderful it felt!

The steed could cover great distances in a heartbeat, its dainty hooves treading on air, floating its way across the length and breadth of time in a flurry of fluid grace. They could have whiled away eternity on his back. The noble steed knew no fatigue nor did he need to feed, and while on his back, neither did they.

The magnificent six-tusked white elephant was another gift from the ocean. Patient and plodding, it was nowhere near fleet of foot as Uchaishravas had been, but it took them wherever they needed to go and helped them savour the journeys they undertook. Placid and blessed with a great heart, he taught them to slow down and appreciate the infinite beauty and marvels of nature.

They returned to the churning with fresh enthusiasm, anxious to see the miracles that awaited them if they persisted with their efforts. The heavenly nymphs were the next to arrive, attired in nothing more than their extraordinary beauty and adorned only with bewitching smiles, bathed in the opalescent moonlight. They brought with them the gifts of music and dance as the Gandharvas followed in their wake. How sweet it was to lie down beside them on the sand and allow them to caress away the aches and pains while wrapped in their silken embraces, which they distributed equally among all who required their services, giving generously of love. To leave behind the pressures of existence in order to lose oneself entirely to the pursuit of pure pleasure. How nice it would be to remain this way forever!

Even their ladies did not object. They were too taken with the Gandharvas singing and dancing in a frenzy of passion, to the rhythms of love, all too pleased to leave behind the tedious humdrum of a hopeless existence. Why care about assorted tasks about the house or for children, when they could sample all things sensuous and sublime at leisure?

Their eyes were glazed as they moved in a frenzy to the thunderous tempo, gyrating and grinding their hips against the pelvises of the Gandharvas. In a state of blissful ecstasy, heads flung back, backs arched, they pirouetted in fluid circles, prancing their way across a sea of sensory pleasure. Some shivered violently, like ones possessed, unable to withstand the intensity and potency of such an extraordinary gift that provoked them to perform acts of violent lovemaking, the exquisiteness of it all being more than they could stand.

Many moons passed. Fighting over the favours freely bestowed by the apsaras and drained by a surfeit of decadent indulgence, they returned to their senses in the cold light of dawn. Sober and somewhat ashamed, unable to make eye contact with each other. The harsh sunlight helped them see. The debauched excesses of those passion-soaked nights was a transient pleasure that would pass through many hands without staying put. But the Amrita was permanent. They needed it to be so. So they left the warmth of soft and silken curves for the stinging rebuke of the enraged ocean, which drenched them with bellowing foam and tremendous waves, laced with salt that tasted like tears.

Morosely, they churned away. Vasuki's appalling breath dulled the pain brought on by excess. Mandara thrashed away at the angry waves in retaliation and the churners awaited with dull impatience for further divine splendours to be driven up from the depths.

The wish-fulfilling gem—the Kaustubh Mani—shone in the distant horizon like a second sun, glittering on the firmament as the brightest among the stars, flanked on either side by Parijata and Kalpataru, the divine flowering trees. Unlike the nymphs, this was not currency made flesh, which could pass from hand to hand. It would have to go to a king. Mahabali shook his head and stepped back. He had always harboured a deep suspicion of all things that were too good to be true.

With the gleam of avarice lighting up his beady eyes, Indra stepped forward. His heart was thrumming with excitement, overflowing as it was with unrequited desire and unfulfilled cravings. Now, with the gem in his possession, they could all be made to come true. He took another step forward, as his needs collided with each other in a frenzy to be granted deliverance.

What should he wish for? Power? More power? Immortality? Love? True love? Success? Enduring success? Gold? Gold and silver? Gold, silver and precious stones? The death of his enemies? Simple pleasures? A quiet place? The lives of fallen brothers and friends? The lives of murdered foes? Freedom from regret? Contentment? Peace? Should he set aside selfish desire and grant the wishes of the less fortunate instead? Could this be the means to end suffering for good with its attendant horrors of poverty, hunger, pain, disease? Could he make a wish and make it all go away?

The gem glittered and he drank in the iridescent hues, looking for a way out of his confusion even as he was mesmerized by the dazzling array of choices it presented. All held their breath, waiting for Indra to make his wish and liberate them from their uncertainty for good. It took him the longest time to do it and they all thought they would die from having held their breath for so long.

But he did do it.

With an almighty wrench that tore out a massive chunk of his heart, he plucked the gem from the heavens, held it in the palm of his hand for a brief, intoxicating moment as a mighty procession of endless possibilities paraded before his inner eye, leaving him paralysed with indecision before he turned to Vishnu. And quietly handed over the gem. Without a word or a backward glance, he returned to his labours. Or he would have, if the effort had not left him exhausted.

The gem shone on Vishnu's breast. He didn't seem bothered by its proximity. Or the widening chasm he had created between them. And there it remained. Where it would cause the least trouble. For there would always be those who coveted the gem enough to pay the price in blood and lives that it demanded.

Mahabali lent Indra his own shoulder for support and led him into the midst of his brothers. So they could all carry on churning. For as long as it took. This time, they toiled with fresh hope, inspired and motivated by the power of sacrifice.

Golden Varuni of the intoxicating eyes, lustrous locks and body made for sin, brought out jars of wine, which they imbibed freely. Mandara and Vasuki sulked as the half-brothers were once again distracted from the ceaseless labour that extracting the Amrita demanded. They drank till they were cloaked in a marvellous state of inebriation that dulled pain and freed them from the unrelenting demands of their own all-encompassing ambition. There was even relief from the effects of the poisonous fugue they had trapped themselves in.

They drifted on a high, the height of their ecstasy marred by ever-present anxiety that it would eventually wear off and plunge them into a low from which they might never recover. So they grabbed the churning rope and carried on churning, because what else was there to do? Once more they went under the enervating clouds of poison and allowed it to leach them off their energy and essence. It was ironic, since this entire enterprise had started when they sought to restore flagging and nearly depleted energy reserves, which was robbing them of the will to carry on.

They ploughed the waters even as the ocean seethed and came to a boil, foam lashing them across the exposed parts of their body, momentarily freeing them from the poison that dulled their senses and muddied up their minds. Doubt besieged them as they wondered if they were not attempting the impossible by seeking to render immortality into a substance that could be contained in a golden jar.

Exhausted, overwrought and distraught, they glanced at each other through a fog of pain, urging themselves to go on because the other side kept at it. And so they drew on the strength of their age-old rivalry to push themselves further than they would have thought possible. How they longed for this desperate quest to end once and for all, even if that meant succumbing to the effects of the poison or allowing the rip tides tugging viciously at their ankles to pull them down into a watery grave!

Death wasn't going to be their lot, they promised themselves over and over again till they had no choice but to believe it. Death wasn't going to be their lot even if torment most certainly was. Was evading death worth enduring such grief? They got their answer after the expenditure of further amounts of dwindling energy as they persisted with their back-breaking efforts.

Shri, the Goddess of Prosperity, emerging on her lotus seat, was borne ashore by the waves that held her close and dear, keeping her safe. One look at her and their aches, pains and killing thirst melted away. Even the memory of their toil and trouble faded. Shri was a beauty who would be celebrated across the annals of time.

Golden of countenance, with limbs and a form that was smooth and shapely, she had coal black hair with hints of honey and gold, cascading in carefree waves all the way to her ankles. Graceful, poised and serene, there was nevertheless an impish gleam that illuminated her striking eyes with their winged lashes, and the corners of her full mouth lifted in a sudden smile that was so radiant, it seemed like the very sun had burst out from behind a storm cloud to bless their lives with all things bountiful and beautiful.

All prostrated themselves at her feet, and without holding back, offered her their very lives. She smiled sweetly and waited. They offered her heartfelt prayers knowing that eternity would be barren without her presence. She smiled sweetly and waited. They gathered together all things bright and beautiful from the three worlds and fashioned ornaments and garlands, which they offered her in worship. She smiled sweetly and waited.

They offered her everything they had. Everything they had accumulated over entire lifespans and kalpas, fabulous treasures and rare valuables they had lied, cheated and killed to obtain and which they had hoarded like misers and guarded with their very lives.

She smiled sweetly and waited. They placed the wondrous things yielded up by the ocean, over which they had toiled so hard and laboured so much, at her feet. She smiled sweetly and waited.

They offered her their undying love and constant respect. They promised to abide by her choices always, never demanding more than she had to offer. They swore on their blood, lives and the lives of all they held dear, that they wouldn't ever try to hold her captive to their will and greed. She smiled sadly and rose to her feet, with movements so sinuous, it was a symphony of pure grace.

Shri raised her hand in benediction and showered them with the full extent of her largesse. Coins of gold poured forth from the heavens in a blindingly beautiful shower that removed want and need from even the most wretched and miserable hovels in the three worlds. The gentle Goddess gave so generously that they were soon buried under mountains of treasure of incalculable value and more gold, silver and precious stones than they knew what to do with. Rare ornaments and caskets crammed with valuables, numerous as the grains of sand on the shore or the drops of water in the ocean, stretched out as far as the eye could see.

Joyously and in a delirium of greed, they counted the coins and measured the extent of her munificence, trying to keep as much of it as possible for themselves, cramming it into every nook and cranny available to them, worrying endlessly about keeping it safe and secure. The women tried on all the ornaments they could get their hands on, and kept at it long after they were bent nearly double from the weight of all the baubles they sought to possess. Soon, they were squabbling and bickering over ownership of the jewels, pushing, shoving, hissing and scratching each other like feral felines.

The Devas and Asuras became feverish in the frenzy that erupted for more gold and even more treasures. Mahabali and Indra wrestled over a crown and sceptre playfully at first, then with lethal intent. Covetousness was a bottomless pit that could easily devour all the gold in the world and ask for more, but it wouldn't deter them from making the attempt to fill it all the way to the top and demand even more. Lusting for the precious metal, they forgot their prayers and promises as they turned on Shri. All wanted the source of this matchless fortune for themselves. They wanted Shri. To possess her and keep her bound to their hearts and by their sides. To hold her captive and never let her go.

There was that sad smile again as she eluded their aggressive advances. She laughed as they sought to chase her down, making a game of it much to their mounting frustration. She ran helter-skelter on winged feet, always a step ahead, even when they gave it their all to close the distance and grab her in their arms. All of a sudden, she disappeared as if she never had been. Her frantic followers rubbed their eyes and looked around in disbelief, with sinking hearts. The largest treasure ever gathered in one place had disappeared with Shri. She had taken back every single one of her gifts. Not one miserable coin remained. All they had was regret and the sobering knowledge that they had paid the price for breaking a promise.

Try as they might, they could not find her again, though many were willing to abandon their quest in order to devote the rest of their existence towards finding Shri and cajoling her to remain by their side. It would have been a futile exercise, for she now reposed in Vishnu's chest, snugly ensconced in his heart forever more, a willing captive to the only one in the entire cosmos who had evinced absolutely no interest in holding her captive. So she stayed and for all of eternity, his heart was her anchor even as she wandered the three worlds distributing her gifts in measures small and great between the worthy and the unworthy, where it was wanted and where it was not.

Shri's loss was felt keenly. She seemed to have absorbed all the light and taken it along during the course of her hurried escape from grasping paws, plunging them all into hellish darkness, rife with recrimination. Steeped in gloom and despair, they took no notice of the dark mass that rushed towards them across the ocean, with menace and deadly intent. It was almost upon them, when realization struck.

'Kalakuta!' they screamed in terror. 'All the venom of a vile world, let loose upon us all!'

There was nowhere to hide as the baneful mass lumbered upon them. It was an amalgamation of their worst fears, conjured out of the debilitating fear engendered by every bad dream and nightmare they had ever had. Blood-chilling screams rent the air as they scattered in blind panic. The thing gathered force then, a malevolent presence that morphed into a violent whirlwind that scattered the clouds, blotted out the sun, covered up the heavens and descended on the rest of the three worlds, tearing apart the denizens as though they were little more than toys of straw.

They fled wildly in every direction but there was no escaping the destructive force they had unleashed. Their worst fears had materialized and there was no outrunning it. No safe space to retreat to. No weapon that could combat it. No time left to those who had sought all of it for themselves. But they ran anyway. From certain death and worse. All except Indra and Mahabali who held their ground and merely watched the unfolding horror.

The venomous, malevolent force was everywhere, swooping down on its defenceless victims, snatching them up and lifting them off their feet, drawing them closer till they disappeared into the killing embrace of the billowing black ether, one after the other. Thousands were caught up and carried far away. Disappearing into the darkness, howling in misery and despair, helpless to stop what was happening to them. Thousands more would be caught up.

'Looks like it will all be over soon. It may even be for the best.'

'It isn't over till it is,' Indra's grin was grim. 'He won't let it all be for nought, especially since it was his idea in the first place. Though I badgered him into articulating his vision. You will see, he will deliver us from harm. He always does.'

Mahabali glanced at his stubborn half-brother who had long been the scourge of his existence. For the first time, he was envious. Jealous of his unshakeable faith, which gave him such reckless courage, conviction and confidence even when faced with overwhelming odds that were insurmountable. If there was one thing he coveted among Indra's possessions, which outweighed his desire for immortality and freedom from strife, it was Indra's friendship with Vishnu.

'Vishnu isn't here now...' Mahabali couldn't help but remark.

Indra was unperturbed. 'No he isn't, but he has gone to get help.'

He had. Vishnu had gone to appeal personally to the Three-eyed God, who alone could absorb the forces of destruction, given that they all originated from him.

'I admire your patience, old friend,' Shiva was saying, 'but surely you are aware that the Kalakuta is of their own making. It emerged from their avarice and their endless indulgence. Their reckless ambition, excessive consumption of Bhumi Devi's bounty and callous disregard for lower life forms factored into its formulation. Perhaps it is only fitting that when they stand on the cusp of eluding death, they are destroyed by a monster they created.'

'Invariably, most will be consumed by their own self-destructiveness...' Vishnu pointed out, 'but the time hasn't come for that. In the meantime, only you can assimilate it, because despite the contempt evinced by your words, you are far too compassionate to leave them all at the mercy of Kalakuta. In return, they will give you their love, worship you for your kindness and build mighty temples to celebrate your magnanimity.'

'A lot of good that is going to do anyone,' Shiva remarked drily as he got to his feet. 'As you know, there is a heavy price to be paid for immortality. By those who seek to win it as well as those who are innocent and aren't even born yet. As for the Kalakuta, it will be awaiting them on the other side, waiting patiently for that which is owed.'

With those words, he strode towards the foreboding mass. It clung to him lovingly, wanting to touch all of him at once, pooling along the shores of the ocean. It washed over him till he was encapsulated in the black glow. He scooped it up in the palms of his hands, eyes shut and with the air of one who was about to partake of his daily refreshment. In a single gulp, he drank it down and it seeped into every pore of his being, filling him up as it was gradually siphoned away from the three worlds and into the empty spaces within him.

He could feel the ripples of Kalakuta's great power as it reverberated through his being. Shattered lives, broken dreams, the detritus of potent emotion washed through him as he felt the acute disappointment of the departed. The jagged edges of so much pain slashed at him. He felt everything they did—rage, madness, disappointment and the rank odour of their fear of endings. Every savage act, every evil deed, every damaging belief and every misguided step that had led them here. Still he didn't flinch.

The Three-eyed God absorbed the howls of their anguish, the overpowering feelings of loss and profound emptiness, feeling it flooding his insides. The destructive power of the Kalakuta filled him up, and Ganga, the Goddess of the Waters, came alive in his matted locks where she had chosen to wander, soaking up the corrosive substance, giving him blessed relief, absorbing the corruption into her own waters to be purified and recycled back into the cosmos.

Shiva bowed down in gratitude and went on drinking as a blue stain spread across his neck, shining and shimmering like a brilliant ornament. And still he drank till all of it had disappeared down his blue throat. Neelakantha. The intended victims of the Kalakuta chanted the name, awestruck, and so filled with admiration they could barely contain themselves.

Only when the deed was completed to his satisfaction did he walk away nursing the black and blue bruise in his throat that would never heal. Parvati spent the eons caressing it gently, her cool and nimble fingers providing blessed relief and her better half decided that unlike immortality, this had most certainly been worth the trouble.

The Devas and Asuras were subdued after this harrowing ordeal. They were chanting as they worked:

Om Neelakantaya namaha...
Om Neelakantaya namaha...
Om Neelakantaya namaha...

With his name on their lips, they drew from the memory of his formidable strength and even greater courage as they went on churning. They were grateful to have been cleansed of the poison that had clogged their pores, clouded their minds and nearly killed their efforts as well as themselves. After all this time and everything they had endured, the end was near. They could feel it.

All the splendours that had come before—the cow of plenty, the flying steed, the white elephant, the nymphs, the goddesses of intoxication and prosperity, the wish-fulfilling gem—all would pale in comparison to what was to follow. All of these things had been there before in various forms as the essential ingredients of creation. But this time, they were the creators—makers of something new, forged from the bits and pieces of something old. Forgers of an extraordinary weapon that would set them free from death and the limitations of a physical form.

A precedent had been set. Creation was no longer solely Brahma's domain. Forever more, those who had the gumption dared to dream big and showed initiative would find a way to prolong their lives and more importantly, enhance their enjoyment of the intense flavours it offered indefinitely. The fence between what was possible and what was not had been torn down and they were stepping forth into a brave new era where there were no limitations, only infinite possibility.

They were drawing closer and closer to the dazzling light, a vast pulsating mass that hummed and throbbed with immense power, struggling to break free. For the first time, they truly grasped the magnitude of what it was that they were attempting. The thing they sought was an inexhaustible source of cosmic energy that could be harnessed to nourish, heal and sustain life or just about anything they wished, if only they could find a way to withstand its uncontrollable power. Mahabali sensed that it was folly to attempt it. Indra's eyes were glazed and he stared at the bulbous light with longing, desperate to wield the magic that would make him the most powerful being in the universe. All would bow before his might.

Like everyone else, I was drawn to the pillar of light too... and strangely repelled by it. A long time ago, Vishnu had become enamoured of its power and engaged in a fierce competition with Brahma, who soared through the clouds and punched a hole through the heavens to feed his need for the magic. The Protector didn't acquit himself any better and had burrowed through layers of rock and darkness, deep into the entrails of Bhumi Devi, forgetting all but his need to draw closer to its source and become one with it. Shiva had hauled them both back from the brink, though Brahma was too far gone by then.

Now the Devas and Asuras were similarly possessed, led thither by Vishnu himself. Sometimes I have no idea what he is thinking. Perhaps he sought to drive them into the very heart of madness in order that they might finally find themselves. His followers were so blinded by its brightness, brilliance, curative powers and unlimited potential that they could not or would not see the rest of it. None had the gumption to recognize the truth about that incandescent throbbing mass of light and energy, which was its capacity to wound, bind and strike down with an arbitrariness that was part of divinity's intricate design and was always a definitive quality of great power.

Unlike the others who were in the thrall of heroic ecstasy, Mahabali did understand something of the true nature of the energy secret they were determined to unravel, but he was powerless to stop them in their tracks. If he had tried, they would have killed him and gorged on his blood and bones, using his essence as an impetus to further their efforts. So he toiled along with the rest of them. What is meant to be will be, he told himself.

The last and most precious of the valuables procured from the fabled Ocean of Milk, Amrita, the Nectar of Immortality, burst free from the ocean in a wild eruption of light. Matter made manifest by their minds. The sweetest gift of them all. The shimmering cloud of gold filled the heavens with its brightness, cloaking them all with its benevolence. Its touch relieved them of all past hurt and trauma, leaving in its place a simple euphoria that obviated doubt, fear and mistrust. The three worlds heaved with the impact as the pulsating mass descended, spreading in all directions.

All of the energy that had been leached off the core of the Earth Mother and the elements and used for unwholesome purposes was restored to the source. The celestial and human races had been guilty of using the resources freely offered by Bhumi Devi so indiscriminately that soon, what she gave was not enough, and they had stolen more and more to strengthen themselves, unmindful that they were weakening their mother in the process.

Parched and barren lands were restored to life as crops thrived, buds blossomed, withered trees sprang back restored to their natural splendour, and birds trilled with merriment. All of the wounded, weary, heartsick and hopeless were cured by the magic as the light touched them and left its warm embers in their hearts. The three worlds were drenched by a profusion of colour and light, with wildflowers blossoming as far as the eye could see.

It was one of the rare moments of pure perfection in the history of the cosmos. All basked in its glory. Only the children ran hither and thither, unable to contain their excitement as they collected the precious drops of golden light from the surface of the ocean in their palms and raced back to fill the golden pitcher, held by the divine physician Dhanvantari, laughing and shouting in glee. When the task was done, he blessed them, 'You will go forth into the three worlds, little ones, as healers skilled in the art and

MOHINI

science of Ayurveda, which you shall master under my tutelage. Share the story of the churning of the Ocean of Milk wherever you go, and inspire people with the mighty deeds achieved by the Devas and Asuras, the great brotherhood who showed by example the heights that can be reached when love, kinship and noble ideals are allowed to prevail.'

Kids being kids, they looked solemn at the onerous responsibility being placed on their shoulder. When Dhanvantari released them, they burst into peals of laughter and ran away to chase after the diminishing droplets of gold, which were placed carefully in the pitcher. He drew them to him again, and they listened. Taking the precious offering he had handed to them, they placed it at Vishnu's feet before clambering onto his lap to examine his fine new ornaments and the precious gem that glittered in his chest, begging to be shown the beautiful lady who now resided in his heart.

The Devas and Asuras watched the proceedings without participating, as if the miracle that had unfolded before their eyes and was of their own making was somehow far removed from who and what they were. Their families, children and allies stood hand in hand, all blessed by the touch of the nectar of immortality, basking in its radiance. All were at peace and filled with calm acceptance. There was satisfaction as well to be had in the knowledge that thanks to their efforts, the three worlds were once again graced with hope.

Ennui and Exhaustion, Inertia and Intrigue

Am I the dream or am I the dreamer? Does it really matter? Either way, isn't it the elusive, ephemeral quality of all things ethereal that makes them so enchanting? It could explain why these things are so desperately sought after and the desperate are willing to give much more to experience it. All it takes is a tantalizing glimpse, or a forbidden taste or touch in a diaphanous dream that ought to be but isn't quite forgotten upon waking. Which lingers long after it has melted away into the nothingness. Because like the Amrita, it is precious and prone to vanish in a heartbeat, leaving only a stray memory of something that was breathtakingly beautiful, heartbreakingly exquisite and almost experienced. It fills one with so much longing and it hurts so badly, that it feels good.

This universe of ours is filled with many marvels and subtle splendours, floating like so much flotsam and jetsam on cosmic tides. There is only one known way to experience them fully, to partake of them so thoroughly that it can fill even the bottomless emptiness of the gaping void within. Throughout time, this has been possible only in the realm of dreams where the stories and the magic are real. Where one can commune freely with nature and the elements, to become one with the currents and forces that determine the nuts and bolts as well as the random rhythms of existence.

When caught up in the flow, which propels one to the confluence of conscious, subconscious and unconscious thought, one is transported to the one place, the only space where it is possible to create things that are of the greatest value not just for the self but for the greater good as well. It is the dreamer alone who can navigate the way past difficult terrains into the remote

MOHINI

regions of the cosmos where boundaries are blurred and even the final frontier finally dissolves, opening up to further vistas where immortality can be churned from an ocean, foes become friends, life trumps death and deceptive hope prevails over deceitful truth.

For as long as I can remember, I have been pursued. Relentlessly so. By those who seek to escape the suffocating confines of reality. There are those who have wanted me so badly that they have wandered the three worlds like madmen, leaving everything behind, risking all, hoping to gain everything, but mostly they have nothing but the fragment of a dream. Which is all they seem to need.

They say I am cruel and capricious. A cold-blooded killer of men. A calculating seductress who would lead her lovers astray, away from their wives, children and the rest of the humdrum realities of the human existence. A fickle creature like all females supposedly are. Which, needless to say, is a surpassingly stupid statement. And the fact that I am the female form of the primordial male galls them no end.

A dream or a dreamer, I traipse along the topsy-turvy topography of spirituality in an increasingly materialistic universe. Sometimes, I have company, inside or outside of my head, and we hold hands and walk together. I like my bosom companions— Shiva, Virochana, Bhasmasura, the ill-fated Aravan, and so many among the humans, Devas and Asuras. And then there was him of course. My heart.

Every one of these has been special and most were left behind, but they all became a part of the stories worth telling. Isn't that everything? A bond thus formed in the rarefied reaches of fantasy is so meaningful and the experience of it is so absorbing, that time and its rigid rules vanish, for good. It may not be immortality, but all agree that it is far superior to the endless corridors of eternity.

The Devas and Asuras knew a lot more than they cared to admit about the endless corridors of eternity. You see, they had gotten themselves hopelessly trapped in it.

In the beginning, it was perfection itself. Which state itself is usually highly suspect. Enveloped in the euphoric state of an Amrita-induced bliss, the half-brothers divided the gifts of the Ocean equally among themselves. Indra got the elephant, Mahabali got the steed, the former got the parijata, the latter got the kalpataru, both got the apsaras and so on and so forth. Contrary to popular opinion, the half-brothers did not get into a tussle over shares of the Amrita. Not immediately at least. It was all very civilized. And so joyful.

Lavish celebrations were held to mark their tremendous achievement, which led to widespread goodwill in the three worlds. There was drinking, dancing and feasting aplenty. Of course, given the profligate quantity of quaffed spirits, it was not surprising that there was some drunken squabbling and the odd bout of fisticuffs over ancient evils inflicted and endured, but that was to be expected. Mostly, it was a joyous occasion and they were all reluctant to pack up, descend from the magnificent heights and return to the dull routine of an existence that now stretched all the way into eternity.

In the early days, they dedicated themselves to quiet enjoyment of the wondrous things that had come into their possession and rebuilding a brand new world, free of the perils and pitfalls of the ones that preceded it. The abodes of the Devas and Asuras were adorned with the marvels unearthed from the ocean. All were involved in noble pursuits that included preservation of Bhumi Devi's resources, educating and taking care of those lower down on the food chain, in order to create a society where all enjoyed equal rights and lived in harmony.

When the commitment to virtuous living, selflessness and righteousness began to pall, some dedicated themselves to the pure pursuit of knowledge while others had less lofty aims and contented themselves with the occasional indulgence in selfish pleasures. The former were seekers of truth who wished to learn everything that could be learned everywhere in the universe.

They journeyed to the distant realms as solitary wanderers or in pairs or groups sharing the extant information, plying their trade and crafts while steadily acquiring mastery over the mysteries that pertained to earth, wind, water, fire and ether, in addition to the subtle profundities that concerned all of existence in its myriad hues.

The secret languages of the plant and animal kingdoms were studied to better record their virtues and properties. They unearthed the secrets of natural as well as occult sciences. Some harkened back to archaic tradition, devoting themselves to preserving all that had been carefully gathered and preserved by the wisdom of the ancients. The lore of the sun, seas, snakes and sorcerers were minutely examined.

They pored over stories and dramaturgical representations from all corners of the universe. Fabulous yarns and epic sagas preserved in scriptures, scrolls and songs about a face that launched a thousand ships, heroes caught between two insurmountable obstacles, fire-breathing dragons, wielders of thunderbolts, magical swords, the tragic hero who accidentally killed his father and married his mother, great floods, life-saving arks, virgin damsels in distress, sleeping beauties and goose girls, gossamer years, the feathered serpent, trickster gods, philtres of love made with chocolate and menstrual blood, horned minions of the dark prince, insatiable creatures of lust that were half-man and half-goat, hermaphroditic gods whose organs fought for mastery over the self, the mystical powers of the eye of the hawk and the virgin's milk, treasure hordes guarded by dwarves and goblins, fortune-telling water spirits, magic lamps, flying carpets, invisibility cloaks, cherubic gods of love armed with flower-tipped arrows, and an apocalypse that saw the destruction of the gods and the burning of the heavens. Before they happily drowned in the sea of stories they were determined to study them, drop by precious drop, while adding to these or incorporating them into their own.

Pursuers of the obscure and profane retreated to the dark,

lonely places in the universe, where they devoted the duration of their years to forbidden rites, rituals and cabbalistic practices to revivify the dead or to summon wraiths from the bowels of hell. They made blood sacrifices to appease the hunger of barbaric deities made in the image of their own misshapen beliefs, who gave them the licence to engage in taboo acts of debauched fornication.

Dappling in the mysteries of mysterious goddesses, they laid bare the finer points of fortune-telling involving hepatoscopy, entrails, blood and spit, spilt the secrets of the stars, and became proficient in the skills of divination and prophesying.

In secret subterranean temples, they imbibed the arcania of communicating with demons in order to better hunt, slay or use them. They were obsessed with the denizens of darkness—spirits, ghouls, suckers of blood, ghosts, witches and the black arts, which would give them the ability to possess the living or animate the dead with the decomposing essence of departed souls.

They studied the boundless capacity of memory, the limitless potential of the imagination and the role of illusion in generating turmoil or influencing the patterns of existence. What a treasure trove of invaluable knowledge and information they accumulated and committed themselves to preserving for posterity! How incredibly unfortunate that next to nothing has survived across the relentless march of time!

Only morsels of the priceless remain. In mouthed hymns and murmured chants. In old songs and stories told by the fanciful with scant regard for fact, given their veneration of fiction. Which, in turn, led to them being rejected as unworthy...probably for the best, since it is better to be dismissed than condemned to death for sedition. In the untrustworthy memories of those who have faith in tradition as well as those who care only about the integrity of fantasy. With those who commune with the spirits of nature and those who are committed to scientific rationale and empirical study.

Soon, even learning lost its lustre. It felt pointless. The more they learned, the more they became aware of their incurable ignorance. Some who knew this became wandering beggars and continued to ponder the mysteries of the universe while engaged in scratching their crotches. Those less inclined to accept the truth donned snow-white robes and pretended to be enlightened till they believed their own lies to the point where it became the truth.

In the meantime, what was immortality without a bit of intrigue? It started innocently enough. Or rather, disingenuously enough. Indra decided to make a statement. Everybody thought the Amrita had dissipated into nothingness after the momentous undertaking had been concluded, which he decided was far from a satisfying conclusion. Of course, the children had made a game of it, offering the holiest of holies to Vishnu. But Indra felt a display of sorts was in order in order to put out the message that it was the Devas who had been adjudged truly worthy and allowed to take possession of the nectar.

Indra decided that a dazzling show-and-tell was called for. At the loftiest location in Amaravati that was heavily guarded, he commissioned the building of a marvellous edifice by Twastha, the Divine Architect, and placed two golden cups, one upended upon the other with serrated edges that fit perfectly into each other as they moved up and down as though unable to figure out if they wanted to lock lips or not. As they flitted between furtive kisses, one could see the elixir contained within, which positively glowed with effulgence. This was placed in the middle of a rotating wheel with wicked-looking spikes that flew hard and fast to cut interlopers to shreds if rumour was to be believed. And two monstrous serpents guarded both. The irrefutable word had it that these beasts could poison you by look alone, and victims would die in an agony of unbearable proportions.

As for the story, it was a remarkable one.

Once the Ocean of Milk had surrendered its sweetest and most valuable offering, the boorish Asuras had attempted to snatch it away from its rightful owners. The Divine Protector had intervened and appeared as the famous enchantress. Mohini. Everybody knew she was the most effective weapon in his almighty arsenal, the best of his bag of tricks.

Clad in the sheerest of silver robes, moistened by the lusty waves that sought to strip her bare, she paraded her wanton wares before the filthy-minded Asuras, distracting them from what ought to have been foremost on their minds. Using trickery and feminine wiles, she persuaded them to allow her to distribute the blessed nectar of immortality. Deeming the Devas to be more deserving, she served generous helpings of the Amrita to them while allowing the Asuras to settle for the opportunity to ogle her bare breasts. By the time the Asuras came to their senses, the deed was done. When the dust settled, the Devas emerged triumphant. Thanks to Mohini.

It was all very ridiculous. But people had never had much difficulty swallowing this load of crock! Ever since, this has been the story most closely associated with me.

'Vishnu has betrayed us...' Mahabali's subjects complained bitterly. 'And Indra has robbed us. The Devas have taken possession of the nectar of immortality. We have been shamefully tricked and deprived of our rightful share.'

'This is foolishness!' Mahabali wondered if eternity entailed being exasperated all the time. 'Indra likes his charades. All of us were blessed with immortality as you well know, when the Amrita enveloped us in a golden mist. What is the point of an elixir that has to be consumed on a daily basis to stave off death? And you all witnessed its dissipation as it returned to the mysterious source from which we procured it. The little ones managed to fill a small jar, it is true, but by my reckoning, in their enthusiasm they scooped up more water, foam, pebbles and sand than the nectar. So what is the point of working ourselves into a frenzy over a non-existent source of inexhaustible energy?'

He tried to make his people see reason and not panic needlessly.

'We have it on good authority that Indra has imprisoned Dhanvantari in a tower at the very summit of Amaravati...' the busybodies insisted. 'He is the only alchemist who has actually succeeded in conjuring up the potion of immortality and Indra has forced him to churn out the nectar in unlimited quantities and now they have enough to drown in!'

'It is Dhanvantari's punishment for daring to teach the humans the science of Ayurveda, which has enabled them to prolong their lives too! As if the three worlds need more humans!' Yet another panic-monger heard from! Mahabali shook his head in irritation.

'Dhanvantari's fate is unfortunate,' Mahabali supposed he may as well go along, 'but it is beside the point! Why are you determined to lose your heads over nothing? Even if all this turned out to be true—which I doubt—we still have Sukra who has returned to us, after the regrettable passing of his wife, with his charming daughter, Devayani, in tow. To the best of my knowledge, he is still very much in possession of the Sanjivani Vidya. I trust time and fatherhood has mellowed him and he is less likely to succumb to the charms of seductresses and sedate husband-hunters. If the effects of the elixir wear off and should the need arise, I am sure he will rise to the occasion. But I doubt it will come to that.'

Judging by their expressions, they did not agree. Not in the least.

'My King! This is no time for a flippant attitude. Did you know that Brihaspati's son, Kacha, has requested admission to Sukracharya's ashram and has been accepted? Indra and his father have sent him with the express purpose of learning the Sanjivani craft…'

'You know that Sukra has never shared that specific piece of knowledge with another living soul, don't you? Others before Kacha have tried. And failed.'

'But this one is wily and has already inveighed his way into Devayani's affections!'

Mahabali shrugged, 'So what? Young love is sweet only as long as it lasts. As for the Sanjivani vidya, it cannot be taught or imparted just like that! Sukra was away for ages and he undertook a quest that was comparable to what we underwent with the churning of the Ocean. It was an endeavour that tested his mettle so severely, it nearly destroyed him! But he prevailed and the fruits of his labours cannot be shared with all and sundry, simply because the nature of discovery calls for a bold spirit and a willingness to suffer.'

He glanced at their brooding countenances. The Asuras were temporarily mollified but he doubted this business was over. And he had a terrible feeling it wouldn't end even after the bloodshed that was inevitable. He sighed. It had been nice while it lasted. Things were bound to steadily worsen from this point on. Mahabali was sure of it.

It was an accurate prediction. Things came to a head quickly after that. Some among his subjects felt his approach was too lackadaisical for their good and had decided to take matters into their own hands. Rahu had been the ringleader. He had tried to steal the nectar of immortality, but Surya and Chandra had supposedly stopped him. Then he had been relieved off his head for his trouble, some said, by Vishnu, for the Sudarshana chakra's handiwork was distinctive and unmistakable. Thanks to the nectar he had been so enamoured with, Rahu did not die, but he had been broken in two. And since he wasn't dead, Sukra couldn't revive him.

Rahu was the first to be condemned to have his bifurcated body wander perennially in limbo between life and death. His fate sent tremors of shock, horror and disbelief across the ranks of the Asuras. The Amrita had protected them from death, but clearly it did not armour them from things so evil they were worse than death. Even the Devas were shaken.

In retaliation, a bunch of hotheads slew Brihaspati's son, Kacha, and did it repeatedly when Sukra resurrected him at his daughter's insistence. Things escalated from there and soon they were at war. After everything they had been through together, things went back to being exactly the way it had been in the past. Brief interludes of peace interspersed with war. And on and on it went in the eternal circle with no beginning and no end. This was their eternity and it wasn't pretty.

And so the centuries rolled on. The half-brothers were

suffering from a surfeit of indulgence in pleasure, learning and even privation. With the passage of time, they found that immortality was not everything it had been vaunted to be. They felt far more wretched than a lowly, disease-ridden beggar who did not have much longer to live. Everything that could be savoured had been savoured and every flavour had been sampled. Everything that could be done or experienced had been done and experienced. Everything that could be said had been said.

They had travelled the gamut of emotions so often, they no longer felt anything. They had journeyed into the remotest outposts of the known world only to find it was more of the same, dressed in exotic new clothes. There were neither secrets left for them to unearth, nor were there unheard stories for them to enjoy. They had seen every dance and its variation, heard every song there was to hear with its never-ending variations. And they were bored stiff and sunken into a state of ennui that promised to persist for all of eternity. Who was the idiot who had thought it would be a good idea to live forever? Was there a more moronic notion in the history of moronic notions?

The morass of monotony left them morose and mired in a morbid muck. They were back to making the mistakes they had always made and fighting in wars that served no purpose besides killing time. Even the dreams and nightmares, though never the same, were starting to resemble one another.

Nobody died. Not the Devas nor the Asuras. Even the humans had made strides in their quest for immortality and lived longer. Bhumi Devi bowed down under the weight of the sudden population explosion as she fretted over her inability to accommodate and share her resources evenly among them. Worse, she was unable to withstand the state of stasis the Devas and Asuras had forced her into, leaving her stuck in place like a damaged wheel.

Mrtyu went off into hibernation and Brahma was furious. How dare they interfere with his design? The fire of his anger spilled over into the three worlds with dire consequences. As past lives persisted into the present and ate into the future, the babies started dying in the land of the humans. The effects wrought by the Amrita, Sukra and practitioners of Ayurveda had prolonged scores of lives at the expense of those that were yet to be. Soon, not only were there no children in the three worlds but none had been conceived in centuries.

All the worlds reeled as souls remained trapped in vessels that could not perish and they clamoured for release, breaking free in bits and pieces, wandering the three worlds as splintered fragments that had nowhere to go and nowhere to be. Spectral apparitions that sought the sweet release of death while scaring the living.

The three worlds were stooped and weary with age and there was no way to end its suffering. Something had better be done. And sooner rather than later.

Weaving a Web of Enchantment

I may have stepped out of a story. Or a dream. A figment from a fantasy made real to serve the occasional purpose, but mostly unreal the rest of the time. Did that mean I was alive or dead? And did it really matter, all things considered?

Now that all of earth was entrapped and left enervated by endless life, death was necessary, even needed. But Death had been beaten, if not completely vanquished. She had retreated, tail tucked between the legs, relieved in part not to be so hated and abhorred. All too soon, Mrtyu knew it would be time to set forth again.

If everything that was happening had already happened and was going to happen over and over again, then all would die eventually. So that they could live again. But in the interim, the chasm between the two widened. Bridging it would involve a spell of enchantment so powerful, it would confound the senses. And set them free. So they could take wing, fly past the abyss into whatever came next.

Having first encountered the enchantress that is yours truly in fables, they found themselves captivated by everything they remembered about me, which was both strikingly clear and hopelessly jumbled. Like a dream within a dream. It clung to their every waking moment, leaving them consumed by thoughts of Mohini.

Obsessed with my extraordinary beauty and special powers. Unable and unwilling to let go, they went looking for me in their dreams, where they realized anything was possible. Searching for enchantment in the stories and making up for whatever was lacking, generously contributing to the myth of the quintessential lover. One of the oldest tales, told of how the Devas, to whom I had supposedly fed the Amrita with my own hands, wished they had forsaken it in exchange for me. They wanted to go back in time, so they could do it differently.

The most ardent of those who loved love and would do anything to become lovers were not content with longing and sighing. They sought to give shape to the shapeless to transmutate into a fantasized reality, the dream they wanted so badly to be real. Chasing after that which they sought in the smoky corridors of the insubstantial and incorporeal, they coaxed me with repeated entreaties and declarations of love. The stories themselves safeguarded the secrets relegated to my keep, but rewarded the relentless with precious morsels that brought them closer, bridging the gap that stretched between us.

Lovingly they gathered every bit, particle and speck pertaining to the one they were determined to love, piecing it together with infinite care, filling in the missing pieces with chunks of their heart and soul, all the love they could lavish upon the object of their ardent desire, and the greatest sacrifice they were capable of making. With aching affection, they murmured into my ears, tickling it with their heated breath, beseeching me to come alive in their arms even if it meant giving up their last breath. They begged me to cast my spell over them.

It has been said that I was little more than a wanton temptress who set traps of honey to seduce the unwary. That I used the love bestowed on me so wholeheartedly to lure men to their doom and gave nothing back. But weaving a successful spell entails giving generously of the heart, soul, mind and body. And while it is true that I might be incapable of the so-called finer emotions, I am also without fear, having never ever been afraid to give or take. So I gave in to all who extended a sincere invitation to make my home in the innermost recesses of their hearts and minds. And my legion of lovers rejoiced. This was the second time they had succeeded in making manifest a fragment of a dream, making it flesh and blood. Having been allowed inside my web of enchantment, they were free to draw from the well of fantasy to mould their own reality and write their love stories with the chosen one brought to life from a dream.

Now they could lie beside their chosen paramour and caress her hair. Massage her shapely shoulders and make her purr with satisfaction. Nuzzle her neck while unwrapping the bodice to free the small breasts. Explore the length and breadth of the wondrous landscape of her body with an inquisitive index finger. Listen to her speak. Kiss the corners of her mouth where she stored her smiles. Time itself slowed to a crawl to allow them to savour the sensuous and wallow in a swirling whirlpool of lust.

Their success encouraged others. More and more dared to forswear their hearts. Even though it was known that the enchantress was heartless. All they wished was to remain caught up in the coils of enchantment forever.

Many made their way towards me to find themselves the perfect lover. Thousands upon thousands allowed themselves to be afflicted with an inflamed imagination and an infection of the spirit. So enraptured were they by my beauty and grace, they were taken aback by the intensity of their feelings and the lengths to which they would go in order to remain entranced. So deep was their love for this otherworldly passion, they had no wish to return to the demands of their worlds. A world without the maya of Mohini was not one that was worth returning to, they all agreed.

As the stories sprouted wings and soared, spreading in all directions, sprinkling the shimmery dust of sorcery, besotted lovers sang lustily and composed magnificent odes to the mysterious beauty of their dreams and how they had breathed life into this bewitching creature with fervent kisses.

Now that my power of enchantment was a part of it, the three worlds were once again enveloped in a golden haze of profound well-being, induced by phantasmagorical visions of the benevolent enchantress, I had become in their eyes one whose extraordinary beauty was exceeded only by innate goodness. As far as my acolytes were concerned, I was their goddess of love, who didn't just sit pretty on a pedestal but was very much a part of their lives. A shield against evil and their promise of light against the encroaching darkness. This was not just a fable, it was their truth. And so it was true.

All who still believed in magic and fantasy or those who were willing to suspend disbelief and those who had allowed themselves to surrender, were more receptive to my advances. They counted themselves fortunate and blessed beyond measure. Even among the sceptics, resistance was scant, and most allowed themselves to be susceptible to the siren's call, even if it meant risking death and worse. So powerful was the allure.

Even later, when some swore that I was a cold-blooded heartbreaker who asked too much of my victims, they admitted that my lovers had been complicit in their own victimhood and all that had been asked, they had been more than willing to give.

Men and women, the rich and the poor, sages and sinners, believers and sceptics, frauds and fools, they were all consumed by my intoxicating presence, gladly allowing themselves to be ensorcelled. They did not mind losing their heads and hearts. Most were happier than they could say, for simply having been given the opportunity to experience such rare sweetness and pleasure.

The docile, long-suffering wife who had taken her courage in her hands and made room for surreal romance in her dreams saw the version of herself she had not dared to love and thereby lost. Having taken a leap of faith, she found she had unlocked the portals to unlimited ecstasy and she couldn't have been happier.

An embittered mother drained of her energy and vitality received a nocturnal visitor, who was a vision of beauty, purity and tranquillity, well-adjusted and accepting of her autonomy. Having denied her feelings for so long, she was happy not just because she could feel again but because what she was feeling was unalloyed joy.

The used-up whore condemned to a semen-stained mattress saw a brazen voluptuary who indulged her bold passions without becoming soured or scarred by them. More importantly, she believed in love and lust again, because neither abandoned her in the morning, provided she had the sense to remain in her waking dream. Lost little girls and abandoned waifs surrendered to a free-spirited sprite who soared across the sky, shrieking with joy, encouraging them to be at absolute liberty to do what they pleased and become whatever they wanted. With her by their side, there was no limit to what they could do.

An old hag rediscovered herself as she had been when she was young and capricious and life had not yet left its mark on her, and was left feeling as though she had drunk deeply from the fountain of youth and once more her world was bright with possibility.

The ancient crone saw a wicked witch and recited incantations to ward off baleful influences. She was mostly relieved when the 'evil spell' eluded her. Sometimes, the magic steered clear of those who wanted nothing to do with bedevilment, wanted it too badly or didn't care either way.

It was even simpler, if equally erratic, with the men. I just allowed them to see me transformed as whatever the chosen ones wanted me to be. There was never any pretence nor any intention to beguile. Merely a fulfilment of a need. Sometimes all they wanted was someone to talk to. Or play a game with. Someone to lie to them and give an assurance that they would be loved no matter what.

So I morphed into mother, maiden, wife, whore, lover, friend, guide, sweet, saucy, sexy, sensuous, nymphomaniac, spiritual advisor, muse, listener, masseuse, healer, princess, prostitute, teacher, rebel, keeper of secrets, soother of woes, patient companion, loving partner in crime, laugher at silly jokes, able handler of odious habits, dispenser of wisdom in a dizzying whirl.

Guards were let down, massive fortifications were disabled and defences were breached to let me in. They merged themselves into my being, pouring secret emotions, the darkest of desires, forbidden passions, taboo impulses, buried yearning, tender thoughts, assorted quirks and idiosyncrasies into the shared spaces honouring me with their childlike trust and blind belief that the best parts of them that had been entrusted to my care would be safe and sound. For the rest of time.

In the embrace of enchantment they found relief from chronic ailments of the spirit and flesh. A cure for incurable loneliness. Blessed release from guilt and regret incurred over foul deeds and lost opportunities. An ointment for the aches and pains of loss and defeat. Healing from a thousand inflicted hurts and traumas. Freedom from fears and insecurities both big and small. A balm for the injuries of the soul, mind and body. Surcease from relentless anxiety, nameless dread and ever-present panic. Answers to futile questions. An easing of the pangs of envy. A negation of the corrosiveness of hatred.

Enfolded snugly in the aura of my presence, some found a quiet place. An abode of tranquillity. A remote haven of wild beauty where they could commune in the resounding silence with the spirits of nature. Go for long walks in the wilderness, easing past the tangled thickets of troublesome thoughts to find their way to their lost selves and get reacquainted.

My voice offered a panacea for a thousand evils. I crooned songs to the tune of love and longing, murmured sweet nothings, uttered charming endearments and a lover's entreaties. Carefully chosen words assured them of true love and fidelity, made it clear that they were needed, that they were worth waiting for, sighing over, living for, even dying for. A lilting tone gently turning the mind's attention away from worry and a ceaseless contemplation of a precarious future. Mostly, I meant it. At least in those magical moments.

I was everywhere and nowhere. Wandering the hallways of the finest palaces with the rich, powerful and accomplished just as freely as I did in the meanest streets and gutters with the poor, wretched and miserable, mingling freely with the celestials as well as humans. Behaving for all the worlds as if it were all just the same. Nobody questioned my loyalty or fidelity. I belonged to them all. Even though I didn't.

They loved me for my generosity and worshipped me with fruits and flowers. Offerings of gold, silks and prayers were made to propitiate my favour. There could be no doubt that I was divinity, an avatar of Vishnu, his most remarkable one. Come to save them from a soul-sapping, heart-wrenching, joyless and treacherous existence.

They talked about the profusion of miracles I wrought. Fallow lands became fertile again. Drought-ridden regions received reviving showers. Polluted water bodies became pure and sweet. Food and grain became plentiful. Every path I took became a slice of paradise and I left contentment, happiness and tranquillity in my wake. Or so they said.

Barren women who received my blessing or simply happened to be in the immediate vicinity conceived that very night much to the boundless joy of their families and communities. Soon the three worlds rang with the laughter of children, born of the bountiful blessings of the good enchantress, if you were inclined to believe the stories. Lepers were healed, the grief-stricken rediscovered happiness, the poor found their coffers filled to overflowing, the blind could see, the deaf could hear, the lame could walk and the disabled were made whole again. Broken hearts were repaired, scarred and stricken souls were restored, empty heads were filled and those wearied beyond hope were rejuvenated. What a magical time it was!

It was like the dearly missed Amrita that the Devas and Asuras churned from the Ocean of Milk, so long ago. Except its powers had been magnified and manifested in a palpable form of divine splendour. Mohini. The Enchantress. The name was on all their lips.

They built temples and monuments in my honour, chiselled and carved sculptures to capture my perfect face and form just the way they had seen it, painted murals to preserve my likeness. They poured their hearts, souls and very essence into their work. Poised delicately on the edge of the world, where boundaries had no power over me, I watched and waited.

Sometimes, I lingered to take in the sights and smells, sample delicacies, eat voraciously, quaff large quantities of drink, dance in the rain with the peacocks for company, sing with the larks, run with the wind, and swim naked in the sea. But I never tarried for long. They tried to make me stay of course, but that was an impossible task. The harder they tried to hold me back, the quicker I departed. The smart ones followed. Without protest or questions. Bereft of enchantment and magic, their worlds were little more than nightmarish realms they had no wish to inhabit. Lost in the labyrinth of love, they succumbed to its irresistible lure, which shattered the moorings of their lives, pushing them into the twisting, tortuous terrain of the unknown. I led them deeper and deeper into the make-belief world they had built for me and away from all they knew. They had built grand palaces using the strength of their love, memories and soaring imagination as building blocks, held in place by a strength of will they had never believed themselves capable of. A safe haven for their souls to retire to once they had departed their bodies.

I myself refuse to be rooted to one spot. It was important to remain on the move. Stagnation was not for me. Neither was the selflessness of a mother. Not when I had the security of the mighty heart that had birthed me and was therefore my creator and self and one true love. I needed nothing else.

I, Mohini, was perfection made possible. And thanks to me, their world was perfect too. Yet, those who had risked everything for my love, stood to lose everything. They had answered a call from beyond and violated every single rule that governed their lives. They loved me so truly and selflessly, they expected nothing in return. Only the honour of loving the Enchantress.

Even when they knew that I could never belong only to one. That I shared my affections readily with all who sought me out without distinction, flitting merrily like a giddy butterfly from one to other, back and forth. That my love was true only as long as it served the purpose of the higher forces I had chosen to serve. Or he had chosen to serve. That I would adore them for only as long as I had to. That I would ask for their lives in return for love. Though I would not do the same if asked. Not that anybody ever would.

I gave you my love. Die for me, I murmured into their ears without a twinge of conscience.

Gladly, they replied without hesitation.

And they did. In droves. Without question. All who loved me enough to lose themselves. Deva. Asura. Man. Woman. And child. They went with a smile on their lips and a fervent prayer in their hearts. Asking only that they be reunited with me. If not immediately, then sooner rather than later. It was all they asked. To be with me again. Even if it was only for all of a moment.

They left the husks of their bodies and their stolen hearts behind to be turned to ash on funeral pyres to the accompaniment of a symphony of bereavement, set afloat on a sea of tears, embarked on a journey from what was known, to what lay beyond.

The Enchantress was the passage between worlds—light and dark, fiction and non-fiction, magical and mundane, truth and lies, real and unreal, old and new, worthy and worthless, mind and matter, life and death. This transition from one state to the next was always marked with violent convulsions. It was only to be expected, since a passage of this nature is bound to leave behind a vacuum. Everybody knows that if there is one thing nature hates, it is a vacuum. It has to be filled with whatever is available. Hence, there had to be struggle involved—theft, toil, terror, fierce fighting, madness, mayhem, mystery and murder. Absolute bedlam. An intensity of expended emotion was involved too.

Grief, hate, hurt and a crippling sense of loss among those who were left behind. The ones who didn't have the courage to leave everything behind. The ones who had been afraid to jump into the yawning nothingness at the penultimate moment. Those who refused to fly without wings or leap without the safety of a security net. Those who had rejected the enchantment and had been rejected in kind.

The carefully constructed state of perfection painstakingly put up with love and faith came apart with a crash. It happened gradually without too much of a hullabaloo, but it did. And then the evil things that had spontaneously generated beneath the gloss and shine of smooth surfaces burst free in a rush of all things terrible and terrifying. Can the stories come to life and harm the living? Something certainly did. And it was something monstrous and noxious.

A number of things went into its making. There was a hint of envy that grew out of all proportion to its original state. A touch of resentment turned rancid. More than a little yearning for that special something, which had been denied to some while so many others seemed to be enjoying it to the fullest. Anger aplenty and hate to taste.

When it broke free, all were contaminated. Discord radiated outward in waves inciting bitter quarrels, jealous fits, accusations, angry recriminations, tearful outbursts, inflammatory words, casual and careful infliction of hurt, dark suspicions, breaches of confidence and broken bonds. Fighting broke out in isolated corners here and there, before it gathered momentum and became full-blown war.

The spell was well and truly broken. After all, all love stories have splendid beginnings and squalid endings. How could this one have been any different? It must have been a mass hallucination, a fever delirium that had caused so many to lose their hearts to an enchantress. The hissing and spitting began in earnest.

'She was a witch and a whore!'

'A fraud and a charlatan, who wasn't even that beautiful, if I remember right. And I do.'

'Why, her lips were thick, not sensuous, and you could see the nasal hair every time her nostrils flared. Did you notice that her breasts had started to sag ever so slightly? And there was a definite touch of grey in her hair… not silver, mind you, but grey like an elephant.'

'Do you remember that poor soul? He was perfectly respectable till the day he wasn't. His old mother wept to see him sit still and unmoving, staring into nothingness as the days, months and years rolled by, lost in visions nobody else could see. Until the day he just stopped breathing.'

'Stuffing the heads of stupid men with stuff and nonsense!'

'Did you know that she is not a woman in the truest sense of what that term implies?'

'Yes, she has the organs of a man and a woman. That is why she can pleasure a man in so many different ways and men being the creatures of base desires they always have been, were reduced to worshipping the abomination's yoni and linga together.'

'No! She is actually a man who lopped off her male organ and drank her witch's brew to grow breasts. It is unnatural and unholy, which is why that indescribable creature is doomed to meet a horrible end.'

'Enchantress, my foot! Filthy fiendish freak is more like it.'

It was too short a distance from Mohini, the enchantress, to Mohini, the pisacha who devoured men, and chewed and spit them out, growing fat on their essence. From a benevolent goddess to a wicked witch with an insatiable appetite for unwary young men, whom, it was said, I lured into the woods. My beauty was a mask and the sinuous curves a cleverly concocted illusion to disguise the unsightly wrinkles and warts of a hag from the wrong side of the grave. They claimed I stalked my prey when the scent of jasmine was in the air to disguise the stench of death and decay, and chose moonless lights to allow the darkness to conceal the maggots crawling out of empty eye sockets.

I supposedly lay with the hapless victims and sucked out their vital juices, leaving only desiccated remains. Feasting on flesh and getting drunk on blood. I survived and went on with my nasty work without a shred of compunction or compassion.

It made no matter apparently, and they threw themselves at the pisacha with the same alacrity as they had done with the enchantress. The willing fools all too ready to chase after a pretty face even when it was ghastly, ghoulish and suspended in mid-air because its feet had rotted away eons ago. The rest of this creature, it was declared, was chewed up by wild beasts when she lay with her legs splayed, alone and abandoned in death for her sins, since nobody wished to pollute themselves by performing the ceremonial rites for one who was both witch and whore and thus, doubly cursed.

Foul spells of enchantment were cast on good men by this evil pisacha, it was murmured in dark corners. To make them take leave of their senses, forget all about their decent god-fearing wives and blameless children and disappear into the woods with a wanton temptress. There they were fed with potions brewed by black arts, whipping them up into a lustful frenzy where they lost all inhibitions and behaved like animals in heat as they spent the nights in orgiastic degradations of the flesh. Having successfully carried out these nefarious designs, the witch, who doubled as a whore, vanished, abandoning the discarded victims. When daylight broke and they viewed the depths of infamy they had fallen into, their poor hearts finally gave out and they died from the horror and shame as well as they ought.

Indra wept before his precious pitcher, which contained the nectar of immortality. It had been a lie made into truth because they believed it was so. Now they knew better. He hurled the thunderbolt at it, shattering the thing to pieces, shocked and hurt anew when he discovered the nothingness within. As he mourned the loss of the Amrita and the brothers he had lost to odious sorcery, he wished I had trapped him in my web. There was some cold comfort to be had from the fact that Mahabali had it worse. Much worse.

The King of the Asuras had become catatonic. He just sat on his throne, his body still and unmoving as a stone, his eyes blank, emptied of all thought and feeling. Utterly oblivious to all around him, he seemed locked away in a place far removed from them all, which he had made completely inaccessible. No healer could find a cure for his ailment. He neither ate, nor drank nor slept.

They said he remained unchanged till a dwarf approached him with the demand for three paces of land. Mahabali smiled in recognition then. And without a word he lifted the dwarf's feet and placed it on his head. 'I am tired. All my life, I have done nothing but do things only to undo them, redo that which was undone and when it is done, undo it all over again to do it over. Over and over again. I had hoped it would be different with her. I gave her my life and love, but she returned them both to me. But she has sent you to me at last. To make an end of it. To wipe out everything I have, so that I can return to the blessed emptiness of the void.'

Indra nearly died laughing when he heard this absurd tale. So his antagonistic half-brother and occasional friend had departed the three worlds after a dwarf tricked him out of his empire and an eternity's worth of accumulated treasure to stomp on his head. It was hilarious. He laughed so hard he was in tears.

Pandemonium reigned on earth. Even in the event of mass death, people found they still couldn't agree on the essentials. The murderous mobs remained convinced that a world without witches was the only one worth living in. They gathered in packs to kill all the whores, witches, fiends and freaks they could get their hands on. Who failed to pass the test which involved a thorough examination of their private parts for signs of anything unnatural or depraved. They saw the Mohini Pisacha everywhere they looked and wielded their weapons freely to show the foul beast what they did to those who dared corrupt the morals of society at large.

Others rose in defence of the Enchantress who had been good to them. As always, each side felt the other was in the wrong and came to blows over it. And people went on killing each other over the veracity of the fabricated stories and the soundness of the principles they had gleaned from them. Which, in turn, had determined their choices and subsequent behaviour.

The fighting, burning and killing wound down eventually, though it had seemed like it would go on till the end of the age when a spectacular conflagration of epic proportions would burn down the three worlds and destroy it for good. Some even hoped it would happen, so fed up were they with a wretched existence.

When the dust settled, the acid rain stopped falling, the fires were put out and the smoke cleared, there was no sign of enchantment. Or the Enchantress. Not even the faintest trace over the vastness of the devastation that had been wrought. They searched high and low, terrified that they would find me lying broken and bleeding in a ditch, with my breasts lopped off and a sword in my womb. But they found nothing. In fact, it became increasingly apparent that their Mohini was long gone.

Had the architect of the enchantment that preceded the killing frenzy even been there in the first place? they asked themselves, but got no answer.

The last dregs of the madness that had consumed them and reduced them to a raging mob hell-bent on killing and destruction had vanished too. They returned slowly to themselves and shuffled homeward, appalled at the large-scale carnage that had been wrought for nought, unable to believe this was their handiwork. Was it the mysterious Mohini? Or was the blood on *their* hands? Shame flooded through them, at war with the burgeoning relief that it was finally over. Returned to waking as if from a dreadful nightmare, they rolled up their sleeves and got to work. To repair and rebuild.

They were consumed by a bitter sense of loss. All had lost so many and so much in the great purge and culling. They mourned the loss of beauty, magic and enchantment from their lives. If only they had known its worth! How carefully they would have guarded those things. Now it was all gone. And so was the Enchantress. As if none of it had ever been.

Bullies and Boors

After the great enchantment was lifted, it was I who was reeling from enervation. Not that it was anything serious though. Merely the after-effect of having expended an immense effort in order to weave a spell that would captivate and hold multitudes of souls across the three worlds in a web of maya over a protracted period, and then with a final burst of power, helping them across the bridge from fear and ignorance to understanding and acceptance. It was draining. No wonder Vishnu spent ages just snoozing in order to recuperate.

There is no rest for the weary though. Even when reposing under the covers in my sanctum, I felt too much like a lonely flame flickering wildly in a rainstorm. But how beautiful the darkness looked against the little wisp of light!

I love few things more than listening to the lullabies of the night with their whispering of innumerable secrets and conveying snatches of omnipresent principles! Is there anything to equal the dark intoxication of the twilight hour? I crawled out from beneath the covers to stretch my tired limbs amongst the chiffon clouds and submit to the soothing ministrations of the silvery moonlight, allowing myself to luxuriate in the comforting embrace of the moon, letting my thoughts drift in his direction. There were too few among the males who knew how to really love a woman and make love to her properly, leaving her thoroughly fulfilled. Kamadeva was one. Kartikeya was another. Krishna was the best of them all. And then there was handsome Chandra.

All must die. All who die are born again. And so it was with Soma. Collector of the sap, which he brewed into a beverage fit for the Gods, which revitalized them and increased their longevity. He had died under dubious circumstances. And his brothers waited anxiously for him to come back to them. With every handful of sap they poured into the Ocean of Milk during their grand enterprise to churn it, they remembered him, chanted prayers to ensure the swift passage of his soul and shared stories to preserve and honour his memory.

The waters paid heed. She was a kindly goddess and she always listened to heartfelt pleas. When they had succeeded beyond their wildest dreams and all were touched by the golden quintessence that had miraculously emerged from the ocean, Anasuya, the wife of sage Atri, found herself with child. She cradled her belly lovingly when she told her husband the news: 'The Trimurti have been good to us. We already have Durvasa and Dattatreya, blessed with the essence of Shiva and Vishnu. Now I am carrying a portion of Brahma in my womb. Since he was conceived in this most fortuitous of times when the three worlds are enfolded by the touch of Amrita, he is going to be a special child, embodying love, truth and beauty.'

Atri's smile was loving. 'A special baby made under the influence of Soma, wouldn't you say?' Anasuya blushed and the great man paused to take note of how pretty she looked before continuing, 'When Shiva's rage proved too much for the three worlds to bear, he sloughed it off and entrusted it to your womb. Not surprisingly, our Durvasa emerged in a fit of temper, a mere seven days later, when the King of the Haihayas gave me offense, threatening to decimate all who stood before him!'

'Now he wanders the three worlds like a thundercloud, but even at the height of his anger, he gives benediction. If it weren't for him, we wouldn't have been blessed with the Amrita or this baby.' Anasuya was staunchly loyal.

'Dattatreya was born of Vishnu's erudition as well as his infinite wisdom and he will be the immortal guru. With regard to the latest inhabitant in your womb, he is a composite of Brahma's forbidden passion for his daughter, the sensitive and reckless soul who succumbed to the miraculous intoxicant he himself had brewed and a little bit of the two of us as well…'

'What are you trying to say?' she pouted. 'Is there something wrong with desire, heady beverages, or us? He is going to be magnificent, you will see.'

Atri smiled and nodded in agreement. He was too wise to speak his thoughts. Their son was going to be beautiful, magnificent and burgeoning with sexual energy. Therefore, he was certain to be a troublemaker of the highest order.

Anasuya's thoughts were elsewhere. Her husband thought that they had been blessed by the Trimurti. Why wouldn't he? She had told him so repeatedly. It wasn't entirely the truth, merely a heavily expurgated version of it. Even with his yogic vision, he had never been able to see clearly where she was concerned. And she had been unwilling to help him. Not because he would have faulted her, but because he would have been too badly hurt on her behalf. Somehow that was worse than being hurt herself.

The Triumvirate had come to her door. But it wasn't to bless her. Anasuya's breath caught in her throat as the memories washed over her.

> They had come when Atri had repaired to the forest to perform tapas, knowing that he wouldn't be back for many a year and that she was all alone. Anasuya had been wary but unafraid. 'My husband isn't home as you probably know,' she had smiled politely, but there was no mistaking the frost in her voice. 'I think it would be appropriate for the three of you to bless us with a visit at a more opportune time.'
>
> 'Do not be afraid. We are not here to endanger your modesty or your chastity,' Brahma said as they forced their way in. Neither their words nor their actions were reassuring.
>
> There was something aggressive and unnecessarily

harsh in the way they behaved and the tone they used with her. Later, they would claim it had all been a test but she knew these males loved lording it over the likes of her a little too much for it to be only a game. Moreover, she was not remotely interested in being involved in sports of this nature.

'Atri is a good man, but he likes to brag about you.'

'He claims that you are the most dutiful of women who keeps herself engaged in useful activities every waking moment. Neither idle thoughts nor temptation can insinuate their way into your life to lead you astray from the path of virtue, because you keep both at bay by the power of prayer and discipline.'

'Unwelcome interlopers of the sort you mentioned are best beaten off with a stick!' she replied. If they heard the edge in her voice they preferred to ignore it.

'You dress with simplicity and modesty. He insists that your heart is the purest in all of creation and that even the name of his beloved Anasuya has come to represent chastity, honour and virtue.'

'In my husband's eyes, I will always be beautiful and perfect, even if time and fate conspire to make me a wrinkled old crone, who has given herself over to idling and indolence. It is a failing the male of the species have— to either venerate their women on a pedestal or tear them down and grind them into the dust.'

Vishnu had the grace to look abashed. Shiva was noncommittal. But Brahma looked outraged. She held his gaze without blinking.

'We have come to put his claims to the test,' Brahma sneered. 'To determine its veracity or to ascertain the actual truth behind claims that your virtue is a carefully fabricated fiction to disguise your propensity for entertaining dozens of lovers while your husband is away.'

MOHINI

'You would dare to make your spurious claims against me under my own roof?' her tone was scathing as she glared at the three of them. 'And you are here to test me? Brahma the rapist who violated his own daughter, Vishnu the murderer who killed a good woman, and Shiva who decapitated his own child because his wife and her creation had bruised his ego? None of you are worthy of sitting in judgement of the lowliest soul in the three worlds and are certainly not fit to judge me even if I were to choose to spend my days in a state of inebriation, while cavorting with the forest-dwellers and its creatures!'

'All males are brutes, that is known,' Brahma smirked. 'It is the female who must be held to a higher standard. Therefore, the best of women strive for perfection in thought, word and deed. She will learn to please her man by mastering the arts of singing, dancing, reading, writing, playing instruments and cooking. She must learn the esoteric language of the stars, tides and weaponry to protect her loved one from harm. The skills of amour she must be proficient in and her conduct must be irreproachable. When she has done all this, she will take her place just beneath the most brutish, poxy beggar of a male in the grand scheme of things. It is known.'

'It is known...' she agreed, 'that a fool of a man would certainly think so. I believe your lot cling to these delusions of grandeur to compensate for paltry proportions and severe inadequacy in all matters that count.'

Brahma flushed but he wouldn't back down, 'You must submit to the test. It has been decided that you must divest yourself of your garments and serve us a meal. If your virtue is inviolate then a golden pelt will shield your nakedness from our gaze. However, if you fail then your infamy will be exposed.'

She turned to Vishnu and Shiva, 'Will the two of

you stand there like logs and allow this travesty of justice to take place? Haven't you a shred of decency? If the foremost of the Gods are this degenerate, I shudder to think of how the humans will behave and the horrors they will inflict upon their womenfolk!'

'It must be done!' Vishnu's tone was conciliatory, but unflinching as she glared at him.

Shiva shrugged, 'He is right. We have been brought here by the tides of fate over which even the Gods don't have control. Wear your nudity with the same confidence you wear your clothes. When something is not covered, nobody will feel the need to uncover it.'

'Is that so? The decision to keep something covered or uncovered has to rest with me. But if you lot are going to persist with your bullying and boorish conduct, then so be it!' Her voice was a whiplash and the Trimurti quailed ever so slightly.

Fools! Did they think she was defenceless because her husband wasn't home? She would show them! Anasuya had always been perfectly capable of defending herself and over the years, under the tutelage of her husband, she too had become one of the foremost practitioners of tapas and her skills in accumulating stores of ascetic merit was unmatched according to him. But the rest had never accorded her the same respect because they had simply assumed that women were not strong enough for such punishing endeavours involving the body, mind and soul. Anasuya would show them all what she was capable of today.

Reaching within herself and drawing from the core of her being all of the hidden reserves of strength she would need, Anasuya used it to siphon away the full extent of her anger and channel it into the weapon she was forging. Stripped of her rage, she felt calm and confident as she

MOHINI

strode forward. Tearing the sari off her body in a swift movement of deadly fluidity, she hurled the garment at them, glorying in the feel of her nudity. The Trimurti quaked with terror, helpless to stop the missile that roared towards them.

Thunder boomed in the heavens, lightning streaked across the skies and the inhabitants of the three worlds cowered in panic as it reverberated from the shock of the momentous events unfolding as a proud woman boldly strode where none before had dared to. She had taken on the might of the Trimurti and she was determined to prevail. Her power lit up the heavens and all who bore witness shuddered in awe.

In the ensuing stillness, three infants lay howling in misery and contrition on the deer skins scattered on the floor of Atri's hut as Anasuya nonchalantly gathered up her sari and tossed aside the garment unhurriedly. Gently, she lifted up the three bawling little ones and nursed them at her breast, till they were all calmer and restored to good spirits. Then she rocked them on her knee till they drifted off towards peaceful slumber.

As the days passed by, she cared for them. Feeding, cleaning and imparting the lessons they ought to have learned but never had. She told them stories of chivalry and valour. Of heroes who fought for equal rights by the side of their women, rather than taking away their agency to inflate their egos and grab more than a fair share of glory and power. They took in her words into the very core of themselves as they suckled at her breast, imbibing it with the life-giving milk she generously gave those who had invaded her home and sought to violate her, feeling themselves filling up with love and respect for all of her sex.

Saraswati, Lakshmi and Parvati, their faithful wives,

found them fighting for space on her lap when they finally succeeded in tracking down their errant spouses.

'They have behaved odiously and we warned them against doing this but sometimes even the Trimurti have to learn the hard way. But now that they have, grant us your compassion and give them back to us!' they pleaded with her.

'Are we sure we want them back?' Saraswati asked Lakshmi and Parvati seriously. 'They have never looked so sweet or appealing and I never did see the point of taking flawed objects and fixing them when they refuse to do it themselves.'

Anasuya only smiled. In a trice, the Trimurti stood before her again, looking suitably abashed, palms folded in prayer. Brahma couldn't look her in the eye and he left with indecent haste. Saraswati stayed behind. She rolled her eyes and winked at her sisters.

Shiva and Vishnu bowed before Anasuya and touched her feet with touching humility and reverence.

'Please accept my apologies for my abysmal conduct,' Shiva was sincere and earnest, a chastened boy who had learned from the whipping he had been subjected to. 'Brahma was wrong. Even the most wretched woman in all of creation is superior to the mightiest god. You have proved that. I solemnly swear that forever more, I will be a good friend to women and champion their rights.'

'Keep your word and you will be revered as the greatest of the gods for the rest of time, for you would have proved yourself worthy.' She blessed him wholeheartedly, placing her palm on his lowered head.

'I apologize too,' Vishnu had tears in his eyes. 'With you as my sacred witness, I hereby take an oath to go to the aid of all women who need me when it is within my power to do so, especially when there is an attempt made to forcibly disrobe them. And as amends for our conduct, we request you to carry our essence in your womb and bring forth children who will serve to make the three worlds a worthier place and one that is safer for women.'

'So be it. Forever more, you shall be the beloved of women who will no longer see you as the one who killed a good woman but as their greatest champion. You shall be strengthened by the power of unstinting love and as long as the three worlds exist, you will be beloved and worshipped with unflagging devotion.'

Anasuya shivered and hugged herself with excitement. They had kept their promise to her. Chandra would be born soon. She couldn't wait to hold him in her arms.

Tara walked out. Nobody noticed. So far so good. From the moment she had married Brihaspati, the Devaguru and piece of turd, having been forced to do so, she had wanted to leave him. And never come back. Not a moment passed by when she did not wish to be saved from her miserable marriage. She hated every single thing about him—his arrogance, faux piety, sterile intelligence, unctuous manner around those in power and contempt for everybody else. His wispy beard, the tuft of hair peeking out from his misshapen ears, the stentorian tone of his voice, his skinny, wrinkled limbs, and rotund belly. She loathed his touch and prayed for death every time he forced himself upon her.

Not that he cared. As far as the purohit was concerned, she was just something he owned and was there to be used as he saw fit.

At one point, she was reduced to fantasizing endlessly about breaking his kamandala on his head before chopping off his offensive head with his own golden axe. She couldn't bring herself to do it and sully her hands with his rotten blood. Instead, she whiled away the hours imagining herself making passionate love to every one of his students who had captured her fancy and even the ones who hadn't. The ones she liked as well as the ones who irritated her every bit as much as he did.

It wasn't exactly the most satisfying or productive way to spend her time, she conceded, but rebellion even when waged only in the head was needed to douse the flames of regret, which had already eaten away too much of her ailing heart and spirits while scarring her soul irreparably.

Why hadn't she given in to her impulse to walk out instead? It would have been more honourable than wasting eternity in the toxic wasteland that was her marriage, spending the days wondering if she hated herself or her husband more. Why had she stayed? She had the worst feeling that it was because she was too weak and had been raised to do as her elders and the man who had taken charge of her person told her to, even if both were more moronic than could be adequately expressed. But she had been the most moronic of them all.

If Tara were honest, she would admit that all she wanted was for one of the males who stepped in and out of her husband's ashram to sweep her off her feet and rescue her from one of their own. None of them could resist ogling her from afar, allowing their lingering gaze to dwell on her gently swelling breasts or brush past her to better breathe in the heady fragrance that emanated from her in a sensuous cloud, or allow their fingers to graze hers while pretending to help with the laundry.

Yet none had the gumption to fight their way past the barricades erected by her husband around his property, the impenetrable fortifications she herself had erected around her person, neutralize her formidable resistance and take her far away. She hated them all for forcing her to remain virtuous when she would have gladly tossed it all away along with her modesty, honour, and just about anything else, for the chance to be happy, feel loved and sexually satisfied. Even if it was only for one miserable moment in all of eternity. Was that too much to ask?

MOHINI

There were other less romantic options too. Brihaspati could drop dead the very next day and she would be a widow who still had her youth and looks, so she could fall in love again with a wonderful man and be as happy as she dared. Or at the very least, be just a little bit happier than she was now. After all, it had happened to more hopeless characters than herself.

Or she could walk out and find a way to be happy all by herself. But that would mean risking the predators who would violate her, before murdering her and violating her some more. Or she would be eaten by wild animals if she was not reduced to beggary or stoned to death for being the whore who dared to forsake her marriage vows. The thought of being reduced to such deplorable circumstances terrified her and she assured herself repeatedly that she ought to focus on the blessings she was privileged to have instead of dwelling on the things she lacked.

The latter was a persistent presence though, insisting that death was better than being forced to live a life that was hateful to her. But it wasn't enough to make her leave. So she decided to stay, forcing herself to falsely hope that her life would get better. Death felt so final and she wasn't quite ready to give up on her wretched life. It was all very frustrating.

Tara had almost given up one time, when her husband went too far and she shocked herself by staying on even after he did what he did. The highly respected Brihaspati, one of the predominantly eminent wielders of power in heaven, had raped his heavily pregnant sister-in-law Mamata. When the child in her womb expelled his stinking seed to register his protest over the foul deed, he cursed the unborn child with blindness and the Gods, led by Indra, bore witness and condemned Mamata for not doing the right thing by carrying the child conceived by violation to term!

'You are a monster!' Tara spat at his feet, tears of rage and misery rolling down her cheeks. 'For the crime of hurting poor Mamata and her unborn child, you should have your male organ hacked off and fed to the crows, before being tossed head first into the thousand hells of Yama for the rest of time. How could you do this to the blameless Utathya who has been such a good brother to you? Indra is a craven and a fool for not punishing the most evil deed in the three worlds! He is not fit to rule nor is he worthy of the worship he demands. Aren't you going to say something? Or are you just going to pretend that I am talking about someone else?'

'Let me explain something to you...' he began sonorously without the slightest hint of remorse. 'You can cry all you want, but the truth of the matter is that nature does not care about rape, love, romance or sex, as long as the virile seed finds its way into the womb to ensure that life goes on. Procreation has always been above principles. The rest is entirely immaterial. Which is why it is better to be pragmatic and sensible about these things, instead of screeching like a hysterical slattern and disgracing yourself! Clearly your mother has failed to raise you to emulate the likes of Anasuya, Vasuki or Lopamudra and I have to pay the price by enduring the hysterical fits of a screaming shrew.'

'I can't describe how grateful I am to you for explaining such profound truths to a poor ignoramus like me...' her voice dripped with sarcasm and scorn. 'It is good to know that you don't care whose seed makes its way into my womb. After all, nature does not care about these things. And I would rather accept the embrace of a diseased donkey than let you lay a finger on me ever again.'

The next thing she knew, Tara was sprawled on the floor, reeling from the blow that had split her lip, knocked her head against the stone wall and left her bleeding. When angered, Brihaspati was surprisingly strong.

'Whore!' He aimed a series of kicks at her ribcage and every exposed part of her body. He may have beaten her to death then, and his students would have let him, for they were watching and listening to the sounds of her humiliation and degradation while pretending to be otherwise occupied. But he got winded and stopped. He was gasping for breath but he gathered himself to aim a few more blows and to fling everything in the vicinity at her, before he stomped away, yelling for his students to attend to him.

Tara hadn't run away even then. Not even when she lay bleeding in the battlefield her home had been reduced to. Anger and indignation left her impervious to pain but when those ebbed away, it was all that was left and she writhed in agony and shame over the memory of being beaten like an animal.

Brihaspati wasn't done with his vileness though. Having gotten away with perfidy once, he believed himself invincible. The Devas had met with a shock defeat to the Asura commander, the mighty Jalandhara. At the Devaguru's instigation, the celestials, led by Upendra, abducted the Asura commander's wife Tulasi and kept her locked up in a secret location where they took turns to violate her. The good woman killed herself and when the news was carried to Jalandhara, he was so distraught with grief and so emotionally compromised he could no longer perform competently. Indra had no trouble vanquishing his forces and beheading their commander.

When she found out that he had masterminded the heinous deed, Tara finally walked out. She was so enraged about the plight of poor Tulasi, Jalandhara and the thousands upon thousands who had been slaughtered that she was nearly prostate with sorrow. However, a part of her couldn't help but be happy that he had finally given her an excuse to leave him.

Under the Moonlight

Chandra found Tara in a clearing, huddled up against a tree, sobbing her eyes out. It wasn't a pretty sight. For a second, he had been convinced he was looking at a Dakini, one of those vengeful female sprits he had been warned about, though his mother insisted that it was merely something men had made up when they were being even more stupid than usual. But he was kind, offering her a piece of cloth to dry her eyes and taking her hands in his to still the shaking.

'I'd cry if I were Brihaspati's wife too…' he told her with a twinkle of understanding that betrayed his own thoughts on the grave business with Tulasi. Chandra, Kamadeva, Agni and Surya had vociferously opposed the grotesque plan of action, not that it had made any kind of difference or made him feel any better about his inability to save the victim in the lamentable affair.

Looking at this frail woman who was dangerously close to breaking, he couldn't help but admire the courage it must have taken to demonstrate her outrage for Tulasi's fate by leaving her powerful husband. None before her had dared to do anything like this before. All of Amaravati was agog about her actions. Brihaspati himself was away performing 'a purification ritual' in some undisclosed corner of Mount Meru and neither his students nor even Indra felt obliged to tell him that his wife was gone.

'Would you like me to escort you back? It is not very safe hereabouts.'

'It would be preferable to be torn apart by wild dogs than go back to that beast of a rapist,' Tara managed to say coherently, though she was having difficulty breathing. Chandra was without doubt the most handsome male she had seen. In fact, no living soul could resist a beauty such as his, even if it concealed a creature no different from Brihaspati, which it didn't. She was acutely aware that she was sniffling and wiping the tears as well as phlegm that was dripping down her face with the torn and dirtied hem of her sari, looking like something nasty that had been expelled by a wild animal.

'Why don't you stay with me?' Chandra said on an impulse. 'I am staying at my father's hermitage. It is not too far from here and my parents have left on a pilgrimage. Once you have refreshed yourself and put away a decent meal, I promise you will feel much better.'

The moment he said it, Chandra felt something give in his head and heart. This was dangerous ground. Very dangerous ground. And he hadn't stepped on it so much as leaped upon it with reckless abandon. It was one thing for him to incur Indra's displeasure by distancing himself from the court over the Tulasi incident and quite another to even give the impression of a dalliance with Tara. The faintest whiff of improper conduct on either of their parts would lead to far-ranging ramifications. They would be courting not just dishonour and disgrace but death as well. He knew all this and yet he was inexplicably attracted to her, drawn to her by a force he knew would be futile to resist.

She was his Guru's wife and the smart thing to do would be to send word to the Devaguru's dogs to come and collect her at once. But he couldn't bring himself to do it. Hopefully, she would come to her senses, refuse his offer and trudge back homeward.

She couldn't bring herself to do this either. The universe had conspired to bring them together for the better or the worse and neither of them could do anything about it.

'I don't want to impose,' Tara's voice was hesitant, 'or get you into trouble.' *Please take me away with you. I have been so scared and lonely. And I am really tired, hungry and thirsty. My mother taught me to obey and be a good girl. She never taught me anything about surviving in the wild and I don't know how.*

'Oh! It is no trouble at all. In fact, I consider it an honour and privilege to be your host,' he lied through his teeth while groaning inside. Anasuya, his mother, was brilliant at handling situations like this before they spiralled out of control. But he himself would be damned if he knew how.

'You are too kind!' Tara took his proffered hand gratefully and hoped he didn't notice the tremor that rippled through her body or the sexual excitement that had stirred unbidden in her breast even as she was tormented by visions of being stoned to death for being an adulterous whore. Silently, she thanked the universe for taking the decision out of her hands and went where he took her, ignoring the trepidation that was bubbling in his chest and which she could feel through her fingertips, in addition to his lust for her.

What followed was the most blissful period in Tara's life. If she had a complaint, it would be that everything passed by in a blur. They hadn't become lovers immediately. It was all very innocent and respectful as they made half-hearted attempts to resist the overpowering sexual currents that surged between them.

He surprised her by foraging in the woods for their meals and cooking it for her.

'My father used to cook for my mother every once in a while,' he told her. 'She liked cooking and made us the most amazing meals. But I have also heard her say that she loved my father the most when he did this little thing for her. He would also encourage me to help in the kitchen. That made her smile too, even when I mostly got in the way. Eventually, I did learn to cook. Mother says it is an invaluable skill that all must possess instead of relegating the task to the ladies and depending on them to assuage hunger pangs at all times over the course of a lifetime.'

'Your mother must be the most sensible person in the three worlds. She sounds so amazing. I would love to meet her!'

Chandra smiled in response and tried not to imagine the look on Anasuya's face if she found out that he was harbouring a married woman under his roof, and his Guru's wife at that. She disapproved most strongly of adultery and was most vociferous on the subject. Her reaction would have been even more vociferous if she had known that her favourite son was risking death and damnation, all for a fallen woman who had disgraced herself by leaving her husband for another. 'The love of fickle creatures lasts only as long as it is convenient and is easily transferred,' she would have said—or were these his own unworthy thoughts? Of course, they hadn't done anything illicit as yet, but they might as well have.

The whispering and nudging had already begun. Who would believe that they were spending their days doing perfectly respectable things of a companionable nature, like going for the occasional ramble, cooking, talking and keeping their hands off each other? Often he would go hunting and his Guru's beautiful wife kept herself occupied by taking care of all the woodland creatures that just seemed to gravitate towards her. He found it hard to believe this story himself. And with reason. He knew it was only a matter of time before they succumbed to the forbidden passion that had bloomed between them.

Eventually they did become lovers. It happened all at once and both wondered how they had managed to hold out as long as they had when they had clearly wanted it all along. Nothing had felt more organic or wholesome or so intensely pleasurable and they chided themselves for wasting so many days tiptoeing around each other, trying to do the honourable thing. Had honour ever felt as good as an orgasm?

Tara had always had a troubled marriage. She had hated the rasping of her husband's breath when he laboured painfully on top of her with the sole view to perpetuate his line. The guttural grunting and the way he held her hip with one hand while clumsily bunching up his dhoti behind him and wedging it in his rear with the other. It was an idiosyncrasy that really got on her nerves. Amongst the umpteen other things she found revolting about her husband. Like the fact that he was a rapist, casteist, hypocrite, wife-beater and a truly evil being with very few redeeming qualities.

Chandra, on the other hand, was everything she had dreamed about in a lover. Their union was not at all complicated. It was so simple yet utterly hedonistic. But more than that, she loved how much they cared about each other. He treated her with so much tenderness and admiration, she thought her heart must surely burst to pieces.

He was a considerate and generous lover. As they spent long days and nights making passionate love, exchanging deep kisses as they devoted themselves to pleasuring each other, all Tara wanted was more and more of the same. She knew that she was gluttonous for his caresses, his touch, the firm yet gentle way he explored every inch of her naked body with his fingers and lips, the manner in which he held her face as he kissed her, and the way he ran his fingers through her hair to yank her head back so he could plant a string of soft kisses on her exposed throat, or the hungry manner with which he nibbled on her earlobe to make her moan in ecstasy.

Tara tried to put off climaxing as long as she could because she never ever wanted to descend from the height of sybaritic excess she was indulging in. But it was never as long as she would have liked, because her body would be convulsing with a surfeit of all things delectable and her head throbbed from the intensity of the experience as their lovemaking grew more frenzied, building to the magnificent crescendo that preceded the grand finale.

As they lay entwined in the bittersweet melancholy that followed their frantic coupling, Tara couldn't help but think that being with him like this physically, even without love or any romantic attachment to sweeten it further, was the fulfilment of a basic primeval desire that was more powerful than the need to eat, sleep, put on clothes or find shelter. Yet this was the one thing she had been taught to deny herself all her life. But all the empty, wasted years and even Brihaspati's abuse had been worth it, if it meant being with one like Chandra. His mere presence could make her heart race and a gentle kiss would leave her beside herself with happiness.

Even now that she had the thing she wanted more than anything else, she was more terrified than happy at the prospect of losing it. Her appetite for Chandra was insatiable and she knew that her hunger and craving for his embrace could never be quenched. All the fire in the world would be insufficient to douse the fire he had ignited in her loins. There was only one thing she wanted in this existence and that was to have Chandra in her bed, even if it meant being his whore forever. She had sacrificed shame, decency, dignity and pride to be with him and she had done so gladly. It was a small price to pay for what she got in return.

As for Chandra, she sensed that he did not love her as fiercely as she did him. But she told herself it did not matter, because she loved him enough for both of them. Of course, he had wanted her and thrived on the danger of luxuriating in a forbidden act. He loved the intensity of her passion for him and her generous dispensation of unconditional love. But he had no wish to lose his exalted standing among the celestials nor face the wrath of his twenty-seven other wives, the Nakshatras, as they were affectionately called.

Besides, of all his wives and lovers, who were innumerable as the stars in the sky, there was room in his heart for Rohini alone. His own heart was entrusted to her care and she cradled it lovingly in her bosom. He would have snatched her fragrance and held it tightly clenched in his fist if he could have, the way her destiny and very soul was locked up in his heart. Her sweet breath steered his wild flights across the three worlds. And he went where the violent winds of his will led him, knowing that every one of his meandering journeys eventually led him back to her.

Tara knew this, though she didn't want to. In the mutual exchange of each other's hearts, the currency was not of equal value. Sensing the discrepancy that gave her sleepless nights, haunted by the monsters that fed on her fear, she tried desperately to tighten her grip on his affections and hold on for dear life. She would not let him go. She could not afford to let him go. No matter the asking price. For doing so would mean a return to the emptiness she had fought so long and hard to free herself from, made even worse than before by his absence. She couldn't do it. She would not hesitate to burn down the three worlds to keep him melded to her if that was what it took.

Every time her fear, dread and insecurity got completely out of hand, Tara would muse morbidly on the unpalatable but unavoidable fact that she was going to lose him, no matter how hard she tried, and even if she sacrificed everything of herself she possessed. Then she would swallow the screams and tears that fountained forth foully from her throat, put on her most alluring garments, adorn herself just the way she knew he liked and entice him to make love to her. He may or may not have had his reservations about the sexual tidal wave and the swirling emotional turmoil that had enslaved him just as much as he had enslaved her but he was too polite a lover to ever deny Tara. Besides, he couldn't resist even when he was repelled by the toxicity of their destructive obsession for each other.

So she hoarded his kisses and treasured every moment he made her moan with a miser's affection, because Tara knew that they would not last forever, even if she drenched whatever it was they shared with all the Amrita in the world churned from the ocean of her love. It would never be enough.

As it turned out, they had even less time than she had anticipated. Tara should have been careful about what she had wished for. All she had wanted was to be blissfully happy for one miserable moment in all of eternity and that was exactly what she had been granted. Brihaspati had returned from his ceremonial cleansing and was informed by his students about the prurient and seamier details of his wife's betrayal, as well as her indecent infatuation with Chandra. He was livid. He sent armed messengers to summon her to his presence, but the trollop had the temerity to reject him outright.

If he was livid before, Brihaspati had become apoplectic with rage. He hadn't expended a tenth of this current feeling when she had been well and truly under his thumb. The cuckolded husband stormed over to Indra's sabha, borne thither in a tempest of rage.

'How dare Chandra do this? Is this the reward I get for serving faithfully as the preceptor of the Devas? He has shamed me and you have been complicit in his infamy, for it happened on your watch. You will all pay for this. I shall depart this very instant, but not before I have razed Amaravati with all its treasures to the ground and plucked the odious moon from the heavens and reduced the lecher to a chamber pot for the rest of eternity for people to dump their wastes into, so that he will be too impure and unworthy to ever be admitted into the ranks of the celestials again.'

Rank terror rippled across the ranks of the petrified celestials. Hadn't they tried to warn Chandra that it would come to this? But he was hopelessly ensnared in the coils of whatever ill-omened enchantment she had cast on him.

Indra was horrified and he tried to find the words to appease one whose wife was living in sin with another. 'Guruji! I am sure this is all a misunderstanding and…'

'Don't you lie to me, oh King!' he roared. 'Those two have been rutting away like pigs in heat and they have been doing so openly. My students have told me everything and your spies have reported back to you. Every single one of you knew all along. But you all turned a blind eye and did nothing to salvage the honour of your Guru, preferring instead to laugh at him behind his back. I can think of no punishment severe enough for such infamous conduct.'

Indra thought quickly, fuming in consternation. What was he supposed to have done? Drag the lovers apart and order them to keep their hands off each other? Cover the naked body of the harlot in heat with wild honey and leave her spread-eagled on the forest floor for the killer ants and predators in the hope that her ardour would be dampened?

All this fuss over a shameless slut who couldn't control her disgusting urges. He would be damned if he and his beloved Amaravati were made to pay the price for the actions of an adulterous whore. As for Chandra, if Brihaspati were to follow through on his threat to reduce him to a chamber pot, or even if a hair on their beloved son was harmed, Atri and his powerful sorceress of a wife who had prevailed over the Trimurti would show up on his doorstep and threaten to reduce *him* to a rock for the crows to shit on. What a grotesque affair this was turning out to be! And how dare they drag the King of Heaven and mighty wielder of the thunderbolt to mediate over their sordid sexual shenanigans?

'You shall be avenged,' Indra declared. 'I swear to you on my honour. I will clap her in chains and bring her before you to face the music for her unforgiveable conduct. As for Chandra, he shall be ostracized and will no longer be admitted to Amaravati, which is the realm of the pious and pure-hearted.' He said this without flinching and caught Kama looking askance at him, no doubt thinking of the romp they had enjoyed the previous night with a gaggle of gorgeous apsaras.

How he hated these champions of female rights! Indra was determined to ignore that reproving look. Would Kama have preferred it if he allowed Amaravati to burn to protect the slut and her lover? At least Chandra was needed. What use did anybody have for a whore?

Brihaspati seemed marginally appeased. Or at least he was no longer spitting fire and preparing himself to curse them all into oblivion. 'She must be stripped of her clothes, branded with irons to mark her as a disgraced whore and brought here in chains.'

Kama made as if to speak and Indra quelled him with a

MOHINI

glare. 'It shall be as you wish, Guruji, and my personal guard accompanied by our finest regiments shall set out immediately.'

Chandra cursed beneath his breath. How had it come to this? Tara had forced his hand and now her husband had done the same. Ever since he had been informed that Brihaspati had returned and was on the warpath, he had been thinking about how to undo the damage he had done and find a way to convince Tara to go back to him. He had broached the subject delicately, trying not to melt when she replied with wounded eyes.

'I hope you know that my love for you means more to me than everything else in the three worlds, but we cannot stand by and allow innocent people to die, sacrificed on the flames of Brihaspati's wrath.'

Tara looked troubled. 'Indra's involvement in matters of the heart does not bode well. Why does he indulge Brihaspati to this extent? He is our king, but he couldn't be bothered when Mamata was violated or when I was beaten to within an inch of my life. If that were not bad enough, he is willing to sacrifice so many to appease Brihaspati's rage, uncaring that he will have the blood of the innocent on his hands. How is this fair? And how can the celestials stand for this?'

Tears would fill her eyes and he would feel compelled to take her in his arms. How could he make her see reason and do the needful to avert the impending catastrophe? Why couldn't she understand that it was easier to blame her than Indra or Brihaspati? Their King and Guru mattered more in the grand scheme of things than a woman who was little more than a caged bird with a broken wing, trilling her song to the indifferent winds.

Chandra tried to make her see the path she must take. But no, sensing his mood and need to talk about their unsavoury reality, Tara would be reclining on a gilded chaise, naked and heartbreakingly vulnerable. Surrounded by her pots of unguents, herbal pastes and potions, she would cover his body in soothing emollients only to lick them off and anoint his member with her concoctions till he was cast into a sea of exquisite sensation where there was no place for worry or unpleasantness.

Slowly but surely, he would surrender as she would devote herself to making him ejaculate a thousand and one times. She was inexhaustible herself and seemed willing to while away their immortality by copulating endlessly till they drove each other mad with desire and leading them recklessly further and further along the path to damnation. They were saying that Tara was an acolyte of Mohini, the Enchantress, and it was from her that she had learned the art of seduction. It would certainly explain why even her broken wing had not stopped her from soaring into the realm of sensual delights.

Now it was too late. With the stalwarts of the celestial army converging on their little hermitage, Chandra and Tara had no choice but to flee like thieves on his silver chariot drawn by stags, fleet as thought. Kama had stolen away on his parrot to warn him of the fate that awaited his paramour. 'You must flee!' he told Chandra. 'Far away where Brihaspati's wrath can't reach you. As for Tara…'

'I cannot abandon her!' he said more firmly than he had intended, because he wanted to do just that.

Kama hesitated. 'There is a way out. Send Tara back with me. I will use two of my most potent arrows. One for him and one for her. They will be consumed by desire for each other and in the fog of their newly discovered love, all acrimony will be forgotten. The three worlds won't have to burn and you will regain your standing among the celestials.'

Damn him! Why hadn't he just used his ridiculously potent arrows without looking to him for permission he couldn't grant and saved them all a lot of heartbreak? Why was it that the decent always did more damage than the devious?

'She would never consent to this in a million years,' he

MOHINI

whispered, 'and her choice matters even if Indra and Brihaspati's supporters think otherwise. Tara keeps saying that she would rather give herself to rabid jackals, wild buffaloes, mad elephants, diseased donkeys and lecherous lepers many times over till there is nothing left of her but her bleeding yoni, rather than return to her husband.'

They both sighed morosely over the unfathomable ways of women. And then went their separate ways.

Chandra and Tara rode a long way, holding hands, transmitting their fear to each other through palms slick with sweat. Hunted every step of the way, they were forced to deal with missiles hurled at them every which way, forcing him to retaliate. Tara cried out as an arrow grazed her ribs, staining her bosom red with blood, and it glistened blackly under the moonlight. Chandra heard the divine astras whizzing towards them and he clenched his jaw in cold fury.

With a clarion call, he summoned the creatures of his beloved darkness to his side. Monstrous beings who answered to none but his own self. Bristling forms of smoke, shadow and steel, asked by their overlord to do the unthinkable. They barred the passage to all who sought to pursue the fleeing couple and dissuaded them using any and all means necessary. Chandra heard the sounds of slaughter and curses directed at him and his lover from the dying lips of his brothers, and felt his heart would burst. As the tears ran unchecked down his handsome visage, he gently extricated her hand from his. And Tara wept with him. For herself.

Sick with grief and regret, they reached the stronghold of the Asura king, Virochana, and sought refuge. Chandra hated himself for dragging him and his people into this, but where else could he go? Tara was bleeding copiously and she needed help. He had to do what was best for her even if it killed him.

As they rode towards Virochana's formidable palace armoured against his enemies with stone and steel, winged by shadowy wielders of mighty weapons, the citizens gathered to watch their progress in sullen silence. Tara hadn't realized it until then, but she had lived in mortal terror of her sins being paraded before prying eyes, in whose unforgiving gaze she would be reduced to nothing more than a bitch in heat. She shrivelled up under the harshness of their anger. A blackness had opened up deep inside of her and it was filled with the sewage of their derision.

'Slut!'

'She has brought war to our doorstep.'

'Thousands will die because of this dirty little strumpet!'

'Whore!'

'Witch!'

'Bitch!'

'Why should we have to pay the price for her promiscuity?'

'Prostitute!'

'If she had a morsel of decency, she would hang herself or leap off the highest cliff.'

'She must consign her body to the flames to atone for the evil she has ushered into the three worlds.'

'Perhaps our King will be sensible and do as her husband demands. Strip her naked, brand her with irons, declaring her to be the cheap slut she is, clap her in chains and turn her over for punishment.'

Tara hadn't felt this broken, not even when Brihaspati had stomped on her chest and back and she heard the ribs crack... Never had she felt more naked or exposed. Faint with self-loathing, she wished Chandra would lend her his shoulder for support, but he had the air of one who knew he had done something disgusting and deserved to die for it. Worse, he probably blamed her for everything. Tara wanted to reach out to him but she knew he would recoil from the slightest touch and then she would crumble in a heap and throw herself under the chariot wheels, exposing herself to the mercy of the sharp spikes, which would hopefully tear her apart into tiny pieces that would be carried away by the wind.

Virochana was icily courteous, but his attitude mirrored those of his subjects. He could not refuse refuge to those who sought it. So he took them in, spoke politely to Chandra, and placed his resources at their disposal. As for Tara, he refused to look at her as though he were convinced that she was little more than a pile of garbage and certainly not worthy of his attention or regard.

She wasn't wrong. As the Asura king issued orders to prepare for war, he couldn't help but wonder if a battle unto the death to be fought over a fickle woman's infidelity was worth anything at all, even by the abysmal standards set by every other futile war that had ever been fought. Clearly, this was proof if any were needed about the hopelessness of existence.

Virochana said as much to Sukra.

'I understand her plight, I do, but if every woman who hated her husband abandoned her marriage to run away with her lover, then this is the kind of shambolic situation that can be expected and the noble institution of marriage would crumble into dust. If the bonds that bind us can so easily be snapped, there would be nothing but chaos and anarchy in the three worlds.'

'You are upset, which is why you want to pretend that bonds that bind are a blessing. As for the institution of marriage, it is an unnatural one,' Sukra remarked. 'I have long advocated a state where we return to our roots and live like the noble animals do. They don't bother with rules the way we do. They eat, sleep and mate. No animal mother has ever bothered to ascertain or even care about the father of her child and in lean times, she may just eat both and eject the remains with nary a twinge of conscience.'

'That is nice,' Virochana was still inclined to grumble. 'So why don't you tell Tara to disappear into the woods to live among the "noble" animals she clearly belongs with? All this trouble because one woman was incapable of fidelity. My troops are on the verge of mutiny because they don't want to get entangled in this business over a wanton whore. Their wives are being most unreasonable and are clamouring that she be sent back to her husband in disgrace. And you are not exactly helping morale by refusing to use the Sanjivani craft, which has given us such an advantage in the past.

Why won't you use it anymore?'

Sukra was silent. He had been a fool to think there would be no consequences to the use of a craft as powerful as the Sanjivani. Of course there had been. Every life he saved in the present was lost in the future. He had finally understood that. Jayanti had helped him see it, by tracking the movement of the planets and linking it to every one of Vishnu's avatars. He remembered his pleasure when he was named the presiding deity of a planet. Bhrigu and Kavya had been beside themselves with pride. But their joy had become diluted when Brihaspati was accorded the same honour.

'Fine company you are keeping these days,' Kavya had sniffed disapprovingly. 'Rapists, gigolos and thieves truncated in half!'

'Don't you see?' Jayanti, who was more philosophical, had spelled it out for him, 'Vishnu in his role as the reliever of pain—Bhumi Devi's and her offspring's—channels his essence through the presiding deities of the planets. Think about it. It was under the auspices of Brihaspati, whom some of the humans call Jupiter, that Vamana destroyed Mahabali. The preceptor's antipathy for the Asuras spilled over into the avatar, wouldn't you say? Which is why a good King died and you lost an eye.'

Sukra nodded, 'That sounds like something that Brihaspati would do when he is not forcing himself on pregnant women.'

'Rama belongs to the Surya vamsa as you know,' she continued. 'And Krishna to Chandra's lineage. The man-lion, Narasimha, channelled the power of Kartikeya, the planet Mangala or Mars. The essence of the Destroyer is said to be concentrated in this particular vessel, which explains the sheer ferocity of this particular avatar. The tortoise carried the baleful influence of Sani in his shell, the boar bore the fury of Rahu, and Ketu influenced the fish. Budha is, of course, *the* Buddha, the Enlightened One.'

'Fascinating!' he murmured, 'And now we come to the planet Venus over which I am the presiding deity. The only avatar that is left is Parashurama, wielder of the fiery axe.'

She didn't have to spell out the rest, for he saw it all in his mind's eyes. Twenty-one generations of Kshatriyas were decimated as the axe rose and fell with rhythmic precision, allowing him to fill the empty sea with their blood. Unlike the other avatars that also saw large-scale slaughter such as Kurukshetra or the slaying of the demon king, Ravana, this time it wasn't arbitrary. Every Asura he had ever saved, he slew again, guiding Parashurama's hand personally. For a debt to Mrityu must always be paid with interest. The sounds of dying and the cries of the bereaved rang out in his ears, and try as he might, he could not dull the clamour. He hadn't used his craft ever since. And Parashurama had hacked his mother to death on his father, Jamadagni's orders. And asked for her to be resuscitated, when he was granted a boon. Sukra shuddered.

'Using the Amrita or the Sanjivani Vidya are not without consequences. One does so at immense peril to the self as well as that of others. Believe me when I say that it is best not to interfere with the natural order. Even this war, pointless as you believe it may be, must be allowed to run its course. For there is always a purpose to be served even if it is not readily apparent to us. And flowers may yet bloom in blood-soaked battlefields.'

'What a poetic bent of mind my preceptor has!' Virochana said with all the sarcasm he could muster.

Sukra was unruffled. 'Besides, haven't you successfully peddled the myth that while you wear the crown encrusted with the rarest and most precious stones that you appropriated from Vishnu after arguing that he had repeatedly favoured the Devas, you will never know defeat. What more do you need?'

Virochana felt a heaviness settle in his chest. 'I hope a myth is all we need to survive. Besides, I hear Mohini plans to relieve me of my head and crown both. In the meantime, we mustn't keep war, death and destruction waiting. Not when the fate of a loose woman and her non-existent honour hangs in the balance.' He felt bad the moment he uttered the words. After all, he himself had a thousand wives and double the number of concubines and he had never felt the need or the inclination to stay true to any of them. *But still, it was different with women. Shouldn't they conduct themselves in a manner that befit their status as the superior sex in order to set an example for men to redeem themselves?* He felt worse now. His thoughts were even more unworthy than his words. So he decided to concentrate on killing the enemies of the woman they had all wronged.

They called the great war Tarakamaya, and it made Tara furious. Didn't the fools realize that she had wanted to make love, not war? This was a useless war fought over Brihaspati's wounded pride and it was typical of them to blame her for it. What crime had she committed? She was not the rapist or killer and yet, it was so much easier for them to vilify and punish her. And all because she had refused to pander to his ego like the spineless lickspittle Indra and his cronies, choosing love and happiness over an abusive marriage that had made her life a living hell.

The Asuras were no different. All of them wanted Tara to turn herself over to the celestial hordes who had been taunting them mercilessly, deriding their decision to fight and die for a woman who was despoiled and disgraced. But she stubbornly refused to do it. And they hated her for it. The unceasing malevolence that buffeted her on all sides steadily eroded what was left of her strength. But she was determined not to give in to their shameless extortionist tactics.

It would have been easier if Chandra would just hold her in his arms and tell her that they were going to be fine, even if it would be a bald-faced lie. He spent the days holed up with Virochana and his generals to lend any assistance he could. Of course, Chandra was painfully polite and solicitous as ever, but he could no longer bring himself to touch her. His rejection of her broke Tara the way nothing else had, and the grief left her physically sick. She withdrew into her chambers, refused audience to all but Chandra and lay in the cold comfort of the darkness. Nobody seemed to mind. Most of her meals were left uneaten and the maids knew she was violently sick on some days. But the general opinion was that it was nothing less than what she deserved.

Tara withdrew into solitude, while war raged around her. Chandra's friends, family and brothers in arms lay among the dead and he knew the celestials would never forgive him for choosing an adulteress over them. They had denounced him as a traitor and would have killed him if they didn't need him to shield and protect them from the darkness. The Moon God was filled with remorse. The killing had been self-defence, but it did not make him feel any better. He couldn't help but wonder if his parents and brothers hated him too.

He spent long hours wracking his brain for ideas to put an end to this bloody business once and for all but he came up short. The Devas and Asuras were evenly matched as always and the struggle could go on for centuries. Tara could put an end to it if she wished to, of course, but for the life of him he couldn't understand why she was being so damnably selfish.

For nine long months, the war dragged on. Neither side showed any inclination to give in. All were tired. All wished Tara were dead. There was even an attempt on her life. Nobody knew if the Devas or Asuras were behind the cowardly attack. Chandra took her in his arms then, and Tara breathed in the scent of him.

'I won't let them hurt you,' his voice was muffled by her thick hair, but there was no mistaking the fierceness. 'From this moment, I will not leave your side and they will have to go through me to get to you.'

She sensed his guilt for having abandoned her, but Tara was pathetically grateful that he still cared and she hastened to comfort him, 'You have given me so much to be thankful for. And I was right to fall in love with you. You won't have to endure much more of this. I promise.'

'You don't—'

She placed her finger on his lips to shush him.

Virochana chose soldiers from his personal guard to protect her. Tara touched his feet in gratitude. There were tears in her eyes.

To her surprise, he bade her rise and blessed her. 'In the beginning, it is true that I did not wish to imperil my people over a domestic dispute, but your bravery and fortitude shames me. Only a despicable craven would seek to attack an unarmed woman or stipulate such shameful conditions for her return. I am proud to have espoused your cause and we will not surrender.'

'You have my gratitude, oh King. A thousand lifetimes will be insufficient to pay you back for the kindness you have shown a wretched woman.' She took a deep breath and signalled to her maid, 'I beg your indulgence one last time, Your Highness.'

Tara took a step back as she gathered herself to address the King. Chandra and Sukra were also present. Both were taken aback by her appearance. Frail and emaciated, she appeared to have wasted away from grief. But she was lit up by an inner spirit of resilience and strength that enhanced her beauty a thousand fold. They watched with worried eyes, as she gingerly accepted an object wrapped in cloth and laboriously made her way back to them.

'My lords!' she began, 'I am happy to be the bearer of good tidings. The war shall end today for I will surrender myself to the celestial forces and they may do as they please with what is left of me.'

Virochana and Chandra shook their heads vehemently, but she was looking tenderly at the bundle in her arms. Sukra noted that it was moving.

'So that is why...' he looked at her with something bordering on respect.

She held up the baby with fierce pride. He was beautiful and they gasped aloud at his splendid curls, radiant countenance and sparkling eyes so like his father's.

'This is your son,' she informed Chandra. 'If Brihaspati finds out, he will stake claim and insist that the baby belongs to him, since he considers me to be his property.' Tara was struggling to find the words as she wrestled with the powerful emotions that were scorching her insides and she addressed Chandra, 'Let the Gods bear witness, Chandra is the father of this special child whom I have named Budha. I entrust him to your care. He is meant to do great things and I have no wish to cast his life in the shadows that claimed mine. I know you will do the right thing by him the way you did with me. And may my love protect you both from all harm.'

Chandra wept. 'I am so sorry, I never did have your courage.'

Virochana looked ashen. 'I cannot, in good conscience, hand you over to that murderous mob. You don't have to make this choice. Your son needs you.'

She shook her head sadly, 'It will be wrong of me to impose any further on your kindness and generosity. But too many have died on my account and it is my turn to make amends. Besides, the choice was always mine to make.'

'I hope you will honour me by accepting this gift!' Virochana removed the crown from his head and placed it on her brow even as his assembled generals gasped in horror. 'Vishnu gave it to me a long time ago. The wearer is granted the protection of every one of his avatars. You may call upon the fish to guide you past treacherous tides, the tortoise to steady your mind and heart, the boar, the half man-half lion, or the wielder of the fiery axe to savage your enemies, the righteous man or Krishna to keep you secure in their hearts, Buddha for enlightenment or Mohini, to reward you with the greatest of gifts. And you have earned the right to wear it.'

Tara was speechless. Ignoring protocol, she threw her arms around him with the greatest affection. Then she pressed her lips against her son's forehead and looked at the dear face one last time. For his sake, she would endure this and so much more. Her heart broke in two as she handed him over to Chandra. She would have liked to kiss the love of her life one last time, but she dared not. Tara needed every ounce of her strength. Instead she sought the blessings of Sukra.

'You were brave enough to follow your heart and may future generation pay heed to your example!'

There was nothing more to be said. It was time to meet her destiny. The crowds made way as she walked towards the gate, holding her head erect and proud. It had been her choice to be Chandra's whore and she stood by it. She regretted nothing. And so she walked to her doom. Chandra held his beautiful baby in his arms and he wept into the hair that was so like Tara's.

I should have left this pathetic tale of rotten love alone, but how could I? Sometimes the stories needed to be rewritten when a tragedy was not warranted. Sometimes people deserved to have their heart's desires fulfilled, especially when all they wanted was a little love spiced with sex. And hadn't Tara suffered enough?

She walked without flinching into the ranks of the Devas, who hissed and spat, brandishing their weapons menacingly as she walked by. To her surprise, Chandra materialized by her side. 'I won't let you do this alone,' he murmured. 'It is the very least I can do.' He held their child firmly in one arm and placed the other protectively over her shoulder.

Brihaspati's cruel face loomed ahead of hers. Indra stood grim-faced and gestured to the troops to carry out the orders that had been issued.

Tara turned to Chandra, 'I am proud to have been yours.' She closed her eyes as she awaited her fate.

At that moment, the skies opened up and rained flowers on the lovers. 'Seize her!' Brihaspati bellowed at the guards, but a ring of fire blazed around Tara protectively. Awestruck, they watched as Tara's crown burst into light and enveloped her in a golden haze. Before their very eyes, she was lifted off her feet and began a slow ascent to the heavens.

Brihaspati stomped his feet in fury and frustration. 'She must not get away! Grab her!' Immediately his troops sought to grasp her ankles but the dancing flames held them back, leaving their flesh sizzling and burning as they screamed in agony.

Chandra was unaffected by the bedlam that had erupted around him. He had eyes only for Tara. Whom he had loved and allowed himself to lose even before he had actually lost her. How could he have been so stupid? He cradled little Budha in his arms and he was grateful for the generous gift she had bestowed upon him. Chandra knew he would move the three worlds to keep him safe, even if it meant facing the wrath of his brothers who were circling him like sharks that had scented blood.

Now that his quarry was gone, Brihaspati turned his wrath upon Chandra. 'Don't let him escape!' he shouted. 'He will pay even if the whore has escaped righteous retribution. His male member shall be chopped off and fed to the flames along with the bastard in his arms.'

Kama rushed to intersperse himself between his friend and the avenging hordes, shouting and trying to talk sense to his fellow celestials. But they pushed him roughly aside and trod the gentle God of Desire underfoot.

They rushed towards him, but Chandra summoned his powers and stood to meet the charge. Fighting single-handedly, he threw back wave after wave of attackers but he was outnumbered. A giant had seized his wrist, knocking lose his weapon. Chandra was on the verge of summoning the darkness, when a blazing trident tore through the heavens and landed with an almighty thud, severing the offending arm that held him fast just beneath the shoulder. The brute screamed and writhed as blood gushed forth from the severed appendage.

The trident returned to its owner and they craned their necks for a look. Shiva strode into their midst, his face darkening with molten rage as he glared at the assembly who had surrounded one of their own and threatened him as well as the infant he carried in his arms with grievous bodily harm.

He turned on Brihaspati, who quailed in the face of the Destroyer's wrath. 'If anyone deserves to spend eternity as a chamber pot, it is you. But you may live with the rot setting in deep within your male appendage, leaving you unable to wield it potently ever again. All will bear witness to your shame and learn what happens to those who rape and raise their hands against women.'

Brihaspati slapped his palms against his forehead to protest the judgement and to his horror, felt the cuckold's horns that had sprouted and which he must bear as a mark of his shame. He sank to his knees in defeat.

Shiva looked away in disgust. His searing gaze landed on Indra, and his features hardened. 'It was bad enough you let your Guru abuse his position of power and get away with his many transgressions but you dared agree to become party to a dastardly plot to torture and humiliate one of your female subjects. Shame on you! Your body shall henceforth be covered with thousands of vulvas to remind you of your duties to the better sex.

As for those of you who sought to ostracize Chandra and do him and his child harm, I have but one thing to say. He does not belong in the sewer that you lot occupy, though you have worked hard to make it look beautiful on the outside. Chandra has proved himself the worthiest among the Devas for helping a woman in distress at great personal cost; forever more he shall remain elevated above you all to remind everyone of his exalted status.'

So saying, he lifted Chandra and the baby with his hand and settled them both comfortably on his head. The silvery, sickle-shaped crescent shone brighter than the sun in his matted locks, bathing them all with its sublime radiance. Kama raised his hand in farewell, tears welling in his eyes, for Chandra had been placed above their reach once and for all.

It may have been the very moment when I felt the first spark of desire for the Destroyer. With one look of withering contempt directed at Indra and his men, Shiva stalked off without a backward glance with the moon ensconced safely in his head.

As for Tara, she had made her choice wisely and she was at peace. Unlike the others, she found herself in my labyrinth of love. Knowing exactly what she wanted, Tara kept it simple. She rebuilt the little hermitage in the woods, filled it with her favourite memories and breathed life into them so that she could reunite with her lover. And so Tara is content to live and relive her one miserable moment of pure happiness throughout the course of infinity and she is happy as can be. Or she will be for as long as it lasts.

One Night of Wedded Bliss

I have always liked Aravan's story. Though for the most part, he himself hated it. Until I waltzed into the narrative, of course…

Aravan had tried to wriggle free but had only succeeded in getting himself firmly enmeshed in the trap he found himself in. He should have listened to his grandfather and stayed away. It was his father's war, not his. He ought to have given in to his original instincts and thrown in his lot with Duryodhana and the Kauravas just to spite his father, the great Pandava warrior-prince, Arjuna. But his mother had made him promise not to do or say anything that would hurt the love of her life.

'Your father and his brothers have right on their side,' she told him with the fanatical glint that came into her eyes whenever they discussed Arjuna, which was nearly all the time. 'Their cousins, the evil Kauravas, stole the kingdom of the Pandavas in a game of dice and now, they will not give it back.'

Never mind that the fools who gambled away their kingdom did not deserve to have it back. What would his mother have said if she had known that the love of her life clearly had no qualms about hurting *him*, her only son? Knowing her, as he did, she would have told him to give up his life willingly if that would make her precious Arjuna happy. That it was an honour to love or be loved by him, to kill for or be killed by him. Thinking about his mother and father made him bitter. And he couldn't help thinking it might have served his interests better had he been born into one of those species of animals that ate their young.

His mother. The serpent-princess Uloopi who had made a laughing stock of herself not by falling in love, but for remaining in love with a man she had coerced into spending one night with her by threatening to kill herself if he didn't. He had done so grudgingly, even though he had a reputation for loving and leaving more beautiful women than could be counted, and left in an unflattering hurry, the moment the Sun God made ready to begin his ascent across the heavens. Arjuna did not look back, in case the besotted girl who had pursued him so shamelessly used it as an excuse to delude herself into thinking he loved her back.

Arjuna may have been an absent father, but thanks to his mother's monomania and penchant for persisting in gathering and sharing every single detail about the great man, he was the ghost Aravan had grown up with. She had been a rigid disciplinarian who was determined to mould her son in the image of his famous father. No matter how much he practised or how proficient he became in the science of arms, Uloopi seemed unconvinced that he would ever be as good as the unequalled Arjuna.

While there was excessive love bordering on obsession on his mother's side, Arjuna had been mostly indifferent about her during the brief period they had spent together, forgotten about her promptly afterward and was entirely ignorant about their son.

Having spent the better part of his young life hating his father more than he could stand, Aravan supposed he had journeyed a long way to Kurukshetra looking for closure. It was far more likely that he sought to make a name for himself, sublimate his darkest feelings of rage and hatred by killing a few people or get roaring drunk and ask his father why, of all his wives and sons, Uloopi and Aravan had mattered the least to him. Besides, his mother had been most insistent, 'You must be by the side of your father as he makes history and earn an honourable reputation for yourself as one of the great heroes of this age, well worthy of being the great Arjuna's son.'

In a war, you always risked dying in a spectacularly gruesome fashion and he had spent eight days evading such a fate on the blood-soaked battlefield of Kurukshetra where he had already seen more bravery, brutality, violence and savagery than most do over entire lifetimes. Strangely enough, this was the happiest and most alive he had ever been. He had covered himself in glory as he established his prowess with the bow and arrow as well as his unmatched mastery of the mystical sciences the Nagas had perfected. Some had even said that his valour exceeded that of his father. This point was endlessly debated, with some arguing vehemently that Abhimanyu, Arjuna's favourite son, was the finest warrior of the age, and most insisting that all must take second place to the legendary archer who had performed miracles with his mighty bow, Gandhiva.

It was a proud moment when he fought and killed the princes of Avanti, Vinda and Anuvinda, who had joined the Kaurava army to get back at Krishna for eloping with their beloved sister, Mitravinda. He had claimed their scalps from right under Abhimanyu's nose, and his victory smelled even sweeter on account of his having shown up as his father's favourite son. All agreed that he was a warrior without equal. Abhimanyu said as much to all in the vicinity because he had to be the annoyingly perfect son, brother, warrior and human being. He just had to. Aravan knew he was being petty but he couldn't help himself.

The nights were even better as he celebrated raucously with the comeliest of the courtesans who had accompanied them to war with boozy abandon, still covered in blood and gore from the day's killing. Even he had no choice but to admit it was a childish effort to grab his father's attention and that it had been entirely ineffectual. Arjuna was otherwise occupied as always. With his dear Krishna, brothers, their offspring, assorted kith, kin and allies, he performed cleansing rituals, attended war councils, offered prayers for those who had died that day, partook of a little fruit, practised his archery drills the way he always did every single day of his life, and spent the hours before dawn resting and meditating in pious sanctimony.

But no matter how busy he was, Arjuna always sent for Abhimanyu to brief him on the happenings of the day and to bequeath gems of practical knowledge, lessons of strategic importance and useful tips. Aravan wished them both the joy of each other and went back to drinking.

All that had changed on the ninth day, when hostilities had ceased at sunset. Aravan received a royal summons to be present at the war council. He considered ignoring it and returning to the arms of his lover for the night, but decided that would be churlish. He was the last to arrive and they were all waiting for him. The mood was solemn.

Krishna smiled at him warmly before getting to his feet to address the gathering, 'The Pandavas and the Kauravas are no different from the Devas and Asuras. In fact, many among you contain the essence of the immortals within, in order to fulfil the dictates of destiny. The way things stand right now, you are both so evenly matched, this protracted struggle could stretch all the way to the end of time.' He paused for maximum effect, 'Which is why I hope you are willing to do whatever it takes to eke out a triumph for yourselves and the ones who have died for your cause.'

Yudhishthira, the eldest Pandava, looked worried. 'We have Arjuna and Krishna on our side. Everybody knows that only Shiva can stop them in battle. We have some of the greatest heroes fighting in our army. Most importantly, our cause is a righteous one. Which is why it is so frustrating that we are no closer to winning back our kingdom than we were eight days ago. The sooner we bring this war to a speedy conclusion, the better it will be for all of us. Tell us what needs to done to secure a victory, Krishna!'

'There is only one thing we can do to speed things along,' Krishna began. 'All it would take is the ultimate sacrifice. Sahadeva, who is an expert in the esoteric arts, will explain it to you with more clarity.'

The youngest Pandava brother pretended to consult his almanac and a bunch of ratty-looking scrolls. You wouldn't have seen the imperceptible look that passed between them if you were not looking for it. Thanks to his mother's relentless stalking of the man who had rejected the two of them, Aravan knew a lot more than he wanted to about his father and all who were close to him, especially Krishna. And of course, all the women who loved him and had been fortunate enough to have received his own fickle love in return.

Sahadeva spoke, 'Krishna is right. If we wish to make an end of things and guarantee a victory for ourselves, we must find a way to harness the power of Kali, the Dark Goddess, and unleash it upon our enemies. She will strike terror in their hearts, strip them of their courage, cause bloody mayhem in their ranks and grind them into the dust.'

'Perfect!' Bhima, the second Pandava brother, clapped his hands enthusiastically. 'Should we hire some brahmins to perform a wish-fulfilling yagna to summon her? But those things take forever and I don't think Duryodhana will consent to sit on his hands patiently while we are engaged in the performance of arcane rituals to kill him and vanquish his army.' Nobody laughed at his half-hearted attempt at banter. He shrugged and returned to the chicken dish he had been attacking with gusto.

Aravan hated Bhima a little less than the rest of his father's relatives because he always had a friendly word for him and insisted on complimenting his 'enormous appetite for the good things life had to offer'. Some evenings he even sent an entire cask of potent drink to his tent with his compliments.

'It would take much more than that...' Sahadeva said with affecting solemnity, 'So much more. The Dark Goddess demands blood sacrifice. A big one.' He looked around meaningfully.

'Shall we sacrifice the elephant corps?' Bhima belched. 'We should get started. Slaughtering an entire division could take a while.'

His younger brother looked irritated. 'It will have to be a human sacrifice. And we can't offer the first person to volunteer either. The chosen one will have to possess every single one of the thirty-two prescribed physical attributes of the truly flawless human being. Only two people in our camp qualify and there

MOHINI

are none who fit this demand in the Kaurava camp. This unique individual, beloved to us all, must be sacrificed on amavasya, the new moon day, in the month of Mirgashirsha. That just happens to be tomorrow.'

Deathly silence met this pronouncement.

'Can you tell us who the two perfect men in our camp are who will appease the Goddess?' Yudhishthira asked hesitantly.

Sahadeva nodded slowly. He seemed unwilling to say the names but he did so anyway. 'Krishna and Aravan.'

But of course, Aravan mused bitterly. Suddenly, precious Abhimanyu was no longer the perfect specimen of masculinity. Neither was Arjuna. Nor any of his brothers or their sons. It had to be someone who was expendable. Somebody nobody would miss when they slaughtered him like a sacrificial goat.

Abhimanyu rose to his feet, trembling with outrage. 'I have had enough of this foolishness! Out of respect to my uncles, Krishna and Sahadeva, I held my tongue, but to do so any longer would be folly that matches the scale of the one that has just been suggested. Let us not talk of animal or human sacrifices on a battlefield that has already claimed more lives than we can afford to lose. By condemning either Krishna or Aravan to such a fate, we will be committing a vile deed. Future generations will spit on our memory and I refuse to be a part of it. With both of them on our side, we need not fear defeat and we will earn our victory the old-fashioned way by the strength of arms. Have you seen Aravan fight? Why, he can defeat the Kauravas single-handed!'

Support from unexpected quarters. Aravan had to admit that he had not expected that. His father's son was so annoyingly perfect and good-natured, he didn't even have the decency to give someone like Aravan a good enough reason to hate him. Abhimanyu came and stood by his side, placing a protective arm around his shoulders with perfect sincerity.

'Do not talk about things beyond the pale of your understanding, nephew,' Krishna said smoothly. 'I gladly volunteer to placate Kali to help you win this war against tyranny and injustice.'

Arjuna leapt to his feet like one scalded. 'Aravan is of my flesh and blood. And he will prove it by volunteering his life for a noble cause.'

'You can't ask that of him, Father! You simply cannot...' Abhimanyu was so incensed, it was truly touching. Aravan nudged him gently to stop the tirade he was about to launch into. *He could fight his own battles, thank you very much.*

He looked straight into his father's eyes, wondering if he could see the hatred reflected in their depths. 'I am happy to do whatever is needed of me, dear Father. If older and wiser heads than mine and Abhimanyu's genuinely believe my death by sacrifice will aid the war effort more effectively than my proven prowess as a warrior, then so be it. Death does not frighten me.'

Arjuna threw his arms around him, his eyes wet with tears. 'You do me proud, son!'

Sahadeva spoke up, 'History will remember your sacrifice, Aravan. Your bravery and magnanimity will always be revered by posterity. As for us, it behoves us to do everything in our power to honour you. Those selected for the sacrifice are always granted one last wish that must be fulfilled at all cost. Name whatever your heart desires and it will be granted to you.'

Sacrifice my father instead of me. Aravan took a deep breath and composed his features. 'Life has been good to me. But I never realized it until this very moment, because I wasted most of it searching for the one thing I couldn't have. Therefore, I won't ask for the things I cannot have. All that I would wish for is the love of a good woman, so that I will not have to depart this world with my virginity intact.' He said this with a straight face, confident that they wouldn't refute the erroneous claim of a man they had just condemned to a premature death. 'It would be truly insupportable. I seek a kind and compassionate woman who will consent to become the wife of a man who has but a few hours to live, who will be a comfort in the end and help me cram a lifetime's worth of happiness into a few moments. Somebody who will be large-hearted enough to weep for me and miss me when I am gone, even though she has known me for only a heartbeat.'

They had all fallen silent. None dared to look at him or at each other. Aravan smiled to himself. Why should he make it too easy for them? The way he saw it, his request was an uphill if not impossible task to try and find a woman who would agree to marry him only so she may be doomed to widowhood on the morrow.

Aravan sneaked a glance at Krishna and wished he hadn't. His blood turned to ice as he realized that he may have escaped death by the skin of his teeth with his hastily conceived plot...if it hadn't been for the god who walked among men.

Giving him a reassuring smile, the greatest trickster the three worlds has ever known said, 'That can be easily arranged.'

Which is how Aravan and I found ourselves in the most luxurious tent of gold brocade in the encampment, decorated with sumptuous attention to detail and festooned with fresh flowers. There were delicacies carefully prepared by Yudhishthira's personal chef and a wide array of the finest beverages to choose from. Arjuna had insisted that the best of everything be provided for his son. After all, it was the very least he could do.

Krishna had officiated at the wedding ceremony. Bedecked in the finest garments and exquisitely crafted jewellery that Arjuna had won as a reward during his victorious sojourn with the celestials, Aravan made for a handsome, if slightly morose, groom. At the sight of me in my bridal splendour, many became so frantic with desire, they fainted. The groom smiled when his gaze alighted upon my features. It was a smile of profound gratitude and it almost masked the fact that he felt like a ship being pulled hither and thither by the stubborn tides and the raging wind.

The severely wounded, disabled and almost dead rose to their feet and left their tents for a glimpse of me, and found themselves restored to the best of health. Doxy prostitutes were not welcome at auspicious events but the petals that were showered on the radiant bride were carried by the cheery wind to the remote outposts of the battlefield where they sat huddled in makeshift shelters that were filthy with use and sang songs to venerate me. On receiving this benediction, the sores, cankers and pustules that covered their bodies vanished and the spark was once again reignited in their eyes. It was most pleasing. I am always happy to help in any way I can.

Hundreds of heads of cattle, gold coins by the bushel and other valuables were distributed among their allies, kinsmen and common soldiers to mark the occasion. Even the Kaurava camp became beneficiaries to Yudhishthira's largesse. This generosity could be attributed partly to his good nature and partly to a guilty conscience that refused to stop chiding him for decreeing that his young nephew die of unnatural causes.

The prettiest maids had been chosen to knead and massage his body with scented oil, bathe and prepare him for his wedding night. They attended to me as well. I was enjoying myself but Aravan was still trying to work through his indignation and rage. Our attendants left us after administering to all our needs.

I looked ravishing, even if I say so myself. A composite of every woman who had visited his dreams stimulating nocturnal emissions, every plain-faced, almost-pretty camp follower and painted courtesan he had romped with in the nights past and his mother, Uloopi of course, with her serpentine grace and a modified heart that only had room enough for him.

'You are beautiful,' he said wistfully, 'but it is too bad that you are not real.'

I said nothing and merely watched as he picked up a goblet filled to the brim and drained it with a single gulp, wiping his lips with the back of his hand, looking very much like the little boy he still was.

'I want to be hopelessly drunk for tomorrow's sacrifice,' he told me candidly, slurring only a little since he was too overwrought for any inebriant to work its magic on him. 'Perhaps Kali will be doubly pleased when I offer her my puke as well as my blood and flesh.'

He drank gratefully from the goblet I had refilled for him. 'Are all the stories I have heard about you true?'

He didn't wait for a reply. 'They say that none can resist Mohini, the Enchantress. That your beauty is Vishnu's deadliest weapon. You employed it to bamboozle the Asuras in order to deprive them of their fair share of the nectar and watched as thousands died begging for a kiss, which you cold-bloodedly refused. During the Tarakamaya, which Virochana was on the verge of winning thanks to the power of the crown he wore, you wove a web of enchantment around him in order to trap him the way a spider would its prey, relieved him of his crown, promising him your love in return and denied him both, leaving him to be butchered. Tara was forced to return to her husband and her baby was taken away from her. They say she tore off chunks of her hair, and then ripped off her breasts, maddened with sorrow over the loss of her lover and child, forced to return to her abusive husband who put her through an ocean of pain.'

It was yet another fanciful, erroneous version of the stories circulated about me, but I did not bother to correct him. Every version of every story has every right to exist. Aravan was looking a little wild-eyed as he poured more of the fiery liquid down his throat where they were soaked up by terror, misery and unspeakable rage, disappearing without a trace.

'Where were we? Yes! We were talking about your perverted ways and penchant for breaking hearts filled with love for you. I have heard that you once rescued Shiva from the demon, Bhasmasura, when he foolishly granted him a dangerous boon and nearly got reduced to ash for his trouble. You are also the Three-eyed God's lover, aren't you? And you made a strange child together. But you broke Shiva's heart as well. And he picked up the pieces of his heart and returned to his wife, hoping she would forgive him for making such a fool of himself over you.

Then there was King Rugmangada who was good and pious. But you seduced the king with your charms and reduced him to a gibbering fool who was so completely enamoured, he thought nothing of murdering his own son because you demanded it of him as the price for your love.'

He was breathing heavily. 'Do you remember King Nontok? Vishnu was jealous because he won a powerful astra from Shiva and used it at his discretion. But you asked him to dance with you and he obliged. How can anyone refuse a beautiful woman who just wants to be held as she sways to divine music? Vishnu seized the moment because Nontok was vulnerable and in love to shatter his thighs and kill him. Nontok was so aggrieved and distraught by the unfairness of it, he took birth as Ravana to vent his rage and spewed it on innocent women like Rambha and Vedavati, because you were responsible for making him hate the wicked wiles of women.

'You see?' Aravan wagged a finger at me. 'I know everything there is to know about you. The three worlds are littered with the broken hearts you have heartlessly left behind in your wake. Strangely enough, despite knowing this, all I really want is to give you my heart for you to stomp under your beautiful feet.'

He raised my feet and placed little wet kisses all over them in the manner of a lost and frightened puppy.

When he surfaced from lavishing his love on my feet, the fear had ebbed and anger had taken its place. 'Why should I be the one to die? My life has barely begun. Arjuna, the so-called hero and my lousy father, has done nothing for me. He didn't even know of my existence, and even if he had, he would not have cared. As for my mother, he does not remember her at all, but she lives for him. Was I given this life merely to provide a receptacle for those two to piss into? Will you be doing the same tonight? Fill me up with piss, because I have no intrinsic value?' He forced more drink down his throat and when it came back up, he choked and coughed. Waiting for the fit to pass, he sipped more cautiously from the goblet he was holding on to for dear life.

He hiccupped noisily, though he was still not as drunk as he would have liked to be. 'I spent all my days and nights practising archery and getting proficient with the use of sword, club, mace and every missile there is. While he was out in the three worlds wasting days and nights, seducing women and breaking hearts like you... I worked hard. It was my intention to become Aravan, the finest archer and mightiest warrior the three worlds have known. The storytellers would refer to Arjuna as the father of Aravan. That would show him! I have my pride too! Who does he think he is anyway?

'Krishna is no better. He is behind all this. Why should I die for their cause? It is a useless cause. Duryodhana is right. They are bastards whose two mothers had them with five different fathers that we know of and they don't deserve the kingdom they gambled away along with their common wife and themselves.

You are no better. Because you are him and he is you. But you are beautiful and I want you so badly. Will you ask me to go to my death with a skip in my step and a smile on my lips? That makes you as bad as them. Even worse. Worse than the whores who pretend to love you for your money. There is a certain honesty to a whore's dishonesty, which is far more acceptable, dignified even, when compared with whatever it is you do.'

As the despair flooded through him again, diluting the liquor he had been imbibing, Aravan was no longer angry. Merely sorrowful. Tears dripped down his face as he wallowed miserably in his anguish. 'I don't want to die. I am too young to die. I don't want to die like this. Weren't you supposed to make my last few hours meaningful and magical? Instead you refuse to take me in your arms to make me forget. Your rejection hurts. One night of wedded bliss was all I asked for, but you would deny me even that. Instead, I am to spend it blubbering and trying to drown my anxiety in drink. Why has this happened to me? If you...'

Aravan had so much more to say but he had passed out by then.

We floated together through space, snuggled up against each other and cradled within the pillowy softness of the cosy clouds as the wind fanned our cheeks. All around, there was nothing but absolute night. Were we trapped inside of a dream? Or were we awake in a dream within a dream? Perhaps it was a series of dreams that we were supposed to experience over the course of a lifetime, one night at a time, but through which we were speeding like the condemned, who didn't have much longer to live. Or dream.

Aravan could feel the burning flesh as he inhaled the smoky fragrance of a body burning, as an unloosed soul took flight into the vastness of the great beyond. He held on to me, grateful for a steadying presence. I spoke to him softly, soothing his fears. Singing songs composed from all the things in a former life that had never failed to make him smile.

Happiness suffused his being. Nobody could tell us apart now that we became one. His groin throbbed urgently with the sheer urgency of his desire. Gently I took his hand and we meandered aimlessly through a storied portal into the labyrinth of fable. We held hands and made our way across the numerous winding passages that twisted and turned across the edifice that was fluid and mobile as a river, its branches opening into one another, moving onward, turning on itself, and then flowing backward.

The best of experiences are the ones that are shared. We explored every nook and cranny of the cosmos that caught our fancy, wandering through breathtaking locales, making love on pristine beaches where the silken sand tickled our bare bodies mercilessly, reducing us to helpless giggling as the waves lapped at our naked bodies with lascivious glee. Lazily, we drifted on cerulean seas allowing the tide to take us where it would, and did little more than soak in the breathtaking beauty of the sun, sea and stars, while great turtles glided by, oblivious to our happiness.

We chased each other up and down over rolling dunes rising majestically from the golden sands, slipping, sliding, laughing and choking on the dust, landing with limbs wrapped tightly around each other, eager to assuage the fires of lust we had successfully kindled.

We slurped up tall glasses of rich milk from the bountiful Kamadhenu and gorged on delicacies from the Horn of Plenty. Rambling around among ancient ruins, we gathered ephemeral fragments of buried civilizations, dead cultures and forgotten histories and reconstructed the whole thing with bits and pieces, watching it all collapse as time tore its way through them in an impatient rush. We gambolled in volcanically warmed hot springs and electric blue lagoons, frolicking with the fish and seals.

We made love endlessly in absurdly romantic settings—under star-flooded skies, on jewelled coral islands, in emerald valleys, on verdant hillsides, on lakes with mirrored surfaces and placid swans, on snowy peaks, under cascading waterfalls, on fluffy clouds and on the broad backs of snoozing whales. Afterwards, we feasted on roasted meat, succulent berries and nuts, and drank wild honey straight from the comb. Then we journeyed on, stopping only to make love, over and over again.

We visited my favourite haunts and I showed him the seat of the ancient friends Nara and Narayana, the two rishis who had taken birth as Arjuna and Krishna, at Badami. In their presence, there could be no anger, hurt, dread or remorse, only peace. He lay at Nara's feet for the longest time and in his silent tranquillity, he found the answer to every question he had ever thought to ask. And by his side was the fulfilment of deep-seated longing that he had erroneously believed no longer mattered to him. Most importantly, he finally arrived at the simple truth, which quelled the crushing fear and doubt that he had carried over from the charred remains of his past: *All of us have something to do with everything, even if it is nothing.*

Every once in a while, over the course of our ceaseless wanderings and endless adventures, we found ourselves with a bird's eye view of the mighty events that rocked the three worlds. We watched the Great Flood, he relived the great enchantment with me by his side, saw the blade of a mighty axe hefted and lowered over and over again, leaving Bhumi Devi drenched in blood. An infuriated woman with unbound tresses plucked out her breast and hurled it at the capital of a mighty kingdom, turning it to ash. An army of monkeys built a bridge across the sea to fight a demon-king who had abducted another man's wife.

He saw a young man with the thirty-two sacred marks that proclaimed him to be the perfect specimen of masculinity, as they led him to a sacrificial altar. There was something strangely serene about him, given that he was about to be decapitated with a single blow. It was almost as if he believed that it was all happening to someone else.

When the deed was done, a beautiful woman mourned the passing of her husband by gently picking up the fair head and kissing his lips one last time before the God who walked among men took it from her. There was no theatrical wailing, keening, beating of the breast or broken bangles. She sat in a corner, with her face buried in her hands, pouring her tears and grief into her palms. The profound misery and aching sorrow that spilled forth from between the gap in her fingers was a palpable thing and his heart reached out to her. She wasn't the only one who grieved for the deceased. He had been more beloved than he knew, and many added their tears into the void left by his passing.

It was all very affecting. But we couldn't linger. He now had the closure he had journeyed through such difficult terrain to find, and it was time to move on. There were so many more journeys to undertake, unexplored places to visit, lives to live, stories to tell and a lover to love.

What Happens in the Forest of Cedars

My journey with Aravan had been satisfying. They all were. But it was time to move on. To the others. The ones who were waiting for me, or perhaps to the one I had been waiting for, for over the entire duration of my existence.

It was like entering a strange new world that, though it resembled the three worlds clearly, wanted nothing at all to do with it. There was something in those dark and deep woods. On the outside, it was a sylvan setting cloaked with an enforced peace. But deep in its bowels lurked a malevolent presence that watched and waited with timeless patience.

It was still and quiet... so quiet that even clamouring thoughts stilled for fear of causing a forbidden ruckus. Powerful vibrations emanated from the epicentre of Daruka, home to the powerful rishis who had committed themselves to the accumulation and hoarding of ancient knowledge, hidden truths, buried secrets and occult lore of immense power. Naturally, there was a solemnity that hung over the place, like the shroud of death.

The inhabitants of Daruka had a fixed way of life. They swore by their rules and lived by their rules and only those who abided by those rules were welcome. They lived in perfectly ordered huts of stone that seemed to have sprung from the fertile ground in perfect harmony with nature. Everything was as pure, pristine and perfect as it could be. The sages and their wives clad themselves in robes of snowy white, did their hair just so, and lived their lives with ritualistic precision. 'Everything had a place and everything was best kept in its place' was their credo.

They did not approve of procreation. It was too unseemly and unwieldy a process. In this world they had created for themselves, they were the gods and kings. They needed nobody else and they wouldn't have it any other way. Men devoted themselves to their all-important studies and women dedicated themselves body and soul to catering to every need of their men. There was no place for bawling infants here. However, male savants manifested by a superior mind and dutiful maids similarly created to be used for the purposes of household chores and virgin sacrifices could be accommodated.

It was a system that worked and many in the three worlds modelled their insignificant societies after Darukavana, but none had the discipline or drive to enforce it continuously over the ages. Things would have gone on in the same way they always had for the forest-dwellers with the superiority complex, if they hadn't been so quick to condemn and punish the failings of all whom they viewed as inferior to themselves. Which was everybody else.

I was one of their pet peeves. The one whose very existence was anathema to them. They were vociferous when it came to condemning everything they abhorred about me. Their hate did nothing to me. As was the case with the excessive love lavished upon me, I was unmoved and so far removed from the implications, they might as well have been talking about somebody else.

The object of their ire consumed their every waking thought and they spat out my name like a curse. Mohini, the Enchantress.

Whatever had Vishnu been thinking when he created a base creature such as herself! All she seemed to do was soil herself and others with seedy acts of seduction. It was said that her lovers were so numerous they couldn't be counted and all were welcome to taste concupiscent pleasures in her convivial company. Any woman guilty of a single one of her multitude of sins ought to have been stoned to death by rights and in the name of all that was holy, or cursed to spend eternity as a stone. This one, armoured in the aura of Vishnu, had gotten away with her misdeeds for too long.

A cautionary tale if there ever was one. The Protector had long remained unmoved by the charms of the wily females. But he had sculpted this enchantress with his own hands and with so much skill, she was physically perfect. He was so enamoured by the beauty of his art, he had become besotted with it and imbued the ivory maiden with the spark of life and a portion of his own power. In doing so, he had created a monster that carried with it every abhorrent characteristic a false woman could have. But he was too blinded with love to take the hammer to his work.

It was a dangerous precedent. After all the efforts that had gone in over the millennia to teach impressionable young women in the interests of upholding dharma, preserving virtue and honourable conduct, and about the importance of denying the itching in their lady parts to keep themselves pure and above reproach, here was this godless creature living in sin and getting away with it. Influenced by her dark arts and debauched ways, more and more women were following in her footsteps, ushering the three worlds into a dark age where sin and vice triumphed with embarrassing ease over morals and virtue. It was high time the problem was tackled at the source.

The latest instance of her immorality was particularly galling. She had consented to marry a doomed man and spend one night with him, initiating him into the rites of her depraved arts. Having been made a widow, one would have thought she would learn her lesson, but the brazen temptress refused to obey the customs of widowhood. Her hair had not been shorn, her bangles were not broken, her anklets, which teased with their beguiling bells were not removed, her silks were not replaced with the coarse hemp more becoming of widowhood, and every one of the markings that indicated auspicious womanhood had not been forcibly removed.

If that were not infuriating and unpardonable enough, Mohini had the unmitigated temerity to carry on with her disgusting conduct and debauchery the way she always had, and had even become the patron goddess of the sexual deviants. This would never do. Gathering together, the good folks of Daruka pooled the full extent of their power, erudition and knowledge to slowly expurgate her presence from the histories, myths, legends, grand epics and sagas that bore the record of her 'distinguished' service to the three worlds.

They were clever about it, taking their time and being careful not to remove her entirely. After all, it was absence that provoked ardour in a heart conditioned to take a faithful presence for granted. In the end, their effort showed results and Mohini, the Enchantress, was reduced to little more than an afterthought, a foolish footnote in the grand scheme of things, a mere whim or a fancy of Vishnu's. A floozy with no substance or depth. Merely a pretty face for men to stoke their heated fantasies with, to be discarded later if not sooner. A silly dream that was not worth remembering, to be forgotten on waking.

Vishnu was unconcerned and happy to ignore the snide nattering of the spiteful and sanctimonious. Shiva was not.

'Saying or doing nothing to avert an injustice, even if it is well within your power to do so, is akin to abetting it,' he insisted when Vishnu was hesitant to release me from the sanctuary of his heart. I don't blame him. At the time he saw something I didn't.

I myself didn't care either way. The opprobrium or censure of others meant less than nothing to me. But on a whim, I sided with Shiva. There was something ridiculously attractive and entrancing about the Three-eyed God. If Vishnu was the tranquil shoreline, Shiva embodied the untameable wildness and violence of the bottomless sea.

So it was with a tinge of excitement that we set out together into the Forest of Cedars. And as our footsteps fell in unison to the tinkling of my anklets, the woods came alive to greet us. The scent of spring hung thickly in the air, and the sentinel trees were laden with fruits and flowers that had ripened and blossomed on our arrival. Shiva plucked them for me, arranging the loveliest blooms in my hair with infinite care and surprising tenderness for one who wielded unlimited power. We shared the fruits, feeding each other the sweetest morsels, as the juices dripped down our chins and stained our chests.

We walked deeper into the woods. Occasionally I stole glances at him. He was so handsome and exuded such animal magnetism, it hurt, and my womb contracted painfully, assaulted by a tidal wave of longing. I wanted to run my hands through those wild, unmanageable, matted locks of his, kiss those sensuous, stubborn lips, lick the blue stain that shimmered in his throat clean and feel his corded muscle undulate on top of me as I took him deep inside. My need for him was so great, it made me blush, and our shared mission threatened to get relegated to the background, overshadowed by relentless desire.

It pleased me no end to note that the Adiyogi was not immune to my good looks, enhanced considerably by the first flush of my attraction towards him. He placed an arm protectively around my waist to draw me closer and I thrilled to his touch.

'You really ought to focus on what you came to do without getting distracted by the astonishing beauty of your surroundings,' I admonished him, sternly mimicking the pious sanctimony of the rishis. In response, he tightened his grip on my waist, mischievously allowing his fingers to wander over my person, delighting in the mounting evidence that I craved to feel him across every inch of my body. I couldn't bring myself to extricate myself from that delightful embrace for long moments.

Mustering all my willpower, I broke free from him, feeling the separation as painfully as he did. But we had a job to do, didn't we? Suddenly it didn't feel that important. Shiva vented his feelings with a few furious beats of the damroo, producing a mighty and mellow wave of gorgeous, full-bodied sound tapping into profound aural memories of every instance of pure feeling ever experienced by anybody across the annals of time. Exulting in the glory of it, he began to dance, beckoning for me to join him. I couldn't tear my eyes off him.

Utterly entranced, my feet moved of their own accord, keeping time with the primeval beats as he grasped my waist firmly and twirled me around with grace and strength. All of creation responded to the unearthly beauty of the heavenly music and I danced like never before, pouring my heart into my increasingly frenzied movements as the tempo soared and increased.

Those magnificent locks bellowed behind him as he moved with masterfully terpsichorean beauty and lightning quick pace as I exerted myself to stay in step with him, lost in adoration, drowning in his vigour and vitality, more enraptured than I ever had been. The ravishing rhythms that held us both in their thrall never let up, even as the achingly beautiful passion we felt for each other rose in an eerie wave that would engulf all in the immediate vicinity.

Drawn to the haunting quality of the otherworldly music and the swaying, dancing forms of the Destroyer and the Enchantress, the rigid male denizens of Daruka rose as if in a trance. Years and years of assiduous labour expended solely for the purpose of study and devotion were forgotten, dwarfed by a bravura performance and the lilting rhythms of lush melody. As they scrambled to the source of that massive vortex of energy, their robes of white were torn to pieces and their hair came undone. They couldn't have cared less. All that mattered were their stiffened phalluses, come to life after aeons of repression, throbbing with an urgency that would not be denied.

Most followed me, the very same Enchantress they had devoted so much time and effort to destroy. But in that moment they would have willingly laid down their lives for me, expecting nothing in return. They lay sweating, grunting and grovelling at my feet, begging to be told what they needed to do in order to win my favour. I smiled and gyrated gleefully, leading them around in circles on a merry chase. Some threw themselves at Shiva, pleading with him to bestow carnal favours upon them, drooling and gibbering like the maddened sex maniacs they had become.

The wives had been busy with the household chores—cooking, cleaning, gathering flowers, washing clothes, hanging them out to dry—the same chores they had been performing ad infinitum—

when suddenly their hips and thighs started swaying sensuously to the cadence of a song so sensuous they felt their nipples harden in response. The very air vibrated with the soulful tune and they forgot whatever they were engaged in and ran in the direction of that irresistible sound. They flocked towards the dancing duo in a frenzy of orgiastic passion, wanting little more than to touch and be touched by the Enchantress. Or the Destroyer. Or both.

None of them could combat the allure of that sublime performance nor resist the incendiary and emotional elements conjured up by the primeval beats. Hearts and loins throbbed, as the sages and their wives in a hypnotic fugue of intoxication and ecstasy swayed and shoved their way forward, straining to draw closer to us, desperate to indulge the urge to love and be loved in return, their excitement at a fever pitch, enveloped in a sensuous smog of lust as the mad revels went on for what seemed like forever. Shiva and I danced on, lost in a world of our own now, flitting, pirouetting, and spinning each other around like dervishes in a dazzling flurry of delectable movement.

As for the good sages and their wives, they found their conscious selves had disappeared, torn to pieces by the primitive beasts they had kept chained in the dungeons of their mind, freed from confinement, eager to feed and gorge themselves silly on a surfeit of sybaritic excess, drawn to the mesmerizing beats that appealed to their basest instincts. Among the dancers, many were engaged in lascivious acts, the numbers thus occupied multiplying and mutating till all resembled one giant vigorously copulating multi-limbed beast.

All of a sudden, just as the magnificent music was building to a crescendo, it simply stopped. Without warning. The silence and stillness of old descended upon Daruka as if it had never been away, sepulchral and suffocating. There was no sign of the Enchantress or the priapic God they had been so mindlessly obsessed and entranced with. The spell was broken, leaving them cold and comfortless in a putrid puddle of shame, self-loathing and a desperate longing to return to the hedonistic delights of mere moments ago.

The sages stared at their wives in horror, the proud, decent and respectable womenfolk of Daruka, in various states of undress with dishevelled hair, lips pursed in paroxysms of pleasure, eyes glazed over with dark desire, bosoms straining with unfulfilled desires that threatened to boil over, hips still grinding slowly as they lay panting on the forest floor, begging to be pleasured like animals in heat.

Outrage restored the coherence of the sages somewhat. 'Rise! You shameless hussies have betrayed your husbands and allowed yourselves to fall from grace merely to get a chance to satiate your lust for a filthy beggar. The lot of you will be punished severely for this lapse. Count on it!'

Still in a daze, their hearts shattered to pieces, their wives allowed themselves to be herded like sheep back to their homes and submitted docilely as they were confined within and left to ponder on their scandalous conduct like caged animals that had lost the will to live. Outside, the sages conferred among themselves, frothing at the mouth, rabid rage having replaced the rousing passion that had roiled through them so very recently.

'We should castrate him, remove the phallus and scrotum that is the source of his power. Without them he will be reduced to nothing.' *But unlike us, even if he were to relieve himself of his genitalia, he would still remain the primordial male principle.*

'He must feel our wrath! Let us perform a sacrifice with our combined powers. From the flames, a giant tiger, a monstrous serpent, an engorged elephant and the deadly dwarf Muyalakan, harbinger of epilepsy, shall arise. They will rip him apart and leave his remains for the carrion birds to feed on!' *Of course not! He will flay the skin off the backs of the tiger and elephant and wear it wrapped around his body with pride. The dead snake will be another ornament to adorn his throat and he will dance on the dwarf's back in triumph.*

'We will bring forth a mighty trident from the flames of our wrath and it will tear him to pieces!' *The trident can resist the Destroyer no more than our wives could.*

'We will summon the eternal flames and order them to consume him. He will die screaming in agony!' *He will gather the flames in the palm of his hands as though they were flowers.*

They would have liked their vengeance, but they had expended their vast reserves of ascetic merits on lustful pursuits and compounded the mistake by venting their rage. There was nothing to be done but to return to their homes, beat the living daylights out of their erring wives, pick up the pieces of their former lives and return to their studies so that they could return to the comfort of their routine and old ways.

The sages didn't realize it then, because their anger and hate was so great, but forever more they were imbued with the essence of the Three-eyed God. He was never far from their thoughts and their every deed was performed brooding over their memories of him and the beguiling being who had tricked them into forgetting their ways. It was but a short step from hate to love, and with time, the sages and their wives learned to venerate the Destroyer with all their hearts and with every breath drawn in the enchanted Forest of Cedars, they relived the magical occasion when he had taken the trouble to visit them and done his utmost to bring about their utter ruination.

Shiva and I were far removed from the turmoil, trauma and emotional upheaval we had so masterfully orchestrated. We celebrated our grand triumph at the Forest of Cedars in each other's arms, expressing our love in all the ways we knew, experiencing its many splendours and infinite forms. During the long reaches of that one night, which passed in a blur of diffuse happiness and sinful indulgence, all that mattered was the bottomless depth of the tenderness and affection we felt for each other.

He stroked my hair as we lay sprawled under the gaze of that old voyeur, the moon, sharing smiles, kisses and stories till dawn broke, upon which we rose to our feet, wished each other well and went down diverging paths.

Neither of us looked back at the clearing that had harboured our love. It was not in our nature to do so. We didn't see the silvery emissions, the tell-tale evidence of our lovemaking either. But Bhumi Devi did. She was a romantic and she spirited away the child of our grand passion in her arms.

She had chosen him to serve as one of her champions. He would perform the greatest of deeds and forever more serve as a beacon of hope for the weary and downtrodden who were forced down perilous paths and hounded every step of the way merely because they were different. The going would always be hard, unendurably so, especially when one belonged to the minority at the mercy of a hostile majority, but these could count on Shiva and Mohini's child to make their passage easier. Even infuse it with all the joy he could bring to bear. For this was no ordinary child, but Harihara putra, born from the most potent of unions.

Shastha's Secret

Shastha was special. His father, the great King Rajashekara, had always told him so. In the early days, he had no wish to be extraordinary. All he wanted was to be exactly the same as everyone else.

'You are the rarest of the rare, a truly unique being,' Rajashekara would ruffle his hair affectionately. 'A gift from the Earth Mother to honour every good deed I have performed over a thousand lifetimes. The moment I held you in my arms, I knew that you were chosen for greatness to make a difference in these troubled times when everything is shrouded in darkness and the future looks so bleak it makes you wonder if there even is one.'

Shastha wriggled in discomfort over the lavish praise but was secretly pleased and had to admit the fulsome admiration warmed his insides, which were usually clenched with a strange restlessness and unease. These spilled over into his dreams, which became a cauldron of simmering angst, and he woke up feeling far from rested.

His mother, on the other hand, made it clear that she felt differently. An extraordinarily beautiful woman, she was nevertheless revolting when her fierce temper was upon her—which was most of the time. Shastha could see it in her eyes, which filled with contempt, disgust and even a touch of fear at the sight of him.

As far back as he could remember, the King and Queen used to fight over something to do with him endlessly and it bothered him no end. He heard words like 'abomination', 'unnatural' and 'fiend' bandied about by his mother to describe him. At first, Shastha had no idea what those big words meant, only that they made him feel awful. Worse, they stayed with him till he was much older and learned their meaning, and had remained his constant companions in the present as well.

Rajashekara would be furious, 'The next time you speak about my son that way, I will have your tongue ripped out from your throat and cooked up with spices for you to choke on!' It was the King's final word on the subject and even she dared not disobey, but there were subtler ways to disobey his orders, and she was not above using them to impress upon Shastha that in her eyes he was worth less than the contents of her chamber pot. Initially, it filled him with hurt and bewilderment simply because he couldn't understand the reason for such caustic hate, especially since everybody else in their kingdom, from the grandees to the common folk, insisted on venerating him on a pedestal and making him the object of their unequivocal adoration.

Things went from bad to worse when his mother delivered another baby boy. Shastha had thought she couldn't be more cruel or malicious, but he had been wrong about that. Her hatred increased manyfold and things became very strained between the royal couple. Soon, they were not even on talking terms.

Outside of her implacable ire, he supposed his childhood was what could only be described as idyllic. Rajashekhara had a few rigid rules he was expected to follow most assiduously. Shastha was not allowed to go swimming in the Pampa with his friends nor would he be allowed to use the common facilities at the ashram where he was being schooled by the Rajguru. His attendants would always be close at hand to take care of his needs and these were loyal slaves handpicked by the King. They were all deaf-mutes. Outside of this, the King placed no restrictions on his beloved son.

'The subjects of a future king must never see him divested of his garments,' he told Shastha by way of explanation. 'It will remind them that their sovereign is a human with the same unremarkable characteristics as them. Which is why a certain air of mystique must be carefully preserved.'

Shastha supposed it made sense, but he knew his father was lying. When he dwelled too closely upon it, the fever dreams returned with a vengeance. The ones with the monstrous deity, who glared at him across the distance, sitting squat and ugly, displaying gargantuan breasts and a vagina that gaped open. Right above was a dangling male member.

Once awake, he would urge himself to forget the monsters that lurked in his head and distract himself with the minutiae of life, blessed with ease, power and privilege. Everything came easily to him and he was considered to be an exceptional child who was running and speaking when infants his age were still learning to crawl. He was a scholar par excellence and learned everything the eminent sages could teach him in a few short years. When it came to the martial arts, Shastha gained widespread acclaim for becoming an expert wielder of whichever weapon he happened to pick up on a given day. Proficient in hand-to-hand combat and a multitude of tongues, he was also a nonpareil charioteer and horseman.

They said he had strange powers over birds and beasts. Tempestuous horses and mad elephants would calm down on hearing his voice and their savage tempers would be soothed by his slightest touch. Tales about his valour were told and retold. Witnesses swore they had seen him tame a man-eating tiger with just a look and milk a tigress while she purred with satisfaction. The entire kingdom celebrated when Rajashekara named him the heir apparent.

It was also the final straw as far as his mother was concerned. She sent word, insisting on an audience with the King in private. Shastha was also commanded to be present. The Queen greeted her husband, reclining on the couch. It meant that her mood was dangerous and combative. She didn't deign to speak to the Crown Prince.

'I gave you every chance to do the right thing but you wouldn't listen,' she began imperiously. 'You have left me with no choice but to do what I must, to make certain that the divine right of my son to sit on the throne of Pantalam is not usurped by a monstrous abomination and the child of a demon-whore.'

Her breasts were heaving. Even the King seemed taken aback by her vehemence. The skin was stretched tightly across his features, which were ashen, and he seemed to be in the grip of a terrible anxiety. 'Please, my Queen,' he pleaded. 'This child is a gift from the Gods. Do you not remember the divine markings on his person, the golden bell that hung from his neck, which has earned him the name Manikanda, or how Bhumi Devi gifted him to me on the banks of the river Pampa?'

She sensed his weakness with a predator's instincts and pounced. 'I remember that this is the ludicrous tale you fed me. At the time I dismissed it as the raving of a lunatic, trying to fob off a bastard, born of his unnatural and deviant fornication with a pox-addled whore, on me. And what you call "divine markings" is in truth an abnormality that is abhorrent to all that is sacred. The royal physician, his attendant and the astrologers were horrified by the evil they had witnessed and insisted that this creature be smothered at once. But you had them arrested and killed to bury the truth.'

Shastha reeled from the shock and confusion. The great King sank to his knees, his head buried in his hands, trembling with agitation. He seemed to be in pain and Shastha rushed to his side. What was the dirty little secret his father was so keen to hide? If it was the fact that he was born on the wrong side of the marital bed, Shastha would have liked to tell him that it made no matter, because a 'demon-whore' for a mother was infinitely superior to this vile creature who was incapable of spewing anything but venom and hatred. He wanted to tell his father to stand firm! His claim to the throne was based on merit in addition to having the royal birthright. What could the Queen do or say to destroy his claim?

He would have his answer soon.

'You cannot silence me like the others. I have revealed the truth to your Diwan and we have made arrangements to expose your sordid secret if you attempt to harm either of us. If word got out, your precious heir would be pelted with stones, cast out from the kingdom or killed where he stands. If people found out that you planned so foolishly to place one such as him on the throne, you would be reviled too and evicted from power if not assassinated overnight. You know all of this to be true!'

'How can you be so cruel and hurtful? What has he ever done to you? When has he ever been anything but a dutiful son despite the countless cruel deeds and insults you forced him to endure? I beg you! Do not do this! It is inhumane and unworthy! He will be the best of kings and my people and this land cannot be denied the benefits of his exemplary leadership because of your petty and vindictive ways. The inhabitants of the three worlds will thank you if only you can find it in your heart to be kind and magnanimous.'

The Queen silenced him with a curt gesture. Shastha couldn't believe his eyes nor trust his ears. Why was the King grovelling at her feet? What was so wrong with him?

'If the ugly truth ever comes out, it will be the end of your precious bastard. But since you have begged for compassion, it does not have to come to that,' she said easily, basking in the power she clearly wielded over him. 'In return for his worthless life, I ask only that you send him into exile. He must never be allowed anywhere within the vicinity of this kingdom. Let him disappear into the remote vastness of the universe, away from decent, respectable people. Even this is a kindness he does not deserve.'

Shastha could only watch helplessly as his father bowed his head in defeat.

The loss of a kingdom did not weigh heavily on his mind. Shastha knew he could win himself an even bigger one if he wished to, but seeing what the crown and throne had done to his parents, he saw no reason to bother with that sort of thing. What did bother him was the fact that his father had refused to divulge the truth. All the way to the bitter end.

'I am sorry I have failed you, my son,' he wept on his shoulder, 'and I know that in the difficult days ahead, the worst part of it will be dealing with something that you do not understand. But you must trust me, neither knowledge nor the truth about your birth will help you. I have raised you to be a man. The best and worthiest of us all. I have to trust that it will be sufficient to help you make your way towards the glory destiny has singled you out for. Nothing else matters.

Remember the things I have taught you and the rules you must strictly adhere to. Stay away from women. You have seen first-hand the cruelty and caprice that characterizes the female of the species. Practise celibacy strictly. These things are important and I beg that you obey my words. It will help you win the favour of the Gods and execute fate's grand design. I hope you will think kindly of me in the future for...' He could not go on.

Shastha embraced him, 'I could not have asked for a better father or a kinder friend. Already you have given me so much, I will never be able to repay the debt. My only wish is for you to reconcile with Mother and find a way to be happy. Don't waste your days worrying about me. Rather than bemoan our impending separation, I would prefer to celebrate the halcyon days of my childhood, spent in your company. And in my heart, I know our paths will converge someday.'

It could only be hoped that the King was feeling better. Shastha certainly wasn't. It was hard to reconcile oneself to the fact that everything one has known and loved has been taken away. Shastha was feeling out of sorts as he trekked through the forest, which bordered their kingdom. As little boys, they had been told it was haunted and not a fit place for humans. Apparently, the Buffalo-Demon's wife had made her home thereabouts and had made it her life's mission to kill everyone who crossed her path.

He made his way past the broad tree trunks, sticking to the shadows as slivers of sunlight helped him navigate. Shastha wasn't sure about where he was headed or what he wanted to do. The trees were growing more closely together, seeming to have doubled in size and the way ahead darkened as the light became ever more diffused under the dense forest canopy.

The surrounding gloom reflected his own mood. His thoughts were chaotic and disorderly. Raw emotion flooded his insides as the questions slithered around his head, desperate for answers, driving him to distraction with their persistent insistence. Suddenly he was too exhausted to walk any further and sat down to rest. Within moments, he was fast asleep.

The dreams were vivid and filled with colour. Visions and images passing through his mind's eye in a dizzying rush, raising an unstoppable clamour in his head. Facts and fiction, heated emotions and cold reason mingled till they were indecipherable.

He found himself in the thick of things yet far removed and disjointed, untouched by their presence and the passions that gripped them. Strange folks danced around him, swaying to enthralling rhythms only they could hear, pelvises grinding so closely they were fused together. Many were copulating on the forest floor with voluptuous abandon. He backed away and stepped on something slick and disgusting. A beautiful woman with hair the colour of grass was gathering the gruesome stuff as if it actually mattered. She looked up at him and tears filled her eyes. Were they tears of happiness or sorrow? He did not tarry long enough to find out.

He was falling into the abyss, plunging into a pitfall, diving headlong into the perilous depths with nothing to hold onto or arrest his fall. During the course of that relentless descent, he was smashed to smithereens against cruel rocks, left skewered and bleeding as sharpened stakes and thorn bushes tore into his innards, without the relief of oblivion or the comfort of darkness that drowned out all else. In the distance he heard the crash and boom of the surging waters that awaited his presence.

The river gathered him in a fluid embrace, pulling him this way and that, cooling his molten disquietude with comforting caresses. Without warning, the implacable tides changed direction, carrying him backward towards the life-giving source, the dual origin of everything. He saw the crystal clear waters gush forth from an engorged male member and the emerald green spouting from a dilated vagina, swelling in a swirling mass of blissful union before he careened into the heart of the ancient deity that combined within itself the warring principles of the masculine and feminine forced into a harmonious truce, with neither straining to subdue or conquer.

Within this cocoon of harmony, the images inundated his mind in quick succession. Amidst the overwhelming flood, he saw the exquisite Enchantress lick the blue stain adorning the throat of the Three-eyed God whose indigo skin was streaked with gold. The sight of her raging, reckless desire inflamed his senses and he could not look away from her. And him. Their desires coursed through him and he felt the naked longing, experienced their all-encompassing love, burned with the heat of the ceaseless craving that drove the duo, leaving him trembling with awe. Above it all was the fervent wish for this perfect fusion of body and soul to never be sundered, come what may, which became his as well.

In the heat generated by an answered prayer, their conjoined bodies convulsed as flesh melted into molten droplets of hot and steaming lava, to be welded on the forge of faith in their love and unswerving belief in forever, till the two of before became the one of now, so that they might live and die together, united by a single fate, blessed never to suffer the pangs of separation.

When they broke apart and dusted themselves off the

remnants of love, lingering feelings and foolish yearning, so did he. He headed north and she made for the south, to the opposite ends of the spectrum they originally came from. He alone remained where he was, on the altar of their love, amidst the burnt offerings and a prayer for togetherness.

Shastha awoke with the gentle prodding of a shard of sunlight. He blinked, rubbing the sleep from his eyes. If he had not been feeling calmer than he had in a long time, he would have been taken aback by the sight of the wizened old man with his bulging eyes fastened on him, squinting in the faint sunlight as he scrutinized his features.

'I am told you have questions...' he began by way of explanation. 'It is why I travelled all this way to see you. What a treat for the eyes you are! You have clearly inherited your mother's looks but none of her angst-free nature. You have your father's strength and raw power, but as yet you lack his ability to veer from one extreme to the other without losing that sense of proportion, which is so essential. Oh well, one can't possibly have everything.'

'Who are you?' Shastha enquired, wondering if he was still dreaming.

The old man settled himself more comfortably against the bole of a giant tree that dwarfed his diminutive form, making his inquisitive eyes seem larger and more prominent. He sighed, 'I am Narada. They tell me you are a remarkable scholar, so I'll put down your slowness to the lingering lethargy that sometimes follows waking. To elaborate about myself, I am something of a scholar myself. A wanderer and seeker, the occasional catalyst to trigger an action or a reaction, speaker of truth and revealer of secrets. I am also a devotee of Vishnu, and therefore a well-wisher of your mother, which, if you haven't surmised by now, is why I am here.'

'I remember now!' Shastha nodded politely. If memory served, and it did, the Rajguru used to refer to sage Narada as a monkey-faced troublemaker whom the mortals as well as immortals he had angered had refrained from killing out of regard for Vishnu, who held all his devotees dear. Even the extremely irksome ones.

He hadn't said the words aloud, but Narada frowned in irritation. 'The problem with storytellers is that they are a jealous bunch who have no memories of anything real that they actually accomplished, because their noses were buried in the stories chronicling the false memories and passive impressions of others just like them. But you must be starving.'

Narada offered him his kamandala, which was filled with milk so thick he felt he had to eat it. But it was delicious and he ate hungrily.

The sage sniffed a little, 'Your mother would be angered by such a statement about stories. She insists they are more real than most things that are actually real.'

'Tell me about her,' Shastha asked eagerly, handing the kamandala back to the sage gratefully. *Please be certain to elaborate on why she felt the need to have me only to abandon me and never come back.*

'Since I have been branded with an unfair reputation for troublemaking, I feel it is only fair to warn you that the things you seek are almost always the things you need least. You chase after the truth and I daresay, nothing I say will dissuade you to do otherwise, but the truth cares nothing for consequences and even less, for hurt sentiment.' There was a sly glint in his eye that knew only too well that all warnings ever did were aggravate hidden fears, which in turn, merely whetted the appetite for the very thing one was being warned about.

'Tell me everything!' Shastha insisted. 'Even if the truth is awful, it is best to have it out.'

'King Rajashekara did not lie,' he began with a gleam of satisfaction. 'Your birth was a divine occurrence. But while Bhumi Devi bore you, she is not your mother. The events that unfolded took place under the most remarkable circumstances. Even in those rarefied realms where anything is possible, especially the impossible, you are a rarity.

'Shiva and Mohini were merely playing at the divine game of Lila when they set off on a mission, but they fell in love, and you were the product of their passion. Nobody would have believed it possible, least of all her, but the Enchantress had become enchanted. And thus was Harihara putra born in a manner of speaking.'

'Shiva and Mohini?' Shastha was thunderstruck as he digested the information and thought of the ethereal beauty who sometimes stalked his dreams with her lover in tow. As for Lord Shiva, he began every single day with the Three-eyed God's name on his lips. Both had been such an integral part of the stories he had grown up hearing.

Mohini was an avatar of Vishnu, his female dimension who stepped forward when all the masculine energy in the three worlds wouldn't suffice for the task at hand. His head buzzed with pestilential questions. Was that why the Queen hated him so much and referred to him as 'unnatural'? The fact that he was the child of two of the Trimurti? It still didn't account for whatever it was that was so shameful and damaging that Rajashekara had refused to tell him about it and that had been the reason he had been denied a throne and driven away from his kingdom. Besides, the King had always insisted on his divine antecedents. What was Narada trying to tell him? And he still didn't understand why he had been abandoned by his divine parents to be raised among mortals.

Narada was observing the myriad conflicting emotions that chased each other across the youngster's face with morbid curiosity and a touch of sympathy. 'Even in the furthest domains where oddities, rarities and all things absurd are accumulated, you are unique. Perhaps it will be simpler if I were to tell you a story from a fabled age so far back in the beginning that it has receded almost entirely from memory and even myth. All that remains is the image of an ancient idol that tells its own story. It was a time when chaos ruled the roost and there was no order. Everything was at odds with everything else and upheavals were endless, leading to nothing by way of tangible results. The pervading feeling was one of hopelessness. It would take something truly special to set it all straight and restore infinite calm.

'That was when Shiva and Shakti—purusha and prakriti—who embody all the equal and opposing forces in nature, which are believed to be irreconcilable, found their way into each other's arms. The two mighty hearts merged into a single great soul—Ardhanarishwara. Suddenly, it was all very simple, sweet and sublime. Their union made it possible for opposites to co-exist in peace and harmony. This was a state of perfection that had gratifying results—light took the edge off darkness without seeking to subsume it, barren lands became fertile, yielding rich bounty, love and compassion, and hope took flight while hate, cruelty and intolerance hibernated. It was the best of times.'

Narada took a deep breath. 'The children of this union were made in the image of Ardhanarishwara. Love had prevailed and the first race was hermaphroditic, combining the best of the two principle genders to evolve into an even better one—Tritiya Prakriti, the third gender. It was a fabulous coalescence, an organic blend of purusha and prakriti's essence, which could not be categorized entirely as one or the other. Which is exactly as it should be, I am sure you will agree. It is why gender itself has far more permutations than people are willing to acknowledge or admit.

Those who study the scriptures in their unexpurgated form will realize that the members of the other gender have been categorized. Men who are sexually attracted to men are kliba, women drawn to women are svairini, shanda refers to men who behave like women for reasons of choice or physical limitations and shandi refers to women who conform to the traditional behaviour patterns associated with males. Napumsa refers to those with ambiguous genitalia. Kami refers to those who love to make love and are indifferent to the gender of the person they are engaged in coitus with.'

Shastha nodded as understanding dawned vaguely. He was remembering his father's rules and questioning his own assumption that he was exactly the same as everyone else... 'I know that this state of perfection that Shiva and Shakti achieved did not last. That it could not last since their union, perfect though it may have seemed, was far from perfect. It is the grandest and most glorious of paradoxes. They are never stronger than when they are together and yet their togetherness neutralizes their respective powers.

'Which is why they had to be relegated to the opposite poles of existence, torn apart by a force greater than even love—practical necessity. But they can't remain estranged forever either and will eventually find their way back to each other to claim the absolute bliss they have earned to make up for, and to endure, the next round of painful separation. I know all that, but tell me what happened to the "hermaphroditic" children of this union as you called them?'

'It was an extraordinary race. They were strong, brave and everything came easily to them. It happens when contradictory urges, impulses, thoughts and feelings have been conciliated. Some blame hubris, but ultimately they could not escape the fate of their parents. Lesser races were fighting for ascendance and the dually sexed were broken apart, if not killed outright, leaving those who survived paralysed and stricken with so much grief they could barely function for the longest time.

'If the legends are to be believed, the fragmented halves of the divine duality have spent the eons frantically seeking and begging to be reunited with their better halves. Most were doomed to die of unrequited love, but some say the children of Ardhanarishwara have never given up searching for the soul mates they lost so long ago. Across time and space, too few met with success and were reunited with their better halves as spouses, lovers or friends. It was even rarer when the original oneness, that state of absolute union, had been achieved. You are young now and yet entire yugas of effort have gone into your making. And of all living creatures, you are the most blessed of all. Two individuals in a single body with their sexes manifested and their individualities intact.'

Shastha nodded thoughtfully. 'The Queen called me an abomination and insisted that I was unnatural. But even at the height of her cruelty there was a hidden depth to her emotions that I couldn't quite pinpoint. It was why I was never angry at her. All I ever wanted was to understand. And now I think I do...'

Narada nodded sympathetically. 'No matter where you go and what you do, all will be drawn to you, Shastha. You represent the ecstatic approximation of blissful unity, the successful merger of two souls, whereas all else are blundering across and bumping into each other, settling for the simulacrum of what they seek, resenting their subsequent unhappiness, goaded by the love they seek, which is lost to them. This is the immortality they seek. No amount of Amrita or enchantment can satiate their misery, which drives them into chasing after one another, only to reject and be rejected in turn. You, on the other hand, have successfully bridged the distance between the seeker and that which is sought.

'As one who is self-sufficient, there will be too many who will be jealous of who you are and rather than work their way to the same state, they will seek to destroy you and that which you represent. King Rajashekhara was wise and he did you a great service in raising you as a boy and doing everything possible to keep you safe till you were ready to learn the truth about yourself. Believe me, hard as your life has been, it would have been worse if you had been raised as a woman.'

Shastha's eyes were wet with tears. 'I thank you, but clearly I am not as self-sufficient as you seem to think. Without my father's help who knows what would have become of me? What would have happened had I been exposed as someone who combines in his body the physical characteristics of both genders? Even so, I am grateful to know the truth about who and what I am. You warned me at the start that knowledge would not necessarily bring comfort, but I am happy that you have helped me comprehend. It will make going forward so much easier.'

On an impulse, he threw his arms around Narada, surprising the venerable sage with the warmth of his embrace. 'You are not a monkey-faced mischief-maker after all.'

'Never forget it, my boy,' the sage admonished with mock severity and hugged him back with a world of affection.

The Buffalo-Demon's Wife

Shastha decided that Narada's view of his 'intersexed' state was a tad too idealized and romantic, but comforting nevertheless. Now that he knew who he was (Shastha had decided to stick to the masculine identity his father had given him for purposes of convenience as well as camouflage till he had figured out what he wanted to do), the next step was to decide where he would be headed next. For the time being, he was still wandering around aimlessly with no destination in mind.

The best part of his life had been devoted to studying how to be a good king and to find the answers to the questions that plagued him. Now that the former option was lost to him and he had a few answers, he supposed he had time to slow down a bit and ponder on a course of action. In the meantime, Shastha had to deal with his shadow, who had been following him for a short while now, a warrior of fearsome attribute who was skilled in the art of the chase and the hunt. Shastha addressed the creature without turning around. 'My name is Shastha. Who are you? Why are you following me? Have you been sent with orders to kill me?'

She leaped down from the branch of a tall tree and stood directly in front of him. It was a woman dressed in the warlike paraphernalia of a soldier. 'I am Leela. But I wouldn't go around introducing myself to strangers if I happened to be the former heir apparent who is currently in exile and whose stepmother wants him dead. Besides, if I had wanted to kill you, it would have been done already. Fortunately, we don't take orders from the Queen. She is no friend of the likes of us. But if you would be so kind as to follow me…'

Leela led him deeper into the forest, picking her way across the non-existent trail with clear-eyed confidence. They walked in silence. The warrior woman stopped at the edge of a clearing. A beautiful stallion lay sprawled on the forest floor. Shastha knelt down by its side. It was dead. And so was the man beneath him, of whom only the broken leg was visible. A short distance away, there were more dead bodies. In fact, there were too many of them, with some lying in a tangled heap. It was a horrifying sight and already the blow flies were gathering en masse, buzzing as they got to work on the putrid flesh.

Shastha noted the blood-encrusted hole where an arrow had punctured its way through, beneath the shoulder blade of a man who lay as though asleep. This one had taken multiple arrows to the chest. There was one with a broken neck. One lay on his stomach with so many arrows buried in his back, he looked like a porcupine. Yet another's body lay twisted at an impossible angle.

There were other women like her, armoured and armed to the teeth, working assiduously across the killing fields. The dead were stacked in rows, and fires were being kindled to cremate them. He saw a young girl dispassionately plunge her dagger into the heart of a man whose thigh had been shattered by an arrow. The others worked just as mechanically, stripping the dead of their weapons and anything else of value, making a quick end to the wounded and clearing away the bodies for cremation. Some of the horses were alive and unhurt; these were being herded away. The women seemed very enthusiastic about the horses.

'They were here for you,' Leela informed him. 'A vainglorious lot who no doubt assumed they would put a quick end to you and then come after us for a bit of raping and looting. We have seen too many of their ilk passing though and we were prepared. Besides, I am in charge here and I decided not to let them kill you till I figured out what you were about.'

Without waiting for a reply she went onto say a few words to her people who glanced at him curiously. 'Isn't he the one from the so-called prophecy?' the young girl glared at him, hefting her dagger menacingly.

'He is not entirely certain about who or what he is. A lost soul.

And you know we don't kill or imprison those,' Leela told her, and the girl lost interest. He watched her assured manner as she went about her business, issuing an order here, sharing a laugh there. Clearly she was their leader and much loved by the looks of it.

As they worked, her followers looked at him with frank appraisal. Some giggled. Leela shushed them and motioned for him to follow as she led the way out.

'What is this prophecy?' he asked her.

'We have a few unusual visitors in these parts,' she told him. 'One of them claimed she was a seer and that she had been alive for thousands of years. There was nothing of the crone about her though. Her skin was unlined and there was always a twinkle in her eye. She said that a son born to Shiva and Vishnu would be the death of me. But she died during a raid and she hadn't seen that coming. We thought nothing of her prophecy till Narada dropped in a while back and told me a little bit about you.'

Shastha had been right about him from the first! He *was* a monkey-faced mischief-maker! Either that or Leela had eavesdropped on their conversation.

'He told us that you were special and we might do well to ally ourselves with you.' She hesitated for a second, seeming to wrestle with her thoughts as a blush worked its way to her cheeks from her neck, and then gathering herself, she walked faster into the woods. He could hear the sounds of other women as she led him to their settlement.

It was a remarkable sight. There were women of all shapes and sizes, young and old, bustling around as they prepared the evening meal. They also paused to take a look at him and call out a greeting to Leela before returning to their chores. Some were dressed in traditional saris while others clearly favoured the attire of men. Incidentally, there were also a few men, some among whom clearly preferred the feminine apparel.

'We are not welcome anywhere else,' she told him simply, 'for various reasons. Some have no wish to share their past and we don't ask. A few are privileged, but have decided that marriage and motherhood is not for them. They miss the silks and comforts they left behind but they have acclimatized and found a way to thrive in these conditions. Others are criminals, who have robbed and killed to reach this place. We don't judge them as long as they abide by our rules here. All who have been ostracized and marginalized by the spite of society drift in here. Some have stayed ever since, but many move on. We have all had our wings clipped or torn off but that is no reason for us to not help each other fly again, isn't it?'

Her disarming smile was so infectious it made him smile too. 'You should be proud of what you have built here,' he said admiringly.

'You haven't seen anything yet,' she said with sparkling eyes as she removed her fearsome helmet with their sharpened buffalo horns, shook her hair loose and tossed it to one side.

'Ladies!' she called out, 'we fought off an armed squadron today and I am happy to report that we have no losses on our side. Prathu lost her front teeth but she claims she has never felt prettier. Sheela lost a chunk of her hair and clothes in addition to sustaining a flesh wound but she has the winning tally for most number of victims claimed and she feels it is a fair trade. Kartika has a broken rib. I was told to inform you that she regrets it, but will be unable to do her chores for the next fortnight and is sorry that she will be cooped up in her chambers resting and recuperating.'

Wild cheers greeted her announcement. She held up her hand for silence. 'It is too early to celebrate, ladies. We must be vigilant as there will certainly be retaliation. But we do have a little respite and we have taken a rich haul and brought in some valuable booty.'

The ladies hooted and whistled at that as they looked at Shastha appreciatively.

An elderly woman insisted that Leela and her guest partake of the piping hot meal that was being prepared. So Shastha and Leela washed up in a little stream and sat down to eat. He had a thousand new questions now and he addressed them to her between delicious mouthfuls of rice and the most delicious fish curry he had ever tasted, with crunchy vegetables. There was fresh toddy too.

'It is a long story,' she told him as she tucked in with gusto. 'I came here after my husband died.'

The others gathered around, helping themselves to the food and sitting in a circle, relishing the prospect of telling the handsome newcomer their stories. 'They called her Mahishi,' said Meena, the lady who had cooked them the delicious meal. 'She hates the name, so don't use it unless you want her to snap at you.' She ignored Leela's frown and went on, 'They called him the Buffalo-Demon and he was a powerful tribal chieftain, but he died under mysterious circumstances. Leela was accused of being responsible for his misfortune and driven out.'

'You could have easily killed them all,' one of them told her.

'What would be the point?' Leela shrugged, sounding very unconcerned about the traumatic past she had endured. 'My husband spent his life trying to improve the circumstances of his people, but when he was crushed by the oppressors, they blamed him for the losses sustained. Now they say he was born to a demon and a she-buffalo. That I was a woman of insatiable sexual appetite in a former life, which was why I am accursed in this one.'

'I got into trouble because of my insatiable sexual appetite in this one. My husband was impotent and my neighbour had a roving eye. One thing led to another and they ruled that I was to be stoned to death, but I escaped in the middle of the night. The sentry placed to guard me was most helpful in return for a few favours he demanded.' She winked at me.

'Everybody has these stories...I had a jealous husband,' the woman seated next to me said by way of explanation, gesturing to her face, which was covered in burns, with one eye sealed shut. 'We cried a lot over them. But then we got fed up. Now we laugh instead. Thanks to Leela, we were able to build a community for people like us, slowly, over the years. The surprising thing is that so many men helped us too, you know, with money, materials or kind words, and not all of them expected "favours" in return. We take care of ourselves here as well as of each other and we are self-sufficient. Isn't that the goal? I certainly think so.'

'We all do our part,' one of the younger ones told him. 'Leela's husband trained her in the martial arts and she used to fight by his side and saved his life on many occasions. She is being modest and rolling her eyes at me to stop, but it is true. And she is training us too to defend ourselves. In the beginning, we had only a small troop to defend against invaders but now most of us can wield a bow or a sword, and we have excellent riders as well, though not as many horses as we would have liked.'

'Those of us who can't swing a sword to save our lives do other things,' another one piped up. 'We cook, mend clothes, clean, weave baskets and make utensils. Sarala there likes to contribute by making sure there are no leftovers.'

'I'll remember that the next time you want me to braid your hair or massage the knots from your neck and shoulders!' Sarala shot back.

'Your father helped too,' Leela told him quietly. 'In the early days, when we were still vulnerable, and undesirables decided that a group of women living alone in the woods were best suited to serve as their sex slaves, the King sent his soldiers to protect us and imprison these men. He has always been kind and we are most grateful.'

'Prince Shastha helped us inadvertently too,' one of them bowed to him, 'by patrolling the borders of your kingdom, and coming down hard on pirates, cutthroats and thieves. You made this land safe not just for your subjects but for us fringe-dwellers too.'

Later, they walked along the stream by themselves. Shastha was silent.

'You don't talk much, do you?' Leela said. He smiled in response.

'Well, given your divine antecedents and all, I suppose there is certainly a chance you will be called upon to fight epic battles on behalf of the Devas…'

'Indra has begged me to become the Senapati of the Devas and help him fight the Asuras,' he retorted. 'He told me not to mourn the loss of my little kingdom in these parts as he will be naming me as his successor and that Amaravati will one day be mine, but I am afraid I turned him down. If you will have me, I would like to—'

'You can stay…' she said quickly. 'Ladies! We have our Senapati.'

Wild cheers greeted her announcement.

'Having a warrior of your calibre in our midst is such a relief. We have done the best we could to repel those who come after us and we have been lucky, but truth be told it would have only been a matter of time before we were completely annihilated. Which is why it feels like today, the Gods finally smiled on us and sent you in their infinite wisdom and compassion.'

'Well, you said it yourself… I was a little lost and I am glad you found me. It is I who am fortunate enough to have found you and be included in this community.'

'But don't you go falling in love with me…' she told him quietly. 'After my husband died, I was captured by our enemies. They kept me captive and tortured me for days. I was starved and half-dead but I fought my way to freedom. But they mutilated my genitals and it was infected. I would have died if some of my husband's men hadn't found me and taken me to a healer. Ever since, it hasn't been easy for me to trust men, but with you it is different.'

She hesitated briefly. 'Nobody knows this story, but for some reason I wanted to share it with you and tell you that I hope you will stay here, and in return, you will have my friendship. All of our friendship. If you will accept it, that is. I was told you too are entirely self-sufficient.'

'Earlier, I wasn't too sure, but now I do feel that way,' Shastha told her. And as he said this, he realized it was finally true.

'This is all working out exactly as I planned when I saw you in our neck of the woods. And there is someone I would like you to meet. He is expected in these parts in a few weeks. He is a Yavana pirate named Vavar, who once tried to rob the settlement. But he is a friend too. We have tried to reform his wicked ways, but have given him up for hopeless. Perhaps you will do a better job.'

They continued to walk by the stream. Talking. And laughing.

Epilogue

'...it was most perplexing and it bothered me that my mind was a blank. That I could not make sense of any of it. The dreams were trying to help. I understand that now, but at the time, they conveyed so much more than I could handle at once. Which is probably why I fled from them. But as you know, fleeing from a dream gets you nowhere. So I was stranded.'

He was a lot more loquacious here than was his wont. But that happened and I listened intently as he unburdened himself. 'Strangely enough, it became clear soon. Learning the truth about who I was helped. I wasn't angry or confused any more. It helped that I was shown my true purpose as well. My father wanted me to be the king of kings, to conquer the three worlds and establish a golden age of peace, prosperity and plenty. The masculine side of me thrilled at the prospect but my feminine nature balked. In the end, the choice was simple. It had fallen to me to work with the like-minded to create a peaceful corner in the three worlds for all those who were not welcome elsewhere. For those who had been written out of the stories and left to die long before they stopped breathing. Helping them a little helped me a lot. And I am happy.'

I was happy for him too. We walked over to the illuminated border between the existing worlds and the universe that lay beyond, which he had finally learned to straddle, and looked over at the little kingdom that had let him go. King Rajashekhara had never forgiven himself for succumbing to his wife's blandishments and had devoted his last years to building an enduring monument to his beloved Shastha's memory. He hired poets, painters, artists, scribes, bards, musicians and sculptors to record the best stories about him and preserve it in his monument to posterity.

They conjured up the stories from what they were told and what they weren't. The child born of the union of Shiva and Mohini, for the express purpose of destroying the wife of the Buffalo-Demon to neutralize a boon she had won from Brahma, according to which only a child born of two males could prevail over her. And Shastha, or Ayyappa (born to two fathers) as he came to be known, had prevailed. Magnanimous and compassionate, he brought tiger's milk for the ailing Queen who had conspired to kill him in order to seat her own son on the throne. A mighty warrior who had saved them from the demonic She-Buffalo, he also guarded the coast against pirates and other inimical forces, before retiring to the abode of celestials. Indra was threatened by his prowess and put up wily Narada into telling him about the unusual nature of his birth. Embarrassed, Ayyappa had sworn to remain celibate and shunned the company of women after his unhappy experiences with his birth 'mother' and stepmother. Therefore, only male devotees would be welcome at the wondrous abode built by his father.

'It is quite a story,' I remarked. 'I am told, Parashurama of the fiery axe personally carved the idol that has been placed in the sanctum sanctorum.'

'Father insisted on doing it,' he shrugged, 'Of course, I intend to visit to make him happy. But I am not going to remain locked up in an altar even if it is the holiest of the holies. Those who want to make my acquaintance can always find me if they look long enough for a safe little haven tucked away on the outskirts of the spiteful society they keep.'

'Have I ever told you that I am really proud of you? An enchantress is no mother, and yet...'

Unlike stories, dreams have neither a beginning nor an ending. I continued to traipse from one story to the next. It was my prerogative, the way it was the prerogative of the God or Goddess who first created something extraordinary from the sweet nothings of a dream, with the independence to exist outside of the creator. I had grown strong on love, faith and an irresistible urge to be captured in the throes of enchantment and become intoxicated with ecstasy, from a foolish dream to elude death forever. I had enjoyed the freedom to choose and be chosen. I flowed across fluid time, wild and untameable as a river, the commander of dreams and conqueror of fancy, who went where the stories led, past even the endings to where new stories were crafted. There is no end to my journey for as long as people dream. And tell their stories. In the end, I found my immortality as others looked for theirs. For I am Mohini, the Enchantress.